GW01458923

GENEVA INTRUSION

BOOKS BY THE AUTHOR

PRIMARY PROTOCOL
Coming in 2021

ISLANDS OF PEACE
Coming in 2021

THE BRIMSTONE OFFENSIVE
Coming in 2021

BEHIND YESTERDAY
"Love, intrigue, and espionage in a time of war."

AT RANDOM
"Thoughts from a marginal mind."

The Geneva Intrusion

A NOVEL
RICHARD D. TAYLOR

Pacific Grove Press

Cover Copyright © 2021 by Richard D. Taylor
Interior Illustrations Copyright © 2021 by Richard D. Taylor
Pacific Grove Press
Printed in the United States of America

For more information on this and other books by Mr. Taylor:
www.richardDtaylor.com

RichardDtaylor@gmail.com
I would love to hear from you.

Version 2021 213.3

I will never know where the urge to write came from,
but neither will I give it up.

INTRODUCTION

Iranian Revolutionary Guard Corps

The IRGC was created after the Iranian revolution, for the protection and survival of the regime. The coup overthrew the Shah of Iran and resulted in the hostage crisis at the American embassy. The IRGC is a big player in Iran's oil, gas, import-export, and telecommunications sectors, controlling from a third to two-thirds of the country's GDP. The Guard is the most powerful security, military, and economic force in Iran and they have used this power to eclipse and dominate the clergy. They commit acts of terror directly and by sponsoring anti-western groups around the world. The Guard is feared within Iran and in many capitals of the world. It's hard to draw an analogy of the IRGC in Western circles, but a corporation with guns has often been used. The IRGC plays a significant role in this story.

PROLOGUE

Fredrik Hald pushed open the door to the Danish post office and entered out of the biting cold. The visit was on his way home from his small appliance repair shop located just three blocks away. He stomped the snow off his feet on the entry mat, then walked over to his postal box and, just as he did every day, he opened it and withdrew the stack of invoices and business mail. Then, as he also did every day, he opened the box next to it. He noticed it had a letter. He reached in and pulled out the letter addressed to him, knowing exactly what to do. At the postal counter, he purchased a slightly larger envelope, placed the original letter inside and sent it Post Exprès to an address he had memorized. He handed the letter to the attendant and went on with his life.

* * * *

One day later, Mr. Seljuk, owner of a small antique books shop in Bettle, Luxembourg also picked up his mail. He also pulled open the postal box door next to his and in it was a letter addressed in care of Dept. 326. He closed the small door and, on his way out, stopped by the front counter of the small postal office.

"You are looking very well today, Harriet," he said. "That husband better be taking good care of you. There are a lot of men out there looking for a good woman." He leaned on the counter, pretending, albeit rather poorly, to be a man of the town.

"Well, after thirty-five years, you would think he's doing something right, but God knows if I can figure it out," she said.

They both laughed.

"Besides," she said, "what would you know about men looking for women? Your days for that sort of thing ended with the last world war."

"Surprises, Harriet, life is full of surprises," he said. "One might be just around the corner, and it could light up your day," he added with a bright shining face. He doffed his hat and with a little skip headed out to his car. He placed the envelope in a leather case and proceeded to drive the fifteen minutes to a large stone castle in a small adjacent hamlet. Upon arriving, there would be the usual thorough security check, and then he would personally deliver the case directly to a man on duty. He would then drive off and never say a word to anyone, as was his arrangement with whoever was sending him the rather generous monthly payment for his services.

* * * *

The communications agent in the basement of the large fortified structure looked at the letter and logged it in with time and date. Then he dialed a senior supervisor. "I have an initial contact letter here from Tangent Day. I am requesting authorization to respond."

There was a pause on the other end as the voice verified the code ID followed by the words "permission granted."

The agent requested a cyber key from his computer and wrote it down on the foil-backed stationery. He then folded it with the foil facing out and placed it in an envelope. He sent it back in a manner—the old-fashioned, hand-written letter—that in every practical sense avoided absolutely any possible digital trail or outside monitoring.

***

IMPORTANT CHARACTERS AND TERMS
On Page 305

***

CHAPTER—1

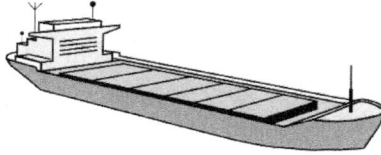

BOARDING THE *MONTCLAIR STAR* — THURSDAY PM

Panama-flagged oil tanker *Montclair Star*
Location: The Persian Gulf, 25 miles off the coast of Iran.
US 5th Fleet in the area

"Pirates, pirates on port side." Juarez, a deck hand, breathlessly shouted as he careened up the stairs to the bridge.

Captain Carlino Bertucci, standing on the tanker *Montclair Star*'s bridge wing, was aware of the situation. A man with twenty-four years' experience, he was tracking the pirates on radar and concentrating on the small boat through his binoculars. He lowered the glasses, walked into the wheelhouse, and quickly radioed the US Maritime Administration emergency group.

"Mayday. Mayday. Mayday. This is the Montclair Star. Hijacking in progress. Request any aid. Coordinates 26 degrees 30 minutes by 53 degrees 15 minutes, course 135, speed 19 knots."

"*Montclair Star*, this is the warship *USS Connolly*. We copy your transmission," said the young ensign on the Arleigh Burke-class destroyer. "Relaying your information to coalition channels now."

"They're on approach, situation is critical, *Montclair* out," Bertucci said, leaving the channel open.

Five men in a small, sea-worn skiff violently attacked the choppy waves fighting their way towards the massive oil tanker in the Strait of Hormuz. The leader, a large man, stood at the front with knees bent, absorbing the powerful surges of the bow as it dove deep into the water then thrust upward. He studied the distance as they approached the plodding behemoth. It required his total concentration to maintain his balance atop the erratically battered boat. Drawing his forearm across his face once again failed to wipe away the saltwater stinging his eyes. A fatigued AK-47, whose violent history would never be known, lay at his feet covered in the spray that filled the air.

"Faster," the leader shouted, "faster." The skiff suddenly shifted starboard under his feet, causing him to slam his foot against the outboard rail to stay aboard. He looked disdainfully at the frail young man soaked to the core, trying to control the screaming outboard motor. "Keep her steady, or we lose speed," he yelled with a wave of his arm. Eyes fixed on the tanker, he waited until the last moment to pick up the semi-automatic rifle.

Bertucci walked over to the wall speaker and pushed the ship's PA button. "This is the captain, pirates alongside, this is not a drill, repeat this is not a drill." With the ship's phone in his hand, he selected the engine room and said, "Banoy, you heard the announcement, pirates will attempt to board. Give me all the speed you have."

Banoy said, "Do you authorize full ahead?"

"Yes," the captain yelled to his chief engineer, "do it *now*."

The radio speaker came alive. "This is the warship *USS Connolly* to the *Montclair Star*; what is your status, over?"

Bertucci looked over the port side wing and saw a man on the skiff below with a gun pointed directly at the bridge. "Everyone down," he shouted, taking an awkward dive for the floor as bullets pinged off the outside of the bridge.

On the *Connolly*, the ensign turned to his captain. "No response, sir, but I heard automatic gunfire."

The *Connolly*'s captain turned to the executive officer and said, "Get a helo in the air, and you," he pointed at another ensign, "turns for flank speed and, navigator, get me to their position."

"Yes, sir," was the reply from each of the crewmen.

The craft was still trying to gain on the tanker as it fought against the dangerous waves generated off the enormous ship's bow. The leader put down the AK-47 and picked up a Soviet-made grenade launcher. Holding it up to his eye, he observed the larger ship move in and out of the weapon's sight and fired.

The unstable platform on which he stood caused the grenade to errantly head for the upper corner of the superstructure, where it entered the side window of the bridge and went out the front without an explosion. Glass rained down on the *Montclair*'s bridge crew.

Captain Bertucci commanded the helmsman, "Hard-a-port," attempting to run into the smaller craft, making it more difficult to board.

Bertucci's voice was tense as he turned to his first mate. "Let's get those jets on." The man moved swiftly to the control panel and threw the master switch. "Jets on," he shouted as the four-inch water jets around the ship created a non-lethal means of making it more difficult for the pirates to make it to the ladder from their small craft.

Just then, automatic gunfire came in the open door. The captain watched as the overhead exploded in a sequential pattern of bullets above him. He looked at his crew face down on the deck.

"Change that order," he said to the first mate. "Get your men to the citadel. Leave the jets on."

The first mate rushed everyone off the bridge and into the companionway.

"All hands to the citadel — *now*," Bertucci said over the PA. He then picked up the telephone. "Banoy," he said. "Shut down the engines and electrical power and get your guys to the safe room."

"Aye, sir," Banoy responded.

Another cartridge-full of ammunition came up from below, pinging off the outside hull and taking out more glass. Bertucci, on his knees, could feel his heart pounding as he turned the dial on the ship's safe. He pulled at the door and grabbed the ship's log. Bent over, he exited the bridge descending five flights of stairs into a room designed to deny the pirates the leverage of hostages. They knew untrained pirates could not start the engines, and short of an explosive charge applied to the hatch, they were reasonably safe. They expected the pirates to leave once they realized time was short, help was on the way, and that they could not navigate the ship to a friendly port.

Bathed in the water from the jets, the leader motioned for a crewmember to throw up the ladder. The third try caught the tanker's bulwark. He and his four men ascended the ladder, all barefoot and dressed in the typical Somali pirates' threadbare clothing. Clearing the bulwark, the men took cover behind a raised oil tank access hatch and, from the duffel bag, unwrapped four KL-7.62 semi-automatic assault rifles from their waterproof covers, several flash/smoke grenades, extra ammunition, and a medical backpack. The lead man felt the engine's muted vibration under his feet come to a stop, and the noise generated by the defensive water jets fade as they shut down. The five men moved quickly towards the main superstructure in practiced precision. The trailing two men concentrated on the superstructure's gangways, with the rest looking for any threat at deck level. Silently and methodically making their way to their destination.

Seconds later, the five men stood on the port bridge wing just outside the pilot house. The group leader, gun at his shoulder, nodded as one of his men pulled open the hatch to the wheelhouse. A second man rolled a flash/smoke grenade into the room. Their backs were against the outside bulkhead as it went off. The leader entered, quickly swinging his gun's barrel into the space, ready to open fire. Two men who covered the right and left sides of the area immediately followed him. It was unoccupied. Not surprised, the leader knew the crew would be locked away but was trained not to take any chances. The smoke that hung in the air streamed towards the broken windows and outside as if needed elsewhere.

Silently he pointed at one of the men who went over to the helmsman's console. Looking at the dark gauges, which showed no sign of damage, the man nodded his head, indicating everything seemed okay. The leader turned to another man also at the console, looking at a sheet with the new coordinates. He motioned for them to stay. Both men pulled on latex gloves before they touched anything. He nodded for the other two men to follow him.

Having previously studied the ship's layout, they proceeded directly down to the engine room, guns raised around every corner, expecting the unexpected. As they approached the engine room, one of the men had another flash-bang grenade ready. The group leader looked through the round window in the hatch and found the room empty. He waved his hand at the grenade, and the man put it away. As the door opened, they all entered the dimly lit, pale green engine control room. There was a shadowy quiet and the thick and stale air smelled of diesel. Large windows overlooked the massive silent engines in the dark room two decks below as the start team technician stood at the engineering console. With an assistant, his job was to start the engines. He surveyed the panel and nodded to the group leader with thumbs-up.

Finally, alone, the group leader turned to the start team and spoke aloud in a Persian dialect. "Time for you to do your job. Let me know when you're ready." The start team put their guns down, and the still-armed leader moved to the entrance door to protect their position.

The assistant pulled on his latex medical gloves as he approached the thirty-foot-long gray control panel that resembled a lineup of ten tall refrigerators, each with a withering array of gauges and dials. He came to a stop in front of the electrical generator module. He pulled open his vest and extracted two plastic-covered sheets of instructions. As he looked at the papers, he flipped the breaker switches in the proper sequence and watched the red status lights turn green. He pulled down on the master handle and heard the generators restart. Their eyes adjusted as the regular lights took over from the dim battery-powered lights.

"Electrical on," the assistant said.

"Check," said the tech as he stared at the control console indicator lights.

More switches set by the assistant started to bring up the hydraulic and lube oil pressure.

"Check again," the tech said, monitoring the pressure gauges.

Moving down the control panel, throwing another multi-breaker switch sequence started the air compressor. The tech watched the indicator on the control panel rise to 128 PSI. He checked the fuel flow indicator and several other gauges and said, "Check, starting main engine one." He held down the large red button labeled "M/E One Start" until the green light above it came on. The deck vibrated beneath their feet as the room filled with the groans and deep moans of a powerful giant awakened. The same sequence was employed to the "M/E Two Start" button and so on until all three engines were idling.

"Normal idle in three minutes," he said to the group leader at the door.

"Good," the group leader said. "Full ahead when you're ready. Lock the door behind me. I will be on the bridge. Don't forget, nothing is to be left behind when you leave. Wipe down any questionable areas."

"Yes, Captain," both men said. The tech looked at his assistant and then put his hand on the maneuvering handle that engaged the propeller shafts and looked at the maneuvering chart that said "Max 105, Full 95, half 65." After four minutes and with full green indicators, he moved the handle slowly, first to 65 RPM. The tech felt the additional vibration on the console and in the room, as the noise level rose significantly. The immense vessel was now ready for its new heading.

CHAPTER—2

KATE IN NEW YORK CITY—TUESDAY AM

Kate Adler, convinced she would have a meaningful impact on the world, knew that to date, her search for the precise path had been spectacularly unsuccessful. Nonetheless, she was determined to make her own choices about her future and not let others direct her way. She would not yield to her friends' well-intentioned efforts and rejected outright the preordained plan of working in one of her father's successful and sometimes mysterious companies.

Kate sat pensively in a white terry robe that hid her crossed legs as she pushed the dark soft hair back from her face. A broad smile appeared when visions of the previous night interrupted her thinking. Having just landed in New York to visit her father, she was standing outside the baggage claim as her college girlfriends arrived, packed into a party limousine. Blaring music and rotating LED lights running the passenger compartment's length entertained them until they got to the first nightclub and throughout the evening. It was a welcome-back party that included drinking, flirting, and more flirting. Through the years, they had remained a tight group. Each of her friends had already survived various life experiences—maintaining husbands, maintaining husbands with kids, and one contemplating divorce. They were a sampling of spoiled, affluent, college-educated women as confused about the baffling process of life as ever.

The confusion extended to Kate, whose experience at thirty-five consisted almost entirely of her work's challenges. Her failed efforts to find her calling had landed her in the national security business. It wasn't fighting global hunger or disease, but it was an area in which she excelled.

The NSA came calling right out of college, but she was never confident if her very influential father had persuaded them, although he denied having anything to do with the offer.

When it came to relationships, Kate wasn't as brave as her friends. Thus she remained single. When her internal stress meter sounded an alarm, the casual male distraction seemed to suffice— infrequent ventures that she kept on her terms. Taller than most women and with an average build, her natural beauty got the attention, masking a keen mathematical intellect.

Kate sighed heavily, focusing on the bed in front of her and wondering what she would do next. Typically she wouldn't have given it a second thought. Cloaked in a night of innocent fun, Kate discovered early in the evening that there was a concerted 'well-intentioned' effort by her friends to match her up, not with a hookup, but a husband. Quietly sleeping in the hotel bed before her was handsome evidence that, despite their sincere efforts, last evening had resulted in a hookup. She let her face blossom with a wide grin at what this poor man waded through, trying to make a good impression.

She got up, walked over to the other side of the bed, and looked down at the attractive face resting on the pillow. In a way, it was too bad because he had been the opposite of a man looking to get laid, which is precisely why he was where he was. A tactic most men would be smart to add to their gaming strategy. However, she soon came to her senses and, in a whirl, pulled off the covers, completely exposing the naked man in front of her. With fresh memories in her mind, she took one last glance and threw the covers back over him.

"What the … ?" he said, coming up on an elbow.

"I'm truly sorry about this, mister, but you gotta go," she said.

He sat up, rubbing his face and hair. "Are you kidding? Why?"

"Why? Now that's a great question. Let's see, how about because I said so, and the last time I looked, it was my hotel room, not yours."

"I don't have a hotel room. I have an apartment in Manhattan, but you didn't want to see it. Besides, we had a great time together last night. I thought we had something going. I know we had something going. Can I see you again?"

"We did, and it's the end of the affair. That's the title of a movie. Life is like that sometimes—taxes, great loves lost …"

He paused. "I don't know your name."

"Jane," she said. "Jane Doe."

"Look, Jane," he said smiling, "are you sure? Because I would like to see you again. Late last night, you thought I was quite a nice guy. In fact, you thought so very late into the night."

She stood over him as he sat on the bed. "Look at those sad puppy eyes," she said through pouting lips, toying with his hair and pushing it to the right across his forehead. Placing a hand on the side of his face and bending over, she said. "They're almost working on my heart—almost."

"Your friends called you Kate last night, if I remember correctly." He stood up and started putting on his things. "They said we were getting married, that we would live happily ever after."

She moved to the dresser across the room and leaned back on it in her best Lauren Bacall sulky style.

Moving toward her with his shoes in his hand, he chuckled, "I believed them because they repeatedly promised all evening long. I wanted to believe them," he said, flashing a phony smile. "Well, okay, not the ever-after part, but at least to get to know you."

"What do you do for a living?" she said, buttoning his shirt.

"I told you last night. I'm an investment banker."

"That explains a lot," she laughed. "You're used to being sold cheap land," she said, gently touching the side of his face. She reached into the mini-fridge and handed him a bottle of water.

His tone turned more serious as he said. "Kate, take a breath here, and let's talk."

"I can't. I'm late to start a full day and then back to Munich."

"Munich, for business?" he said, throwing his tie around his neck.

"No, I live and work there."

"How about some coffee first?"

"What's your name, big boy?"

21

"Darren. Darren Winton. You knew that last night. How soon they forget," he said, pointing in her direction. "I gave you my number, and you promised to call." His smile betrayed his sincerity.

"Darren, dear, oh, that's cute. It's not going to happen. I'm already late, and you're making this dull thing in my head think it's alive.

"How about your heart? Is *it* alive?" he said.

She didn't respond but placed both of her hands on her hips.

"All right, my ladyship, seems you've made up your mind." He pulled a card out of his wallet and handed it to her. While putting on his jacket, he said, "Call me next time you're in New York. I promise we will go somewhere without blaring music. Someplace quiet like the library. No entourage, just you and me."

"Funny boy." She put his arm over her shoulder and walked him to the door. She gave him a brief hug and, pulling back, placed a kiss on his cheek. He reached for her, and she said, "Bye, Darren, and thanks for a lovely evening; I will send you the divorce papers in the mail."

He was standing in the hall. Bowing to the inevitable, he shook his head, looked at her, and said, "It was a great time. You have a bright mind, and I have to admit there was something that got me a little too attached." He grabbed her hand and, squeezing it as he walked away, said, "Bye, Jane Doe, have a nice flight."

Kate swung the door closed, then stared at her side as if she could see him walking down the hall. Kate turned, then leaned up against the door, thinking about the different decisions she had made in her life. Finally, taking a breath, Kate turned around to face the door and tapped it mindlessly, thinking about reaching for the knob. Instead, she headed for the phone, telling herself to get a grip. She dialed and heard someone pick up.

"Dr. Arsdale, it's Kate. I'm in the States, in New York. How is my father doing?"

"Ms. Adler, how nice to hear from you. Nothing much has changed, which means he is fine," the doctor said.

"I would like to see him today; will that be a problem?"

"Well, of course not, Kate. We all would like to see you."

"Can you have a car pick me up? I'm at the Grand Westland."

"Of course, Ms. Adler. It will be about an hour. Is that all right?"

"Perfect," she said.

"Excellent. Cory will be your driver, and he will call when he is downstairs."

CHAPTER—3

PRESIDENT'S DAILY BRIEFING — TUESDAY AM

Martin Perez, President of the United States
Dennis Corwen, Secretary of Defense
Royce Wakefield, Secretary of State
Dr. Stephen Devroe, Director of National Intelligence (DNI)

It was 7:30 in the morning as Dr. Devroe, Director of National Intelligence, approached the entrance to the Oval Office protected by its Marine guard and Mrs. Hayward, secretary to the most powerful man on earth.

"Good morning, Mrs. Hayward," he said.

"Is it, doctor?" she said with an expressionless face.

Devroe smiled. She always seemed to know more than she should and less than she admitted. She was the purest example of how much you make in this town, does not equate to how much power you have.

"Well," he mumbled, "I have to admit I have experienced mornings with greater promise."

"I would agree," she said, "it's a rather tense atmosphere except for the fact that the last time I was in there, they were talking about baseball."

"They?" he asked.

Ignoring his response, she pushed the intercom button, "Mr. President, Dr. Devroe is here."

"Send him in."

Devroe entered the Oval Office and found the Secretaries of State and Defense in attendance.

"Am I late?" he said.

"No," said Martin Perez.

The president followed with, "But you missed a highly technical and secretive discussion concerning last night's Nationals baseball game."

"You guys have time to watch a game?"

"Actually," the president said, "I was in my top-secret sports briefing before you got here." He shifted in his chair, indicating a change of subject. "I wanted State and DOD here this morning, given recent events. What do you have for us this morning, Stephen?"

"Unfortunately, I have more of the same today, Mr. President," he said, handing the president an iPad. Addressing Wakefield and Corwen, he said, "Sorry I wasn't expecting you, gentlemen. What you see is a report from the 5th Fleet of another hijacking. And to address the problem directly, no, we still don't have any intelligence indicating for certain who is behind the attacks."

The president silently frowned. "That's the second one in two weeks."

"Yes, this time it was the *Gran Prince*, and it's another hijacking under the noses of the coalition charged with deterring exactly those kinds of threats. These incidents are driving the markets crazy. As we well know, that waterway is one of the most important in the world, with 90 percent of Persian Gulf exports and 40 percent of global consumption flowing through daily."

Royce Wakefield, Secretary of State, added, "You don't need to attack; you only need to threaten to disrupt that much of the world's oil supply to declare economic war on the Western global economy. The price of oil could rise as much as ten dollars in a day, not to mention marine insurance rates and a cascade of other things."

"Where are the markets today?" the president asked.

Royce responded, "So far, down 7 percent, and they have only been open an hour. That's 28 percent in the last three weeks."

The president spoke. "The markets need something to hang their hat on, something that says there is an end to these incidents, giving us time to turn this around. Until then, we have a population that's at best uncertain and at worst completely terrified of losing their retirement accounts."

Devroe nodded. "After making visual contact, the *USS Chafee* followed the tanker to within twelve miles of the Iranian coast, but without a good reason, they couldn't get any closer without being the aggressor. As you know, twelve miles is the territorial limit in the Persian Gulf."

"That's the problem," the president said. "*They* are the aggressor. Common sense says the Iranians are hijacking tankers and allowing all the blame to fall on the Somalis, who could care less. The Somalis are not about to attack Iran to defend their honor. There isn't a damn thing we can do about it without being able to pin it directly on them.

"Stephen," the president's voice had acquired a more serious tone, "you're telling me that the best surveillance network in the world can't come up with a damn thing connecting Iran to the hijackings?"

Devroe responded, "Worse than that, we can't pick up anything at all about any part of the operation. They're completely silent. The only case we have against them is circumstantial, but only a moron wouldn't see the logical connections. We had a team go into Somalia and hire some locals to contact the pirates to see what the talk was on the ground. Most of the pirates weren't even aware of the hijackings. They said it was suicide to work in the Gulf."

"I'm sorry to say this," Wakefield said, "but I appreciate anything done well, and, if it's them, you have to give the Iranians credit. They have perfected the art of the indirect effect. Being able to get the effect they want without revealing the fact that they're responsible. If they looked harder for a better disruptive target than shipping right off their coast, they couldn't find one."

Dennis Corwen, Secretary of Defense, said, "The Iranians are saying they cannot control a ship that 'requests' harbor safety and, of course, denying any involvement."

Corwin showing his frustration, said, "Once they're safely in port, the Iranians then say the hijackers broke international law, and they must be imprisoned and face Iranian justice. Ironically, by prosecuting them 'in-country,' they claim they're assisting in policing the pirating problem and, with indignant arrogance, ask us to step up our efforts to prevent further attacks. The Iranian court held the hijackers, denying any request to interview them, saying it could affect the hijackers receiving a fair trial. It leaves us with no path to discredit the Somali hijacking story. When they finally release the ship's crew, they will have seen nothing but a ragtag group trying to board the tanker. That's because the hijackers make sure the crew is in the safe room when they board and the whole time until reaching port. Every ship so far has conveniently had a safe room. It's quite brilliant."

"So," the president sighed, "if we cannot take them out committing the act, then how do we stop them? We need to stop them."

Dennis, in his signature monotone delivery, said, "Unless we can catch a known member of the Iranian military on one of those ships, we are, I'm sorry to say, dead in the water."

"Or," Devroe followed, "produce an incriminating radio intercept. Unfortunately, there is absolutely no chatter, which means they're staying away from any electronic communications. We can only guess their objective is to keep us out of the Middle East so they can control that part of the world. We need the same kind of real evidence that we had in '88 when they mined the Strait of Hormuz. Short of that, we are without political and legal cover."

Wakefield broke in. "At State, we are perplexed at the regime's boldness, given their recent peaceful overtures—peaceful for the Iranians, anyway. The mullahs have made signs they want discussions on the original sanctions that came with the nuclear treaty. They might see the hijackings as creating a lever in those discussions. They're excellent negotiators, but they have always played the long game. This 'gun to your head' tactic has never been their style."

"Okay," the president said, "let's wrap this up. What now?"

Royce shook his head, "Well, Mr. President, if State pursues the traditional options of a strong public protest to the U.N., they will only deny involvement and point out our usual anti-Iranian agenda. As to the use of force, I think Dennis should address that."

Dennis looked down at the blue and gold carpet before saying, "Overtly or covertly, even SEAL Team Six needs a specific objective. Without political cover and a defined target to destroy, given their indirect approach, there is little the Pentagon can do."

Royce's voice sounded frustrated, "Well," he added, "we are certainly not going to violate their sovereignty publicly; it would eliminate any high ground we can claim internationally. That's playing right into their hands. I received a message from Ambassador Telling, who heads our Iranian special interests section at Tehran's Swiss embassy. He has gotten some signals that the mullahs are not in on this, and the Revolutionary Guard is creating its little personal war. I have to say, it seems an improbable scenario."

"What's his proof?" the president asked.

"Do you mean actual proof? He has none. All he has is some well-placed bar bills and whispers. The Revolutionary Guard was mainly in charge of the nuclear program, which, in their opinion, the clergy gave away with the nuclear treaty. They were not shy about showing their unhappiness with that result and their belief the theocracy has gone soft."

"The Guard tried the direct approach in 1988," Dennis said, "by mining the strait, and we kicked their ass. Back then, we could prove the mines were theirs as, incredibly, inside, they were marked 'Made in Iran.' They should have tried this indirect approach then, and the Revolutionary Guard would not have lost some vital ships. I don't see any other option besides hoping they make a mistake so we can strike them. Other than that, they're playing with bows and arrows, hiding in the shadows, and we only have nuclear bombs. You could call it a 'ghost war.'"

Before he even got the words out, the president's body said it all. "So, you're telling me we have an entire battle group in the Gulf of Aden and an unparalleled intelligence capability and cannot do a damn thing to stop this phony war they're waging? Are you telling me the markets are falling around the world, and we must sit here? In days it could be worse than the crash in '08 when we came close to a bank run."

"No, Mr. President," Devroe said, "we are merely pointing out that you've no political or legal cover to do anything. But we cannot *make* you sit there and do nothing."

"A fascinating distinction," the president said, "but I'm not sure it helps." Almost annoyed, he waved his hand in an unmistakable gesture meaning the meeting was over.

As the group stood and started to file out of the Oval Office, the president said, "Stephen, can you hang back for a second?"

"Of course, I can, Mr. President."

President Perez asked the last man filing out, "Dennis, could you get the door?"

"I will get it, Mr. President," Mrs. Hayward said, entering the room. "This envelope was inside a letter addressed to you. It says it's for your eyes only. I checked the return address, and it doesn't exist, at least not through a search. The toxic scan was clean, and it only contains opaque paper. Would you like me to open and log it?"

"Thank you, Harriet," Martin Perez said, reaching out for the envelope. "I know what it is, and it's personal and no need for the formality."

She handed the envelope to him, adding, "President Buhari is here for your meeting."

"Yes," he said. "Get me three minutes."

"Yes, Mr. President," she said and left the room, closing the door behind her.

Devroe and the president stood in front of the Kennedy desk. Perez was silent for a moment before saying, "What's your unvarnished opinion?"

"Like when we were drunk in college? No lies?"

"Give it to me, no lies."

"It's a goddamned disaster. The Iranians have us by the balls. They're creating an international crisis without taking the heat. There is no doubt that eventually we will find out the whole story, but the clock is ticking, and there isn't much time left. That's my sober opinion, and it scares the living hell out of me."

"Look, I have to meet with President Buhari. I can't postpone as I must keep to a regular schedule as every person in Africa knows about his visit to D.C. Go back to your office and double down on finding out anything you can about this operation. We'll talk later, so don't fill your evening."

CHAPTER—4

MEETING WITH FATHER—TUESDAY PM

Kate Adler sat in the back of the dark gray Bentley thinking about her life and her father. She pulled the vanity mirror up from the tray table, and as the lights came on, checked her face and hair. Why was it important? Father wouldn't care. Somehow, she did, and it was symptomatic of the problem. Kate always wanted to please him but couldn't in the ways that seemed to matter. He wasn't disappointed, and he said so, but she knew this was a little like his having wanted a boy. The expectation was enough to lay the groundwork for a lifetime of wanting to prove herself but in her way. They had been so close emotionally all her life, but they just seemed on opposite ends when it came to his interests and hers.

Father's business was his life's blood, and it encompassed areas and interests well beyond what she knew and wanted to know. All she had to do was show up at a board meeting, start asking questions, and that wall would drop in an instant. It all seemed preordained and out of her control. Now that she had just the slightest inkling of curiosity, it appeared to be too late, as his failing communication skills were now almost non-existent. If she were suddenly to become the person he wanted, his acknowledgment would be the primary motivating factor. It seemed now that important reward was out of her reach. Life is what it is, she thought, you're here, you affect—you die. She had avoided her father's corporate world and struck out on her own, seeking a purpose in her life. She craved an essential reason for her existence but could never figure out what path held the answer.

Cory, the driver, brought the car to a stop and patiently waited for the gates to open. They separated the general public from the Tudor-style mansion and the large circular drive surrounded by tall, mature trees that blocked the late sun this time of day. The gates opened, and Cory pulled the car up to the front entrance.

A stiff breeze blew leaves all over the area. A young man, alerted by the gate, opened her car door and said, "Hello, Miss Adler, coming to see your father today?"

"Yes, is he awake?"

"I believe so. If Dr. Arsdale knew you were coming, I'm sure he has worked it into the schedule."

Kate entered the familiar entry, complete with the memories it held. She placed her purse on the round table centered in the room that once held her collection of random things she found in the surrounding yard as a child. It now supported a massive arrangement of flowers. She heard the familiar click, click of her heels on the patterned marble floor. She proceeded down the hall, as always, toward her father's office. Jake, her father's nurse and orderly, joined her from a side room.

"Miss Adler, this is a surprise."

Kate gave him a sideward glance, a 'can't you remember' look with a frown.

"I'm sorry, I mean Kate," Jake said, grinning. "It's hard to break the habit."

"Or teach you new ones, apparently," she said playfully, hitting him on the arm.

They both continued toward the office.

"How is my father doing, Jake?"

"Oh, he is doing fine as long as we keep him calm. He has his schedule and lives mostly within it, except for constantly watching the news. Just because you can't remember most things doesn't mean you can't participate in the world. Dr. Arsdale said we need to keep him in a stress-free environment, but he will just turn on the news again. We are doing our best."

"I know, Jake. I have complete faith in you. It's tough when we get to this stage. Sometimes I don't know what to say."

"Don't refer to anything that will make his heart get excited, and we will be okay. Those are my orders. Recently, he seems to become clear and occasionally makes lucid comments. He is very different when it happens. His posture changes, his head is erect, and his speech pattern is different …" Jake paused. "Miss Adler, ah, he has been with me for four years now, and I know him pretty well—"

"What does he say?"

"He mentions something about a group. Sometimes he will ask for Avery, and then he is gone again. He says it's urgent, and sometimes he will repeat it several times and other times just once, and he is gone again."

"Thanks, Jake," she said. "I appreciate the personal interest you have in my father."

"It's all part of the job, but you're right. Your father is special to me, actually to all of the staff."

The orderly escorted Kate into the room her father occupied in the thirty-five-room house. It used to be his office, still filled with memorabilia from his business life. They hoped the items would trigger his memory. The coffered ceiling and wainscoted walls provided an old-world European atmosphere that her father held dear. As they entered the room, her father watched the news on a television mounted to a movable bracket on the wall. Transfixed by it, he didn't acknowledge their entering.

The television announcer said, "Western capitals and financial markets around the world were on edge today as reports surfaced of yet another hijacking in the Strait of Hormuz area just off the Iranian coast. Our own Scott Essen in Tehran has more details. Scott, what do you have for us?"

"Hi, Brent, some alarming news coming out of the Middle East today concerning yet another hijacking of an oil tanker. We cannot verify the exact location, but it's in the Gulf of Aden, possibly in the Strait of Hormuz. Some call it the chokepoint of the world's oil supply as a large portion of all oil delivered by ship from the Middle East must transit through the narrow passage. It would be the third hijacking in two weeks. Certainly, the bigger story, Brent, is the reaction of the world's financial markets to the threat to the oil supply. Both Germany and China have suspended trading, and the US exchanges are in full retreat. The SEC has indicated it will release information later tonight on whether trading will open tomorrow."

Kate caught herself paying attention to what the broadcasters were saying for a second. Her work's secluded nature, her recent travel schedule, and a general lack of interest had caused her to miss this particular story.

"Here in Tehran, Brent, it's relatively quiet with their news agency releasing a statement confirming the arrival of another tanker in its ports and specifically stating they were responding to the internationally recognized 'Request for Safe Harbor Provision.' Further to that, they pointed out that if the coalition cannot control the hijacking with their massive sea power, how can Iran be held responsible?"

The orderly lowered the TV's volume using the remote. "Mr. Adler," Jake said, "your daughter is here today to visit."

"Who?" her father asked.

"Your daughter, she will stay a while. Is that all right with you? I need to have your permission."

Mr. Adler looked at Kate and nodded hesitantly.

Kate looked at her father sitting in the bed with a stand supporting a table over his lap. He held a pencil and had drawing paper on the table. There were scribbled images that meant something to him, but left the regular world in the dark. It seemed that was what he was doing until his attention turned back to the news.

"What are you drawing, Dad?" Kate asked as she took a chair next to him.

He looked at her without answering. He put his pencil down. "What is your name?" he asked.

It always hurt. Every time they went through the same dance, some variation of Kate repeating her name and telling him she was his daughter. Then he would say he didn't know anyone by that name, but she could stay.

"How is your food?" she asked. "Jake says you still like spaetzle."

He looked at her kindly. "Have you been here before?"

"Yes, Dad, many times. Your memory has slipped a little."

"Is everything all right, Miss Adler?" Jake said before leaving the room.

Kate turned toward the door and said, "Yes, Jake, thank you." When she turned back to her father, he again became transfixed on the news.

"Thanks, Scott," the anchor said. "I have to interrupt as we are getting a State Department update. It's Darren Wilcox, the department's spokesperson. Let's listen in."

"Good evening, ladies and gentleman," Wilcox, standing at a podium in front of blue drapes, began. "I will get right to it. We are monitoring closely alarming reports that another hijacking has taken place off the shores of Iran. We are still collecting information about Somali pirates boarding a ship and heading for an Iranian port. This is probably because they don't believe they would make it through the Strait. We have chosen to wait until a clearer picture has emerged to make a formal statement. But we will request Iran, in accordance with international law, disallow these vessels access to their ports given their unlawful actions in international waters. The hijacking is a fast-moving story." Addressing the media in the room, he added, "I would suggest staying at your posts. Sorry, but that's all I have right now."

Kate picked up her father's water cup. "Would you like a sip, Dad?"

He continued to listen to the television without responding. Kate spent a lot of time thinking when she visited, time she would have preferred to spend hugging her father. Nevertheless, here he was, and his only reaction to her being here was emotionally reacting to the news. It's not like she completely ignored the world's problems or how they looked to be getting worse, spiraling out of hand. She wanted to do more, but working at Dad's company just seemed the wrong way to go about it. Who wanted to be the 'boss's kid' and put up with people dancing around your every move? Besides, she didn't see how she could help the world from a platform based on shipping and electronics when her goals were focused more on helping starving children.

When she was still in college, a man approached her and offered her a job. He turned out to be with the CIA; the agency had noticed her overall test scores and natural aptitude for mathematics. She ended up going through the CIA training, thinking she would be contributing to IT, but that was not the case. They indicated her 'farm' grades and language abilities directed her toward the field. She ended up in Denmark, eventually concluding that given the low-level assets she was monitoring, her job was the equivalent of babysitting. She suffered for two years before applying to the NSA for some genuinely challenging work utilizing her math skills. She thought being a "white hat" in network security was a way to ensure the right people were winning the information war. It was her best chance of stopping terror around the world. Again, it wasn't helping starving children, but it was a constantly challenging job.

"Dad, would you like to talk? Do you remember Mom?" she asked. She figured there was nothing to lose. Dr. Arsdale said that sometimes reflection would activate memories, as the real problem was short-term and not long-term memory, although it rarely worked.

Her father looked at her and said, "Mom? Your mom? Where is she?"

Her hopes rose as she at least got him away from the television.

"Do you see her often? Does she live close?" he went on.

Kate's hopes nosedived at the realization he was not talking about anyone he knows or knew. She touched his arm as he turned back on the television.

CHAPTER—5

POTUS TALKS TO DEVROE—TUESDAY PM

The president walked into his private residence and closed the door. The family was back in their hometown celebrating an engagement, so the large rooms with very high ceilings seemed a lot more empty than usual. The briefing this morning detailing the *Montclair* hijacking yesterday had set the tone for the entire day. That was the elephant in the room, and he had to do something, as doing nothing just wasn't an option.

He pulled off his coat and threw it on the sofa, and walked over to the bar cart. He poured his usual Canadian Scotch whiskey with a splash. Holding it, he looked through the bottom of the glass down to the silver tray. The drink acted as a filter, changing the color of the tray. Whatever you put into the glass would change the color of whatever you could view through its bottom, he thought. It seemed symbolic that whatever was in America's glass would color the world—and *he* held the glass. Raising the liquid to his lips, he tasted and smelled what signified the end of the day. Confidently, he walked over to the phone and called his friend Stephen Devroe.

"Hey, where are you?" he asked.

"I'm in the damn shower! I mean, Mr. President, I'm presently detained."

Martin laughed. "Well, get your ass over to the residence, pronto. I'll tell security to allow you upstairs. I'm in the Treaty Room."

"Right, be there ASAP. Are you hungry?"

"No, and neither are you."

"And how would you know that? Hello?" Stephen put the phone down feeling privileged: how many people in the world does the President of the United States hang up on?

* * *

Martin Perez was now in the Treaty Room in residence. He walked over and opened a lower cabinet door constructed to appear to be three sliding drawers. He entered a code and then placed two fingers against the lit panel. It scanned them, and the display turned green. He opened the door, reached inside, and withdrew a worn box. It contained a phone former President Kenneth Harper had given him. Other than his wife's jewelry, it was the only thing inside the safe. He put the phone on the table and sat down to read its instructions. Moments later, he thought it was a hell of a complicated way to place a secure phone call.

He went to the front door of the residence and said to one of the Secret Service agents standing guard, "Doctor Devroe is coming up. Can you let him in and tell downstairs to be expecting him?"

Downstairs Stephen flashed his creds to Andrew, the Secret Service agent standing in front of one of three elevators that accessed the residence.

"Andrew, how are you?"

"Fine, Dr. Devroe."

Devroe thought, Even the president's daughter would need identification if she tried to access the second floor. These guys are robots willing to die for what they do, but can't they at least have some personality?

"That's it?" Stephen said. "No 'how are you? How is the missus'?"

Without a smile, Andrew replied, "You're not married, Doctor."

"Well, Andrew, I guess that lets you off the hook, but I'm still reporting you for lack of humor." The door opened. "So, I'll be off then."

"Yes, Doctor."

He went upstairs, and an usher held the door as he entered the Treaty Room.

"Stephen, how nice you could make it to our important meeting. I hope I didn't keep you from anything important."

"You mean like dinner?"

"You can eat anytime."

"Martin, I have an important question. Have you ever gotten Andrew to show any emotion—ever?"

"Yes, when that Piper Cub flew into White House air space. He was quite animated."

"That doesn't count."

"Is that the same suit you had on today?"

"Yes, if you must know, but the body underneath is clean. You keep strange hours."

"There are no hours. Every president thinks he can come in and own it, but eventually, it owns you. Get a drink, and I suggest you sit down," Martin said.

"You're kidding?" Stephen said, walking over to the drinks cart.

"Not in the slightest, my man. You're going to remember this conversation for a long time."

The president started. "Did you uncover any new information regarding the recent hijacking?

After shaking his head, it hung low in defeat. "I'm sorry Martin, it's a complete black hole. We have not gotten a sniff, and we can't explain it."

"The last few days have not been the more enjoyable of my presidency. The Iranians have created a situation that dictates our having to play by new rules. Do you remember when President Harper tried to stop North Korea from supplying Syria with weapons-grade uranium? State had already applied every sanction we had available, and our protest in the U.N. was pissing in the wind. Other than sink the ship, there were few options."

"Sure, I remember, but I never heard how that came down. When you gave me this job, I was overwhelmed and didn't have time to look into it."

Perez set his glass down under a lamp. "Connecting a couple of dots and going around you, I called Dan Tilde directly over at CIA and asked about the incident. He said there wasn't any direct or indirect involvement by the CIA. He insisted it wasn't our operation on any level."

"So it had to be us but wasn't?"

"Right you are," Perez said. "So how did Harper make that happen with his hands tied, much like ours?"

Devroe's eyebrows went up, creasing his forehead. "Magic?"

"Late one night, after work, I invited Harper over for a very private drink."

"Your days actually end?" Devroe said. "That's a surprise."

"Remember in Tuesday's meeting you said there were absolutely no digital-signals intelligence and thus no warning? Well, that's unprecedented. I think you will agree.

"So, based on that, and the fact I was sure that wasn't the last hijacking, I had nothing to lose by arranging a meeting with Harper to see if he had any advice. His initial reaction was very evasive. He talked around the situation and agreed that it was unprecedented. He was so busy dancing around in circles I knew something had to be in the middle, so I pressed him. 'What are you not telling me?' I asked, 'I need something other than the normal beltway crap that won't get us anywhere.' He reiterated the North Korean story about the ship headed for Syria with a load of uranium. It eventually turned back, and right after, the Israelis bombed a Syrian nuclear reactor in the desert. There was nothing new there, but then he let out the secret: The operation was in cooperation with Israel and a shadowy organization without a name. 'Some,' he said, 'referred to it as the Cartel.' I said I had never heard of it. He indicated that was because their desire to remain secret was somewhere beyond paranoid."

"That could describe a lot of organizations. Who are they exactly?" Devroe said.

"I don't know. Harper insisted their agenda played a part in his foreign policy efforts but wouldn't divulge the extent."

"It's a good thing I'm sitting down," Devroe said. "Thanks for the warning. Did you say agenda?"

"He described them as a group who addresses issues that normal law abiding countries, like ourselves, find problematic for one reason or another."

"Problematic?"

"According to Harper, problems that can't be addressed because of treaty obligations or just plain political correctness."

"Not sure what you mean. The U.N. does the same thing with a massive budget but doesn't seem to be able to reshape events on the ground," Devroe said.

"Perhaps it's because they lack the singular focus the Cartel possesses. A group of billionaires who have chosen the Cartel as their philanthropic vehicle provides ample funding. As a result, it seems they have a tactical element they can employ."

"Is that PC for guns?"

"Yes, they have been known to address what they see as problems kinetically, but in general, they have a more deft hand. However, my friend, as head of a billion-dollar agency, you're not going to like this. There was a time when it cost billions getting supplies to the space station through NASA; then private companies did the same thing for millions. Harper indicated that, without any government infighting, oversight, regulations, and the need for constant change, this organization developed a data and communication-surveillance system on an unprecedented scale. Well-funded and able to focus, uninterrupted, on a single task, they were able to do it on an accelerated timetable and a commercial—not governmental-size budget."

Devroe put his glass down. "Now, this is getting scary. If I had not heard it in this room, I wouldn't believe it. If this Cartel thing existed, if this surveillance capability existed, it would have some visibility in our systems."

"I will take your word for it as soon as you provide some proof. Harper said the group consisted of *very* powerful people who banded together to promote their agenda, and in doing so didn't exactly play by the Geneva Conventions.

"I have to tell you, Harper was not at all comfortable talking on this subject. When he was out of options, he enlisted their help in dealing with North Korea. Specifically, Kim's group of leadership cronies who benefit most from the kleptocracy rampant in the regime. This Cartel group made it known they could touch each of them directly and threatened to freeze their bank accounts in the West. It seems the leaders vehemently denied any accounts existed, then, in typical North Korean bluster, threatened them and called the groups bluff. According to Harper, in less than an hour, two of the leaders' bank accounts weren't just frozen but completely disappeared. The group then said one more account would cease to exist every six hours the ship remained on course."

"Fantastic, I love it," Devroe said. "It's like a spy movie. But how in the hell were they able to pull it off?"

"As Harper said, they don't exactly play by the rules. The operation involved their technical abilities. However, does it matter? In four hours, the ship came to a halt in the water. In another two hours, we detected it was turning around called back to a North Korean port. Shortly after that, the Israelis bombed a reactor in the Syrian Desert. The Syrians said they bombed open desert. The Israelis said they destroyed a reactor. Then the story just went away."

Devroe's face didn't look happy. "To answer your question, it *does* matter. We can't have this kind of power, just able to enforce their will through dubious channels. We could be the next target. It's our job to make sure the country is safe from just this kind of influence."

"For the moment, I agree with you. However, does an organization that helped a president to curtail a rogue nation's proliferation of nuclear materials sound like the bad guys?"

"I get it," Devroe said, "but stranger things have occurred."

CHAPTER—6

KATE'S LIFE CHANGES

Kate looked at her father lying on the bed, seeing the man of her youth, not the frail, distracted person before her. Kate, looking at the wilted figure wired like a robot to various electronic boxes, felt sad and powerless. It contrasted sharply with her memories of a giant in the corporate world after they escaped from East Germany. When she was a child, he would take her along as he traveled the world. She met heads of state, as well as business and political contacts.

He was all she had as her mother had suddenly disappeared the day before the family's planned escape from behind the wall in East Germany. Her father believed a last-minute change in his schedule had avoided a similar arrest attempt on him the same day. Father and daughter narrowly escaped to the West the next day before the Stasi, the East German secret police, could foil their plans.

Since then, the burden of Kate's mother's death weighed heavily on his shoulders. The incident moved him to dedicate his life to reducing the effect governments had on ordinary people. As close as they were, there were certain things he didn't share.

After establishing shipping and transportation businesses in Europe, they came to the States. They settled in San Francisco, and Father threw himself into becoming a success in the electronics industry, creating Adler Electronics. Unlike similar businesses, he was able to retain controlling shares in a company worth billions. Considered a trusted asset by more than one high-ranking official and by two presidents, her father loved his adopted country. Later, they moved to New York, where he set up the now formidable enterprise's headquarters.

Kate had always held ceremonial director's positions in all of Dad's companies. She received all the minutes and reports ignoring them all. Upon his diagnosis, the businesses moved into a trust managed by Avery Stanton, a longtime friend and his closest business associate. Avery had been active being in charge of the organization for three years now. He made it clear she could take over the organization at any time, but she was happy to leave it to Avery.

Kate felt the warmth as she grabbed her father's hand. She looked out the window at the expanse of lawn and gardens and the shadows from the trees. The huge house was old and had been home during some of the most wonderful years of her life. The wooden floors creaked, it was always cold, and the pine trees dropped their needles, making a mess. Nevertheless, she thought, you could go home again, and here she was. She looked at her father lying on the bed surrounded by the displays and beeps. It seemed so ironic that electronics still played an essential role in his life.

"No," Mr. Adler shouted, bothered by something.

The sound startled her. "Dad," she said, "would you like to go outside in the sun? It will help you relax. This television is not good for you."

He made several noises and pointed at the screen.

"Dad, did you hear me?" She was worried and pushed the button beside the bed that summoned Dr. Arsdale.

Her father quickly turned onto his side and went up on one elbow. "Jake!" he yelled.

Kate made note that he knew Jake's name and had forgotten hers a long time ago.

Her father leaned toward Kate and made direct eye contact with his daughter. It startled her, as he always seemed to be somewhere else during her visits.

"Bunny?" he said clearly and softly. She pulled her head back at the sound. Her eyes filled as she heard and saw the man in her memories.

"Daddy?" she said, grabbing his hand.

Her father looked at the TV screen and then back at her, squeezing her hand tightly, and said, "You can't let them get away. Everyone suffers. It was all for you, all of it. I did it for you. Make

43

peace with it and make a difference. Only you can keep those in the castle together, and they must continue the work."

"Daddy, who are they? What do you mean? Who, how can I help …?"

"Tell me," he said, "promise."

Kate felt his grip start to fade. "Yes, Daddy, yes, what do you want me to do?"

A loud alarm sounded in the distance and then another. Kate's father collapsed, exhaling an ominous sound. Standing, she tried to roll him from his side to his back. She heard footsteps.

"Daddy," she cried. "Daddy, no, no."

Then it hit her like a wall. "Daddy!" she screamed, bringing the back of her hand to her face.

"Help me!" she shouted into the air.

Dr. Arsdale and a nurse ran into the room. They came up alongside Kate, immediately lowering the bed to the flat position.

"Kate?" Dr. Arsdale said. "Kate, I need you to move."

She felt Dr. Arsdale nudge her over, and she reluctantly gave him the space he needed.

He raised Mr. Adler's eyelids and flashed a penlight into his eyes. "It's slow, but it's there. He's not breathing."

He pulled her father closer to him, adjusted his airway, and started CPR.

"Start the BVM; he's Agonal," the doctor said. The nurse reached behind her and grabbed a bag ventilator mask. She attached it to oxygen, inserted the ventilator tube, placed it over Mr. Adler's nose and mouth, and started squeezing the bag.

"Jake," Dr. Arsdale called loudly.

Jake ran into the room, holding a cellphone up to his ear, and saying, "Already on it."

Kate was crying profusely, alarms were blaring, and the room was moving. She reached in, trying to touch his arm but had to settle for a fistful of his robe.

Jake said, "This is the Adler residence on Woodland Avenue. I'm declaring a cardiac emergency. Please send help immediately."

Jake rushed to Kate's side. "We are going to take care of him. An ambulance station is only a half-mile away."

Kate didn't hear what he was saying. The room now started to disappear. Bending over, she grabbed the low railing on the bed in front of her as she began to fall. Jake placed an arm around her waist and moved her to a chair before she completely lost her balance. Trying to focus on the array of alarms and lights, she could make out the monitor lines. Concentrating on them, she made a valiant effort to will them off their current mark, to no avail.

Dr. Arsdale looked up at the ICU monitor. "Get the crash cart," he instructed. "Two hundred joules."

The nurse holding the mask looked up at Kate and said, "Hold this."

"It's all right, Ms. Adler, I've got it," Jake said, touching her shoulder, keeping her in the chair.

"One-milligram epinephrine IV push," the doctor said.

The nurse moved the cart toward the bed while opening the top drawer for the medicine. After filling the needle, she inserted it into the drip. Now beside the bed, she set the levels on the touch screen. The device started making a sound that gradually increased to a steady tone as it reached the prescribed level. "Two hundred joules, ready to deliver, doctor."

"Ten more compressions," the doctor said, applying pressure to Mr. Adler's chest.

"Okay," Dr. Arsdale pulled open Mr. Adler's robe, reached for the paddles provided by the nurse, and said, "Ready?"

He looked up at Kate and said, "Stand back, please. Clear." Her father heaved on the bed.

Dr. Arsdale looked up at the monitor and waited a few seconds. He handed the paddles to the nurse and started CPR again.

"Come on, Helmut, you can do it. We have a color change," the doctor said. The defibrillator was recharging; the ICU monitor kept up its shouting and, after a few seconds, he said, "Let's try again. Clear."

Again, the voltage surged through her father's body. Again, the doctor waited a few seconds and, with no change, restarted CPR. Dr. Arsdale could feel his muscles objecting to the physical exertion as he repeatedly pressed on Mr. Adler's chest. He paused, looking up again at the monitor.

"One, two, three, four," the doctor started again on his way to thirty. They waited, all looking at the lines that Kate couldn't move. With her eyes flooded and face streaked with tears, she moved closer to the bed, staring at Dr. Arsdale for signs of hope.

He stopped the CPR and again flashed a light into Mr. Adler's eyes. He paused for a second before closing the man's eyelids. He shook his head and said, "I'm so sorry, Kate."

"Doctor?" the nurse quietly said.

"I'm declaring it at 2:48 p.m.," he said.

Kate put her hand on her father's forehead. The nurse turned off the alarms, and the room fell into a deathly quiet. Kate placed her head on her father's chest, crying.

"Daddy, I love you. Bunny loves you," she said.

CHAPTER—7

DEVROE MAKES THE CALL

Devroe had just listened to the unlikely story of an organization that could do what the lone superpower in the world could not. He was more than skeptical. "Wait, Martin, are you suggesting we contact these Cartel people?"

"Not exactly," Martin replied. "However, given the third hijacking and the imminent possibility of a fourth, I *am* asking if you have any better ideas."

"Well, even if we could go in guns a blazing, we can't prove we know who to shoot." Devroe enacted several signs of frustrating body language. "I would say no, I don't have any better ideas. But contacting a third party and telling them that the most powerful country on the planet is powerless and needs help doesn't quite strike me as the answer, either."

The president was silent for a moment; he looked at his friend who was experiencing the same annoying dissatisfaction that had filled his thoughts the last two days. Indeed, just punching the schoolyard bully on the nose would be the most gratifying. But they were not on a schoolyard. "My friend, I recognize the power of the presidency. Especially *this* presidency. However, there is often a great disparity between having power and being able to use it indiscriminately. Power always comes with the need to act within acceptable patterns of behavior."

The president, having stated his position, got up and walked over to his desk. He opened an envelope and unfolded its letter.

The side opposite the foil contained numbers, letters, symbols, and a request code.

He held up the piece of paper, saying, "Harper finally came clean with the details, and I followed his detailed instructions. I sent what he called a 'request for contact' letter to some P.O. Box in Denmark. He told me I would receive an access number for a unique encrypted phone. Harper came back later and dropped off a device he said was a phone."

"Martin, listen to yourself. We have a world crisis, and you write a letter to a P.O. Box in Denmark. Really? Is that how you contact them? By letter, through the US Post Office? There is something here that doesn't sound completely kosher."

"No, I'm not kidding, and as Harper said, they're beyond hyper about security, hence the unconventional approach. They won't accept anonymous open communication with their organization. Once the introduction is made, accepted, and verified, they access a private network using the phone to maintain contact. Harper said their internal network was off-the-charts secure. We haven't tried to crack it or don't want to."

"What the ... Martin, I'm the director of National Intelligence, which is over the CIA, the NSA, and Homeland Security. How can I not know about this? On top of that, I know we have cracked anybody and everybody to a certain extent."

"The explanation I got from Harper was they're below the radar and not considered a security threat, or we tried without success, or didn't try. I never got a straight answer." He held the paper up again and said, "Isn't it interesting that in this electronic world of ours, the most secure manner of communication is the written letter?"

"Martin, Jesus Christ, you're going forward with this, aren't you?"

"As you said so prophetically, Doctor, no one can make me sit here and do nothing."

"I knew the minute it came out I would regret saying it."

The president was silent again. "Look, Stephen, I don't see we have many choices or much to lose if we get them involved. The reality is they don't need our permission to get involved; I would not be surprised if they were on this already. They can't make it worse, and if they're found out, we deny our involvement. If you and your departments can't tap into their communication, then there is no record of our having contacted them."

"You will forgive me if I say the jury is out on that claim."

"So, after careful consideration of the options—basically none—I've decided to make that call. Well, in truth, I've decided *you* should make that call, off the record—*way* off the record. Am I clear here? You will report only to me, but if it gets out, you're on your own. I can't offer any cover. There is no way I would ask you to do this if it wasn't so damned important. Do you understand what I'm saying?"

"Yes, you don't need to explain," Devroe smiled. "Remember, I'm a valuable, trustworthy, and reliable member of your administration."

"Yes, when you're sober."

Devroe laughed. "Ah, yes, those were the days. It's different now. I wish I had the time to get sloshed once in a while now." Devroe looked at the president; they had come a long way. The man had the gift of understanding people and what's important to them. His part of the package was organizational. The primary reason they had won the election was that they had a better organization, and he had worked his ass off to build it.

"In fact, Mr. President, it wouldn't be the first time you threw me under the bus. Remember, the time I had to take the fall for the flag heist all because you couldn't have a ding on your future 'presidential' record?"

Martin lifted his arms and looked around the room. "Did we make the right decision or what?"

"Give me a break. When do we make the call?"

"Now," Martin said as he walked over and picked up the box with the phone and held it up. "Harper told me he had complete confidence in this device and the people behind it. He said many were fellow 'Bonesmen' from Yale."

"Oh, and I guess that makes everything just fine. What am I going to say? Actually, who am I going to talk to?"

"You're going to talk to the contact desk, wherever that is. It seems the code ID will convey who you are representing."

"And ..." Devroe said.

"Bring up the hijackings. The first thing we want to know is if it's on their radar. Do they know any more than we do? After that, outline our position about our believing it's the Iranians. However, without proof, we cannot act. Indicate we will offer any assistance we can within our limits and even if we had to push our limits. I must approve any aid we extend. If we decide to take any action on our side, we must present the concept properly in the event it hits the light of day."

"What then?"

"I'm not sure."

The president picked up the phone that was about half the original Motorola Series brick phone size. "It certainly wasn't designed as a consumer product, that's for sure. It looks like you could throw it off a ten-story building. Harper told me it utilizes their private network based on 256k key size, and the network behind it will encode and decode in real-time."

"No way." Devroe's voice had a hint of "yours is bigger than mine." He went on. "Nothing that small can chunk that much code. You're talking about needing clustered IBM Blade Servers. If, in reality, it did that, it would heat the entire room."

The president smiled, "I love it when you talk dirty. I detected that deep-down, Harper is a geek waiting to come out, and he was more than excited about their communication security. However, it is not exactly user-friendly." Martin turned the phone on, and its large screen lit up. It paused for a few seconds without any further attention and then produced a series of numbers that rolled up the screen, pausing after every fifty rows or so with a "Please Wait" on the screen.

The president looked at the screen as a logo came up, indicating a connection directly into the private network. "Harper said it was NSA-proof due to using a private protocol that existed in a part of the internet not indexed by search engines known as the dark web." With a smile, knowing he was going to rile up his friend, the president said, "Harper, almost with joy, indicated it was so secure even NSA couldn't trace it or monitor its transmissions."

"Now it's you talking dirty, but it's still bullshit. Was Harper drinking at the time? Oh, yes, you said he was, and, in my opinion, that lays waste to his credibility. How does it make the wireless connection?"

The president responded, "I have no idea. If you don't mind, I will do this. The fewer people that know this number, the better."

Typing on the keypad, the president entered the character sequence he had received in the letter, then hit enter. A full-color "G9" logo appeared on the screen with a progress bar. The logo disappeared, and two buttons appeared on the small touch screen, one labeled "Text" and the other "Voice." He selected text and typed TANGENT DAY >REPLY REQUEST ^7R800KV5.

"We need to wait for a callback. Stephen, can I get you something?" the president asked.

"Yes, you can get me something for my stomach. I'm pretty good in a stressful situation except when I'm hungry."

"That's a change. If I recall, you had a cast-iron gut in college."

"I had a lot of things in college, like more hair, personal time, and a life."

"Are you seeing anyone? What's your love life like?" the president asked.

"My love life? I have regressed to the point I have a heart attack when I kiss a woman."

"Pity, you were always the go-to guy in the dorm for lonely women."

The phone lit up and buzzed. The president picked it up, and the touch screen provided two buttons labeled "Voice" and "Disconnect."

He handed the phone to Devroe, saying, "Just do the best you can. Is there a speaker button?" Devroe selected "talk" on the screen and then touched "speaker" on the row of buttons below.

The voice on the other end just said, "Front desk, please place your thumb finger on the square provided."

Stephen pulled the phone from his ear, eyed the screen, and, sure enough, there was a square. He pressed his thumb on it, and, in a second, the square lit up.

"Thank you," the voice said.

"Yes, my name is Stephen Devroe, and I would like to talk to a principal."

"Of course. There will be a transfer and a tone," the voice said.

Devroe said into the phone, "What if we get cut off?"

"We won't," the voice said confidently. The agent phoned the principal on duty and connected the call.

"Hello," a voice said, "am I to understand this is the president's requested call? We have been waiting for it to come through."

Devroe listened to the man, who had a thick British accent. "Yes, I'm representing the president on this phone call. I'm the ..."

"Mr. Devroe, no introduction is necessary."

"What?"

"Dr. Stephen Austin Devroe, forty-one years old, born in Salem, Oregon. Attended ..."

"Okay, I get it," Devroe said. "Look, I'm not sure who you are, but ..."

"Mr. Devroe, for future reference, I'm Agent 2116, and you can contact me on this number any time it's important. This conversation is being recorded and is available only to the steering committee."

"Thank you. At least that's more than I had at the beginning of the call." Devroe looked at Martin. "This call is to address a dire situation developing in the Middle East. We are positive the Iranians are behind a series of hijackings but cannot prove it. You are aware, I'm sure, the state of the world markets and the potential for disaster. Not only is there not enough time for sanctions to take effect, but a more direct military strike also requires proof we do not currently have. The president has asked me to make contact to obtain any other information and to extend our offer of assistance should it be appropriate. The president wants you to know that he will provide any help within his authority and political cover. Do not hesitate to ask as we will consider all requests and do what we can." Devroe looked at Perez and added, "However, I must emphasize this phone call did not occur should it come to light. Sorry, but that's how it has to be."

"We understand completely. Such is the situation on our side. We also believe it's the Iranians and have detected an anonymous intrusion into our system but haven't traced the source. Earlier, we picked up fragmented information from a source on the ground of a possible move on the world's economies by creating panic. Still, we didn't pick up any tactical information. We believe the hijackings could be part of that plan."

The agent continued, "This has become a top priority as our interests, as well as yours, have been threatened. There are, at this point, no definite plans in place on our side. Shortly a meeting will address the situation."

Devroe interrupted. "We would like to be in the decision-making process."

There was a noticeable pause in the cadence of the conversation. "Mr. Devroe, I must be clear. We welcome your offer of assistance, but any decisions regarding any action, if required, are made by the Cartel's chair and the steering committee. The result will stand on its own, not affected by any outside influence. This format is essential if we are to maintain our independence and still cooperate."

Devroe, taken aback by the comment, looked at the president, who smiled at the rebuff. Martin nodding in agreement.

"Dr. Devroe, are these acceptable terms on which we can move forward?"

"Yes, these are acceptable terms, and we greatly anticipate moving forward." Devroe gave Perez a look that said, what's this?

The agent continued, "Marvelous, what conclusions have you come to on your side?"

"Well, as I said, we believe it's Iran, but they have been cautious not to use electronic communication. Our contacts with allied governments confirmed they also have failed to uncover any connection. Without proof it's them, we lack a legal base for recourse."

"Well," the agent said, "you seem to have summarized it nicely. As I said, we are at the front end of this with a meeting scheduled in a matter of hours to determine a course of action. Please check this phone for text messages that will only refer to scheduling future calls. Your character sequence is the only way to activate the phone, and please keep it safe. I know, given the size of the phone, it's not easy but important. It's challenging to reduce the size due to the amount of computing power we need to encipher the signal to make it undetectable."

The president saw his friend's face wince with the term undetectable. "No problem. Can I get in contact if needed?"

"You can contact an authority on this side at any time. All other agents will be fully informed. We feel this could be very serious. After the meeting, we will share what we can. Goodnight to you, Mr. Devroe."

Devroe selected "disconnect" and looked up at the president. "'We will share what we can?'" he said. "What the hell does that mean?"

"I guess it means what it means. We are not the lead on this. This Cartel may or may not need our help. Also, I think they're not going to tell us anything that would place us in the position where we would need to react to or condemn their plans. It's obvious this is not their first rodeo."

CHAPTER—8

IRANIAN REVOLUTIONARY GUARD CORPS

Sunday

Major General Vahid Khiabani, Commander in Chief of the Iranian Revolutionary Guard Corps (IRGC), and his inner circle met secretly in the secure situation room, waiting for news of the latest hijacking. The guard station outside rang the access line. Vahid hit the speaker button. "Khiabani here. What do you want?"

"Major General," the guard at the station said, "we have a Quds Lieutenant Abedini with a message for Admiral Shahbazi. His papers are in order."

Khiabani looked up at the group and asked, "Do we know him?"

Admiral Shahbazi replied, "Yes, he is one of mine." The admiral stepped closer to the telephone and said, "Let him in."

Shortly there was a knock, and the internal guard opened the door.

A Quds lieutenant stepped into the room, stood rigid, and said, "Message for Admiral Shahbazi." He handed it out with a stiff arm, spun on his heel, and went back out the door. The admiral stepped forward, unfolding the open paper. He looked up at Khiabani with a smile.

"The *Montclair Star* is within our territorial waters and has requested shelter. The *USS Connolly* shadowed the tanker, stopping twelve miles offshore. There were no casualties. The latest hijacking went exactly as planned. Another successful step in our A'rafat faRdā (Blessing Tomorrow) operation."

Everyone in the room cheered but Khiabani. He did not see the step-by-step sequence that the others did. His was an all-or-nothing effort to save his country from the corrupted path on which its leaders had placed it. Their complacency and acquiescence to the Great Satan brought shame to those who fought in the revolution. From the very beginning, the Guards protected the roots of the revolution and the theocratic government itself. The clergy sold its soul to the West in any number of ways to insinuate themselves into the Western economy. All while trying to maintain their form of Islam. Attempting this was heresy, as the two were beyond incompatible. Their path demanded concessions once thought unthinkable. The revolution required sacrifices from everyone, making it pure and of the people. Now a small cadre of very capable revolutionaries had banded together under the leadership of Khiabani. They intend to bring their country back to the untainted clarity the rebellion promised. He pressed hard, putting his cigarette out, holding it down for an extra second.

"What about the 'detained hijackers'?" Khiabani asked forcefully.

"All procedures are the same as last time. The *Montclair*'s crew cannot identify our Special Forces who boarded the vessel as anything other than pirates. When they reach the port, and before they dock, we replace our Special Forces team with handpicked agents posing as the pirates. They're taken to a special section of the prison with comfortable accommodations. The *Montclair*'s crew will then be released from the safe room, having seen nothing. This way, we can claim we arrested the pirates. We also say they cannot be released or interviewed, as they must receive, as the Americans say, a fair trial through our justice system. Later, the verdict will be secret, as the crew is released with a 'pardon' and compensated. Our lawyers will question the original crew looking for any details that might lead to their knowing the boarding party's nationality. After the questioning, the original crew is free to go. The ship kept as evidence in the trial of the 'pirates.'"

"What do the Special Forces replacements know of the story?"

"Nothing, I can assure you they know nothing. They're soldiers following orders, knowing their stay will be short and the rewards will change their families' lives."

"Who was that with the message?" Vahid asked.

"He is Quds, sir. I will swear for him. He is my courier."

Vahid glared at the Admiral. "What does he know?"

"Nothing, absolutely nothing, he believes this meeting is normal and nothing out of the ordinary. The sealed message is from our contact in Asuluyeh, who is also one of us."

Khiabani looked around the room. "We are taking the precaution of not using any electronic methods of communication. Do I have to remind everyone that if one piece of the wrong information gets out before we complete our task, we die? Do you all understand—dead? Worse, we will have failed, and our beloved country veers off into collaboration with our sworn enemies."

The room grew tense even though those in the room knew of Khiabani's direct tone. In the last few years, he had grown into a man to be feared. Khiabani had always been a hardliner, to the extent that executions under his command rose to troubling levels until current plans dictated a lower, less controversial profile. Some of those gathered believed in the general's cause. Others feared to displease the man known as 'the sword.' Rumor had it that, in a rage, he executed one of his commanders for incompetence during the Iraq War using a sword. He then personally pulled the man's body into the desert to die. Returning to his troops with bloody hands, he grabbed the lapels of the next officer in charge. Standing face-to-face, he shouted, "You are in charge," and, pointing to the desert, added, "Don't fail."

Khiabani got to business. "Do we have our next target?"

"Yes, sir," the Admiral responded.

Moving over to a separate table in the office, Khiabani said. "Good, then let's see what you have."

CHAPTER—9

FATHER'S MEMORIAL

Kate had spent the last two days wandering around in a fog similar in opaqueness to what enveloped the Golden Gate Bridge every evening during part of her childhood. In the preliminary reading of the will, everyone learned her father had dictated no memorial service and almost immediate cremation. Avery Stanton stood by her side as they stood before the urn in the softly lit chapel. Music came from somewhere, floating over everything like a damp blanket. She asked them to turn it off.

Without looking at Avery, Kate said, "I can't believe we didn't have a memorial or funeral service. There are so many people in the valley and here who will feel slighted they didn't get a chance to say goodbye."

"I'm sorry," Avery said. "It's what he wanted. No one was to participate except you and me. Memorial gifts to his charities will be substantial, and that's what he would have wanted."

Kate was upset in a way. "You mean that's it? He's gone and nothing?"

"There was no changing his mind. He wanted no undue attention brought his way. He wanted his work to be his legacy. Next to you, it was the most important part of his life. The funeral home will keep the ashes until we can come back and distribute them as he wished."

"It just doesn't seem to be enough," she said. "Not for someone like my father."

Kate had accompanied Avery as he took care of the details per her father's wishes. She stood in all the right places and said the right things, but nothing cut through the fact that her father was gone. Kate floated in and out of reality, trying to grasp living without the core force that had dominated her life, the single rock she had always depended upon for everything. Even in the last year, there was a comfort in knowing she could see him whenever she wanted. Now he was gone. Life must now be lived without the lifeline that brought her comfort and made her who she was. Her world would never be the same.

Avery asked, "How are you holding up?

"Avery, you've been a godsend. I can't thank you enough."

"Well," Avery said, "regardless of how much I might have done, it would never be enough. Your father was my friend. It wasn't all for you, you know."

"I know, just the same."

Avery opened the door to the limo and, when they got inside, he brought his coat together. It was a sign the topic was going to change.

"When we get back to the city, we need to go over some things, but we needn't bother with them now. Due to events, there is a board meeting scheduled for late tomorrow morning. I'll get you the details later, but it's essential you attend. Kate, are you listening?"

"Yes," she said, still looking out the window. When they arrived at her hotel, they had dinner. In some ways, it was a good thing. Avery tried to bring up some of the lighter memories and was great at making her not feel alone. He was as close to a second father as any other human could be, and she appreciated him dearly. They said goodbye in the lobby.

Walking away, Avery turned and said, "The meeting is at eleven tomorrow morning. I will have a car outside waiting at ten-thirty to take you there."

She smiled, "Avery, you've been terrific. I want to thank you again for everything."

Avery studied her expression and noted her tone of voice. "That sounded like a daughter who just said, 'Dad, I'm going to the library—honest.' What does that mean?"

"It means there is a crucial meeting tomorrow at eleven and you will send a car for me." She stepped forward and gave him a customary hug and an affectionate peck on the cheek. She watched him walk out the door and into the city. She needed to escape and began by looking around the lobby until she located the lounge. Wading through the lobby traffic, she made her way to a seat at the bar. After setting her purse down, she spoke to the bartender standing in front of her: "Vodka martini, perfect, and a twist."

"Shaken?" he said.

"Just up would be fine. Thank you."

It was late, and there were only a few people still hanging around. She sat there in a black skirt and white blouse with black accents. She liked how she felt when she wore them. Gazing at the colored bottles and mindlessly playing with her napkin, her thoughts wandered to nowhere in particular. She was adamant about not being pressured into Avery's or the corporation's agenda; it was just too early. Avery was more than capable of managing the companies, and they didn't need any input from her. Besides, they were all very accomplished people. They would figure out a way to continue the transition that had been in effect the last three years or so. Besides, back at work, she had her hands full trying to catch people intent on doing harm. It took a certain amount of smarts and she was proud to be one of the best. Sitting in the corner office of a corporation reading balance sheets and hearing complaints about HR just wasn't her cup of tea or her cup of anything.

A man dressed in the required Manhattan Italian suit left a table against the back wall where several guests sat and stopped at the bar a couple of feet away from Kate. Addressing the bartender, he said, "Kevin, can I get another round, and can you go light on the gin for Linda's gin and tonic." He looked back at the table as he spoke.

"Again?" The bartender smiled. "No, problem, but it will be the same price unless you get your friend in the blue blouse to come over here so she can meet a real man," he added light-heartedly.

"Kevin," the man said, "what I like about you are your sense of humor and misdirected self-confidence. You *do* know being young doesn't solve everything."

"It solves enough," the bartender said with a broad grin.

The man turned toward Kate and, leaning on an elbow, said in a soft voice, "Let me guess: sunsets, palm trees, and distant horizons?"

Kevin placed the martini in front of Kate, and she said, "Sunsets?"

"Yes, you are a million miles from here, and I was just hoping you had landed in a nice place."

"Was it that obvious? I usually try to hide my penchant for disconnecting."

"Hide? I would call it a rather important skill. Want to talk to a disinterested party about the reason for your disconnecting?"

"Not really. Those things are generally pretty personal."

"Of course, they are. That's the reason for a disinterested party."

Kate looked at the man without showing any interest or offering a smile at a line that deserved one. "What about your friends?" she nodded toward the table.

He looked over. "A rather loose use of the term, if you knew them."

Kate gave in and laughed, then took a healthy sip of her drink. "Okay, you made me laugh, and I will play nice. What do you do for a living?"

"I own a monkey circus. It's the only one on Wall Street."

Kate laughed again, only harder. "That felt good," she said.

He removed the napkin from under his drink and turned his glass several times on the bar. "So I take it the sunset was because you are down—it's a start."

The bartender, hearing the start of a conversation and sensing an opportunity, said, "Dave, you want me to take these over?"

"Yes, and I'm sure you won't mind, will you, Kevin? Thanks."

"Nope, not a bit," Kevin said, eyes on target.

Kate tilted her glass up, purposely not looking at the well-dressed and well-mannered man next to her. She then contemplated the situation and a comfortable start to a conversation. Putting the now-empty glass down, she said, "What's your name?"

"I'm glad you asked. Dr. Freud, with an F."

He was interesting and not into himself. It was a pleasant deviation from the average, run-of-the-mill man on the make. For just a second, she had escaped and was wondering if she wanted it to continue, but her plans would bring it to an end.

"Well, Doctor, while you've been charming and I appreciate the lack of a lame pick-up line, I'm afraid it's the end of the night for me," Kate said. She could see his disappointment. "Honestly, it's a matter of timing; I'm off for Munich tonight. I'm escaping the clutches of those who wish me ill, but at the same time want only the best for me." Imminent departure was an excuse that always worked when she was in town, but this time it was true.

"Sounds like you need a knight in shining armor."

"What happened to your being a doctor?"

"When one finds himself in this situation, it's usually advantageous to be multi-dimensional," he said, holding his arms out.

With somewhat of a giggle, she grabbed her purse off the bar and, stepping off the stool, said, "You're charming; I will give you that, but I must be off just the same."

"What's your name?" he asked.

"Jane."

"Well, Jane, do you want a brief assessment from the doctor?"

"Okay, I'll bite."

"I see you as intelligent, confident, independent, and exceptionally attractive with a tendency to fly solo most of the time," he said. "How did I do?"

"Don't give up your day job," she said. "I have enjoyed this, but it's time for me to leave." She looked over at the table of his friends and added, "You have yourself a nice evening." She put a hand on his shoulder as she walked past him toward the entrance, aware of the fact he was still looking at her. She was also mindful of the fact that she liked it.

Once upstairs, she closed the hotel room door behind her, pulled her cellphone from her bag, and quickly dialed the concierge. "Hello, this is Kate Adler in Suite 1209."

'Yes, Ms. Adler, it's Jamison. How are you enjoying your stay?"

"All of you are wonderful, as always. Jamison, I know it's late, but can you get me on a commercial flight to Munich tonight? Any carrier will suffice if it's before tomorrow morning. Charge it to my bill."

"Of course, Ms. Adler, are you sure you want a commercial flight and not private?"

"Yes."

"Just give me a few minutes."

"You're a dear," she said, "thank you." She would be off, leaving Avery to pick up the pieces, but it was vital that she get back to normal, back to a routine, her routine.

CHAPTER—10

MUNICH SECURITY ALERT

Monday

In the monitoring station's cafeteria, Brad Danner watched Kate Adler seated across from him, staring at the surface of the table, and lost in thought, as she was prone to be. Remembering the cup of coffee before her, Kate slipped her fingers into the handle. Her gestures fascinated him; they seemed to be an integral part of whatever she was expressing at any given time. The vessel rose to her face as her other hand wrapped around it, tilting the coffee slightly forward as she lightly blew on the dark surface. She was, as always, oblivious to the effect she had on the immediate space around her.

Brad and Kate were coworkers, and two years ago had become friends when they were both transferred to the NSA field office in Munich. Kate's gift was in computer science. Brad was a type of analyst, but, according to him, it was under a cloak so dark it was beyond any of their clearances—so don't ask. They shared many of the typical workplace frustrations, and Brad understood her work. During their time together, Kate knew she could change the tenor of the relationship, but Brad was a coworker, which disqualified him from being a casual male distraction in her mind.

The work they performed, and even the existence of their team's office, was a tightly protected secret. All communication had to be through the established covert channel to maintain the cover. The workers could not, under any circumstances, contact the NSA or any official in the US or any foreign government. The non-disclosure agreement they'd all signed was airtight, with a 'state's secrets' act thrown in to scare the hell out of everybody.

The purpose of the station and its team was to maintain and

monitor the output product of a system called Geneva9, the most extensive worldwide data monitoring and communication surveillance system ever developed. It was, by order of magnitude, more ambitious and complicated than any coding effort attempted. Given it acquired and decrypted, in complete secrecy, most of the data it targeted in the world, it was likely going to stay the largest. It was a dark secret that existed outside the awareness of any governmental oversight.

Building on this capability, Geneva9 was now capable of controlling many real-world systems such as surveillance systems and radar installations—anything that connected in some way to the networks that encircled the globe. As at Natanz, it was capable of penetrating private, off-line systems using a vulnerability algorithm that searches for any part of a network that touches the outside world, even momentarily. Geneva9 was the world's first truly digital weapon.

Previously, the power of a surveillance program was restricted to the size of massive data centers operating at cutting-edge speed around the globe. Geneva9, affectionately known as Mom, was not a typical computer; its architecture was a decentralized software program, much like Torrent and peer-to-peer file sharing systems. Its program utilized the combined fractional power of a massive number of commercial servers. Its first technical breakthrough was masking its presence; its second was compiling the different packets of data back into the original problem along with its answer.

G9 operated mainly in the non-indexed part of the Internet called the darknet. It's a space five hundred times larger than the regular Internet indexed by the conventional search engines we use every day. G9 constantly monitored itself through sensors and beacons placed around the world, reporting any anomalies that were then to be followed up on by the team. At least that's what the members of the group knew. Actually, no one ever saw anything but the module assigned to his or her workstation. That is, except Brad, Kate, and Marc, the station manager. However, that did not ensure they knew the full extent of the program. Kate thought perhaps Brad knew more, but he wasn't talking, despite her frequent attempts at solving the mystery of his silence.

The station, located on Munich's outskirts, occupied the bottom floor of a nondescript brick warehouse, built well before anyone toiling inside was born. The building's appearance from the outside belied its high-tech interior, layered with eighteen inches of concrete and lined with materials to block radio waves and prohibit external audio recordings, all of which, according to at least one of the workers, lowers your libido.

There wasn't a single piece of data or shred of paper within the station that referenced its links to any organization. Their badges identified them as employees of a false-front company. In addition to the team, the office staff included six very gifted computer geeks.

Brad studied Kate's silence. Ignoring the usual lunchroom distractions and with her lips touching the heavy lunchroom mug, Kate said, "I know for a fact it was there, Brad. It was there on the screen, and then it disappeared. I ran it three more times with the recorder on, and I couldn't duplicate it."

Brad was sitting across the coffee room table, his eyes still on Kate's hands.

"How did it go, back in the States?" he said. "Do you want to talk about it? I think it would be good to talk about it." After waiting long enough to know she wasn't going to answer, he changed the subject. "What were you running?"

"I was compiling the input from the ASTOR system test that ran last night," Kate responded. "Mom's internal safety systems obviously detected something that required tracing outside the master application. A ticket came in this morning from the compliance officer confirming Mom also flagged him."

They always referred to Geneva9 as Mom, as it was apparent she ran the place, and they were just there to polish the brass knobs.

"I forwarded it to Marc," Kate continued. "I'm supposed to know this stuff."

"Well, if anyone knows their stuff, you do. Why did you end up with it?"

She looked up at Brad with a half-smile. "Because, Mr. Danner, I was, as usual, the first person in this morning, and it was at the top of the priority list. Some of us take this job seriously. In fact, some of us," referring to his mysterious job, "actually have a job."

It was a point she had humorously made several times before.

"Hey, I'm not read in on that test. Besides, if you didn't get in so early, all bleary-eyed from an all-night flight, perhaps you wouldn't see things that don't exist," Brad replied. "Really, Kate, why don't you take a few days off? That's what normal people do. It's just a thought."

"This coffee's hot, Brad Danner, and I'm already in a bad mood. Don't tempt me."

"Okay, don't get so over the top. I was trying to pass along a little obvious advice that you are ignoring," Brad said, sitting up straight and putting a hand over his heart.

"If you're trying to act sincere, it isn't working."

"Kate, you lost your father; you don't have a mother. What could be more devastating in a person's life?"

"Dwelling on it, and it's something I intend not to do."

"This stuff tends to park itself in our minds, and it's affecting us, whether we like it or not. It always helps if you talk about it. I'm trying to be a friend here."

Kate looked at him with patience and compassion. She knew he was trying to be a good friend.

"Thanks, Brad. It's appreciated."

The office intercom came to life. "This is Marc. Full team meeting in the Turing Conference Room immediately."

Kate turned to Brad. "When I handed Marc my ASTOR log with my suspicions on the anomaly early this morning, it looks like it lit up the higher-ups. We have a meeting to attend. Let's go."

Brad pushed his seat back. "I have to pick up some materials. I'll meet you there. Save me a seat."

Kate walked across the lunchroom and turned into the hall. There she found herself in lockstep with Nathan Stillman, the last thing she needed.

"Well, well," he said. "What's America's favorite brunette doing this morning? Oh, are you following me? Have you finally decided …?"

"Zip it, Stillman," she said. "I can't make it any clearer. Find another female to hit on. If we weren't in Europe and sworn to secrecy, I would have had you legally nailed to the wall by now, via your private parts."

"I suppose I have successfully asked a few ladies out on occasion, but you're like this huge stone wall that I cannot get over. I want to show you I can be a nice guy if I want to be, and I want to. What do you say?"

"You're so full of it. Why do you even bother?"

They entered the conference room and moved to the other side of the large oval table. Kate sat down next to Thomson and put her hand on the empty seat next to her; she looked up at Nathan and said, "This seat is for Brad."

Looking hurt, Nathan said, "What do you see in that Boy Scout anyway?"

"A gentleman. Aren't you glad you asked?"

Kate started counting the faces of her team members, and all were present. Marc took the front of the room, looking around. "That's eight of us," he said. "Where's Brad?"

"Right here," Brad said, walking in the door and heading for the open seat next to Kate.

Marc Henderson closed the door and entered a keypad code, activating an electrical field surrounding the room. Called a Faraday cage, it completely blocked any signals from entering or escaping the room. That was a little unusual as they were in the middle of a building that was already secure.

"All right," Marc said, "this is a Level 4 security meeting. Does anyone need to be reminded of the rules?"

Brad looked at Kate and raised his eyebrows while chewing on his pen. There were five levels, and it was the first time Level 4 had been used. It set a tone in the room.

"All right, everyone, I will get right to it. One of Mom's tap sites registered an unknown origin on her OLA—Observe List of Attacks. The Astor test she ran last night came up with some intermittent anomalies and recommended outside observer status. This is where human brains come in. That's you, people, in case you need reminding. Kate picked up the test and experienced some unrepeatable events."

Marc turned to Kate. "Kate, disperse the workload over your team. This project is the hottest thing in the building, folks, and I need something solid before kicking it upstairs. All the related historical data on this occurrence is located on the Delta drive under," he paused and reached down to read off a slip of paper, "E-92."

"Each of you has been given temporary clearance to these files.

Each task will run a full set of threat kits. Kate, I will need a summary at our six o'clock."

Marc held up a piece of paper. "I'm going to have to file a damn D38 by the end of the day, and you are going to give me something to say. Meanwhile, Level 4 protocol is in effect until further notice. That's it, short and sweet. Let's find out how and who has Mom worried and get it plugged or bring your sleeping bags."

Stillman walked up behind Kate, who was now standing, and said, "I forgot my sleeping bag. I was wondering if I could share …"

Kate pressed her heel down directly on Nathan's big toe.

"Ouch!" he yelled and bounced on one foot. "Damn, that hurt. It was just a joke."

Kate looked up at him. "And to think it's only the beginning, big boy. I have no sense of humor," she smiled. "It seems some catch on faster than others." She proceeded out the door without looking back.

* * *

Kate had tasked assignments to each of her team members with a target time to get together and compare notes. The teams worked all afternoon, running the standard diagnostics, progression filters, and threat cycle analysis.

Brad stopped by to ask her if she wanted a cup of coffee. "You've been at that desk all day, and I guess some of the night. Come on; let's take a break and get a cup."

"We're on a Level 4 alert, and you want to drink coffee? Don't you ever get sick of it?"

"Why should I? It tastes good."

"How would you know, with all the stuff you put in it? I'm working, waiting for a report from a test and—Brad, look, there it is again. Just like this morning. That's a strange progression sequence."

Kate was running a log and immediately trapped the sequence and started a trace. The program started running with lists of addresses flowing down her screen. She nervously stood up and started pacing back and forth inside her cubicle.

"I know that walk and look," Brad said. "What is going on in that mind now?"

"I'm waiting for the results of the trace."

"What's the trace going to do? Whoever it is will hide behind a ton of anonymous servers. You'll never find them. On top of that, with the IP-spoofing built-in, they will never find us. Are they running a TOR browser?"

"No, it's straight encryption and damn good. Nothing says this is a normal threat profile. Something is wrong here. I sent it through the known threat signature list, and it doesn't generate a match. It's not standard. You're probably right, but I have a hunch. Remember the incident last week when Mom detected an Iranian probe that bounced all over the globe and ended up at some Internet cafe?"

"Yeah, but it was just a query. Wasn't it contained and quarantined?"

"Maybe it was. Or maybe not," Kate said.

The screen stopped scrolling, and Kate sat back down. She saved the current trace in another quarantined folder.

"I need the previous file," she said.

She had the history log on the screen with a couple of keystrokes, but it was thousands of files. Using the find function, she searched the plain text description attached to the data for the words "Iran, ASTOR, active" followed by the date bracket. She entered the terms, then hit return. Scrolling down the filtered list, she eventually found it.

"It's at IROI-8783/TS," she said. "What was the network file number again?"

"E-92," Brad said.

Kate pulled up the log file from the drive and copied the trace log portions Mom had captured. She then opened an application that compared the similarities between any two or more files. She pasted the two log files together and tapped the return key, lifting her hand slowly, expectantly, as if something big was going to happen.

Brad was now standing with his arms resting on the top of the partition, staying out of her way.

"Well?" he said.

"Don't know yet," she said. The program started painting lines in yellow on both sides of the split screen. It continued similarly for most of three minutes until …

"Bingo," Kate said. "Eighty-seven percent match. Except for the random bounces, both trace back to the same computer cafe in Hamedan, Iran."

With excitement building in his voice, Brad said, "Can you reverse ping it to see if they're still on?"

"Doing it now." Kate pasted both bounce patterns into a skip trace generator, running both searches at the same time.

"Holy shit," she said.

"Hey, watch your mouth, young lady, or I'm going to tell your mother."

She looked up at him

"Oh, God," he said, holding his head with both hands. "That was not the right thing to say."

"I got a hit," she said. "Whoever it appears to be is still on and at the same terminal at the cafe. That's just plain dumb."

"Get the credit card info," Brad said a little loudly.

"Bang, it's gone," she said. "They saw it."

"That will teach him to spy on us."

"Come on; we have to tell Marc."

* * *

In a small Internet cafe in Hamedan, Iran, Nazari was trying to penetrate a system that had hacked the IRGC network and determine what, if anything, they pulled out. He had been trying to discover the physical location of this system for months. However, the masking produced multiple locations requiring physical observation to determine whether it could be a data center.

No one in all of Iran knew how hard this was. They all acted as if it was just throwing a switch.

Nazari's fingers flew across the keys, entering symbols and characters with impressive speed. The command-line interface had appeared and was starting the run when Nazari quickly pulled his hands back as if someone had electrified the keyboard. On the screen was a closed pattern search back to him. That's not supposed to happen, he thought. He looked around the room, pulled the USB stick, and quickly power-cycled the computer, causing the DNS server to assign a new IP address.

He sat there for a few seconds, wondering what had just happened. He couldn't believe someone had not rebooted this computer since he was here last. It made the backtrace much easier than it should have been, revealing his exact location. That was sloppy. He was by far the most astute person in Iran concerning security systems. He had been educated in the US by the IRGC and then sent to work for various companies in Europe, including Oracle, SAP, Adler, and a stint with the DGSE in France. It had been a long journey, but the result was that he was a highly skilled programmer schooled in the West's methods in managing security.

Nazari had just made a rookie mistake, but only he knew about it. He stood, pulled his backpack onto his shoulder, and proceeded towards the door. Nazari crossed the street to a man who stood casually smoking, leaning on a wall. He was the Qud's handler monitoring the fieldwork.

Looking at his feet, Nazari said, "I think they saw me. They quarantined me in the system."

"Who saw you?" the man asked. "What do you mean? They saw you?"

"I think their monitoring software picked up my tap, and they logged off."

"Did they determine where you are?"

Nazari thought for a second before replying. "Yes."

"Are you sure?"

"Yes, I'm sure, but we can change cafes, and they will try to connect back to here and find nothing."

"You fool. You stupid little fool."

"Look," Nazari said, "my code is the best, but trying to penetrate this system is different. These people are working with something that I have not seen. For instance, they did a brute force hard trace that should take days, and they did it in seconds."

"It doesn't matter," the man said. "Don't you see?" He thought for a minute. "You need to find out their location and fast. It might just save your life."

Nazari's body stiffened. "What do you mean? We all agreed we would try that penetration tool to determine if they harvested anything from our network. It didn't work."

The man grabbed the programmer by the shirt.

"Listen to me, you idiot. You need to find the location of that group, or you and your family will find themselves covered in sand. Disappear, just like that." The man snapped his fingers. "Now, what are you going to do?"

The programmer looked at the man grabbing his shirt. The urgency in the man's voice betrayed his fear, and Nazari realized his handler was also at risk.

"What is going on here?" Nazari asked, pushing his handler back. "What have you gotten me into?"

"You knew the risks when you accepted this job."

"No, I didn't," Nazari said. "You're talking about my family. The risks you outlined were for me. I'm military, and I accept that, but not my family."

"Listen, I'm just trying to tell you the way it is. Our objectives are much bigger than you can imagine. Failure is not an option. That's all I can tell you."

"Promise me," Nazari said, "if I can physically locate them, you will keep my family safe."

"Yes," the handler replied, knowing that decision was well above his authority.

"Finding out the location should be easier than trying to break through twenty layers of security to monitor their data flow," Nazari said, "but I will need help."

"What kind of help?"

"People on the ground. I need someone on the ground to verify it's the right physical address. But first, we must go to another cafe. I know where one is."

"Good," the handler said, pulling out his cellphone. "You flag down a taxi while I set up the inspection team."

CHAPTER—11

IRGC MEETING

The intercom on the general's desk came alive. "General," a voice said, "Captain Musa Abasi is here with an urgent message for you."

Vahid moved over to his desk and pushed the intercom button. "Send him in," he said.

The chief of intelligence entered the room, stopped, and stood at full attention with a formal salute.

"At ease," Vahid said. "Captain, please tell us, what is so important?"

"Maj. Gen. Khiabani, I need to bring to your attention an incident that should be of great concern. Before the beginning of the day, we received intel regarding a penetration of our security network."

"Which network?" the general asked.

"The one normally used in day-to-day IRGC business," Abasi said. "Of course, all communication regarding Operation A'rafat faRdā has bypassed all normal electronic channels. No information regarding our plans ever existed on the network. Thus, we feel nothing of our efforts to cleanse the Republic of Western corruption could be compromised.

"We established a profile of the penetration, and the trail led us to this office—your office. We do not know if they were looking for information on A'rafat faRdā or just a random hack. If they were looking for specific information, then we may have been compromised.

"We have developed a special agent with unusual talent in this area, and our abilities exceed what our enemies believe are our capabilities. Without going into all the details, we have checked multiple addresses in four countries. The highest probability is a building in Munich, but it will need to be verified by someone in person. It is unmarked and occupied by six to eight people. No one in the area knows what is going on inside. We tried to contact the property owner, but a shell company privately owns the building. There isn't any contact information on city forms. The payment was in cash, so there are no mortgage records. In addition, the owner used cash to pay the taxes for the upcoming two years. We did determine a T4 trunk line runs into the office."

"Please, what does this mean?"

Abasi took in a deep breath. "That's a huge amount of bandwidth. Due to this level of security, we think it's an NSA monitoring site."

The general was visibly agitated. "As I understand it, this should mean nothing. Even if they manage to acquire information, it would be about the normal business of running the organization. There would be nothing that qualifies as top secret."

"I know, general. We both know this is true, but those at the NSA do not. The fact that they targeted your specific server leads me to, in the environment of absolute security, suspect they're looking for information on Operation A'rafat faRdā. Information on this program would be limited to your offices. Our best man was attempting to break into the Munich network trying to anonymously obtain any material substantiating this theory when a reverse trace revealed his physical location."

"Please, you must get to what this means to our efforts."

"It means they were able to retrace the signal to an Internet cafe we use in Hamedan. That's all they will find out, but it is an important piece of information to them. I'm sure their procedures are the same as ours, which dictate obtaining more solid proof before submitting a report higher up the chain. They do not have enough of this information, but it could be just a matter of time. It is an unacceptable unknown."

Khiabani sensed something was not under control. "How much time do we have?"

"This cannot be known. But given the efforts to keep this secret we cannot afford that even the slightest detail might emerge. For this reason, I'm recommending immediate action."

Vahid turned to the others in the room. "I need recommendations now," he said.

Gen. Karim Nabavi of IRGC Ground Forces, one of the senior IRGC officers and assumed second in command of the IRGC, exclaimed, "We must send a team to eliminate those involved. We have no choice. That requires inserting a special operations team into a foreign country on a deadly mission that cannot be traced back to Iran, let alone the A'rafat faRdā effort."

"If that's what must be done, the question is, *can* it be done?"

"Actually," Nabavi said, "I know of a sleeper cell in Germany, specifically Munich, that's already in place."

"What kind of sleeper cell?" Vahid asked.

"It's a group of contract mercenaries that exist for operations in Europe. Because they're through a private contractor, if discovered, there is no chance they can trace it back to us."

"How soon could they be deployed?"

Abasi broke in, saying, "Sir, we must verify if it is the correct site."

Khiabani ignored his comment. "How soon?" he repeated.

"Immediately after their briefing," Nabavi said.

"Can you deploy them without revealing A'rafat faRdā?"

"Yes, we can transfer funds from France, and there will be nothing tying it back to us."

"Make it happen," Vahid said. "Quickly. Get back to me with specifics as to when it will take place and real-time reports."

"Yes, we should have news back in a matter of hours."

CHAPTER—12

Vianden Castle Luxembourg
CARTEL SITUATION CENTER

Dan was one of the Cartels analysts who worked in a Medieval castle that served as the organization's headquarters in Vianden Luxembourg. He was the agent on duty and approached Dr. John Wilkerson, head of intelligence and analysis.

"Dr. Wilkerson, I think you should see this."

"What is it?"

"Mom has generated a POC8 (Pattern of Concern level 1-10)."

"Can you bring it up on Screen 3?"

Wilkerson started reading the report and started to get concerned as a serious picture began to form from the information provided. They usually received several POCs in a week, but they were not all on the same level of concern. A Level 8 got everyone's attention.

POC8-121

Pattern Progression Table

1. **INFO** - The submarine *Yunes* (Kilo-class Iranian diesel electric submarine) departed the Bandar-e Abbas naval yard at

1325 hours seven days ago.

2. **Anomaly** - *Yunes* - Non-scheduled deployment date.
       Deviation: Schedule disruption.
3. **Anomaly** - Normal deployment/return cycle - five days.
       Deviation: Exceeds normal deployment cycle.
4. **Anomaly** - *Yunes* - Communication blackout.
       Deviation: Non-standard communication profile.
5. **INFO** - Kilo class range: seven thousand miles.
6. **INFO** - Nominal speed and range max operational area.
       West: Antisiranana Urban Madagascar
       -12.310658, 49.281834
       East: Batam City, Riau Islands, Indonesia
       1.086804, 104.043187
       South: La Roche Godon
       -37.822435, 77.551801
7. **INFO** - Commerce choke points within operational area:
       A. The Strait of Hormuz - DISCOUNT
       B. Port of Singapore (Malacca Strait)

8. **INFO** - Malacca Strait: Possible high-value targets
       Items weighted 1 - 100
       10   HLV Typhoon   Heavy lift vehicle
       11   MT Forester   Motor transport
       79   LNG/c *Serena*   Liquefied gas tanker

9. **Target Conclusion** - *Serena*
10. **INFO** - Targets scheduled arrival: Singapore within 8 hours
11. **Analog**: Navigation options from Bandar-e Abbas place the *Yunes* within a six-hour intercept window of the *Serena* at normal cruising speed to Malacca Strait. The operational area contains no other high-value targets.

12. **Analog**: Iranian submarine could attempt to capture/destroy *Serena* within the Singapore port range.
       -Items weighted 1 - 100-
       27   Sink transport
       32   Hijack to a third cooperating port.
       92   Destroy ship
       Likely execution methods to include
       -Items weighted 1 - 100-

5	Torpedo attack - (fuel ignition doubtful.)
5	Board ship - hijacking
92	Board ship - Rig for explosion.

Estimated time to boarding = 8 hours +/- 1 hr.

Estimated Probability of action   87%

Response Recommendations
Action Item - Deploy defensive boarding team - *Serena*
Available Assets
        Boarding Team: Alpha Team 4
        Current location: Kuala Belait facility, Brunei
        Transportation: Sikorsky UH-60 Black Hawk
        Equipment location: Kuala Belait facility, Brunei
        Egress: Mark V special op craft
        Equipment location: Kuala Belait, Brunei
        Evacuation and Support: Lockheed C-130

Deployment Estimate: ETA boarding 6 hours +/- .5 hr.

Wilkerson turned from the screen and said, "Danny, get me Penn in operations on the phone. We have just hours to avoid disaster."

CHAPTER—13

MUNICH STATION

Kate, Brad, and the rest of the team came together in the conference room for the six o'clock EOD (End of Day). The team heard a light thud on the other side of the wall coming from Marc's office.

"What was that?" Sally asked.

"Marc is pacing again and forgot to stop before hitting the wall," Bill said.

Everyone laughed as it was a well-known trait of Marc's to pace when faced with a problem. It had been a tough day, and everyone was ready to leave.

Eric, the resident database guru, was sitting with his feet on the table wearing a hoody and tennis shoes. "What's keeping him? I'm tired."

"He's only a few minutes late," Ann said. "Be patient."

"I've got a date," he said.

"Eric?" Ann said on an empathic note, "The only date you will ever have in your life will fall off a tree."

Everyone in the room started laughing hysterically as Eric pulled up the hood and crossed his arms. "Haha," he said. "That hurt."

"I'm sorry," Anny said. "That was rude, untrue, but really, really funny."

Brad waved at Kate. "Come on; let's get a quick cup of coffee."

"There isn't any," Kate said.

"I know, that's why you have to come. You do know how to make coffee, don't you?"

"You are so hopeless, Brad Danner; it's enough to bring out the mother in any woman, you should use it to your advantage."

"Come on, there's not much time," he said, waving toward the door.

Kate didn't move. "It could start any minute, you fool."

"So what? We can hear it start from the coffee room and pop back in an instant. What's the difference between potty break and coffee? Come on, I need a cup," Brad said, as he started to roll Kate, still in her chair, out of the room.

"Okay, okay, at some point, you need to look out for yourself." She looked over and, with her hand on her bag, said, "Nance, can you keep an eye on this? There are some very shady types in this room."

Eric looked around the edge of his hoody and Kate said, "Not you, Eric, you're just a sweetie pie."

"See?" he said, looking at Ann.

Twenty steps later, Kate and Brad stood in the small nook that serviced the conference room. Kate opened a cupboard door and grabbed a pre-made coffee packet. She slapped it right on Brad's chest, and he instinctively grabbed it.

"You see this, bozo? You put it into the top of the coffee maker. No muss; no fuss." She then started filling the coffee pot at the sink. "This is the tough part, so watch carefully."

Brad purposely moved in too close, and Kate gave him a shove in the hip. Immediately, their heads snapped toward the open door at a staccato sound. She turned off the water, and they both listened—four staccato sounds were followed by four more, a shout, and then another sound. Kate instinctively turned and moved towards the unusual noise. Brad yanked at her arm, pulling her around. With a stone face, he repeatedly tapped his lips with his finger, signaling for silence. They stood frozen, looking at each other. After a second without another noise, she grabbed the coffee packet, placed it in a drawer, and quietly emptied the coffee pot, gently putting it back on the burner.

Brad silently pointed toward the other door in the small space and quickly started out of the room. The door opened into the programming area. Brad bent over to stay below the cubicle partitions and looked back to see if Kate was following suit. He motioned for her to stay close as he paused at a corner. Across the aisle was a restricted-access door with an electronic lock.

Kate mouthed the words, "Do you have your card?" She made a swiping motion with an invisible card.

Brad reached into his back pocket and held up two cards. He looked around the corner one more time, then started across the aisle toward the locked opening. Kneeling in front of the door, they looked at the reader; Brad swiped the card, and nothing happened. She looked up at him, worried. Quickly Brad tried the other one, and it worked, to their deep relief. They opened the door and slipped inside.

They were in the back-office server area, with the muffled sounds of a hundred cooling fans and other equipment. Brad finally felt safe to speak. He stepped in front of Kate, blocking her path, and whispered, "What the hell do you think that was?"

Kate's face was alive as she said, "Those sounds were gunshots."

"Yes," Brad said. "Gunshots from guns with silencers. Someone wants us all dead."

"We need to get out of here and disappear," Kate said in an urgent whisper.

"Right," Brad said. They looked around the room and located a large roll-up service door. Brad tried both his cards, and neither worked. They anxiously ran toward a hall leading out of the place and past some offices. At the end was another door, painted red with broad yellow strips, a crash bar, and a bright red round bell mounted just above the upper right-hand corner of the opening. The meaning of the German words written on it was apparent: An alarm would sound if they opened it. It would alert whoever was in the building that not everyone was dead.

Brad looked around and grabbed some paper towels used to clean the glass on the copier. He felt behind the bell and located the clapper. He crushed the paper towels and stuffed them between the clapper and the bell.

"There," he said, "but it won't last long."

"We don't need long," she said.

He whispered, "This looks like it opens to the outside. If it does, and these people know what they're doing, they will have it covered as an alternative exit. We could be walking right into a trap or worse, gunfire."

"I don't see we have many choices," Kate said. "We've got to do something, or it's just a matter of time."

Behind them, they heard several muffled bangs. The noise was heavy and unfamiliar.

"What was that?" Kate asked.

Brad paused a second before responding. "Smell that?"

"No. Oh, I mean, yes, smoke," she said. "It's coming out the ventilator."

"I think they're torching the place."

"As I said, we don't have much choice," she said.

He looked at her. "Ready?" She nodded, and he stepped back and hit the door and the crash bar simultaneously. The metal bell started its muted clamor as they started out the door, which moved about a foot before coming up against a tall hedge growing right up against the building.

"Jesus," Brad said as he forced the door open with his shoulder. There was barely enough space to squeeze out. "I'll go first," he said.

"No," she whispered. "I don't think I can hold open the door." The hedge was solid; Kate dropped to her knees, looking through the door's opening and out to the street from beneath the bush. A car passed by directly beyond a wide sidewalk, but otherwise, nothing else seemed out of place.

"We might be in luck; it looks safe," she said. Kate squeezed through the opening as Brad pushed against the door.

"Wait," she said. She saw the problem was a vertical sprinkler up against the outside of the door. She steadied herself against the wall and kicked it several times before she could push it over.

"It's clear," she said.

Brad emerged and started through the bush. Kate put a hand out to stop him. An approaching Chevy Suburban would have to slow to a stop at the light, just fifty feet away.

"Stay here," she said, as she was pulling her neck scarf from around her shoulders. She wrapped it loosely around her right hand several times then rushed out toward the slowing car.

"Wait," Brad said, and she was gone.

As the Suburban rolled to a stop, Kate stood close behind the driver's window, out of the driver's sight. She held out her arms straight, her hands cloaked by the scarf, and yelled, "Holen Sie sich jetzt aus dem Auto" (Get out of the car *now*!). She motioned to the man inside the car to get out.

"Schnell Schnell," she yelled. The lone man strained to look back toward her, not getting a clear look at his assailant. He slowly opened the door, stepping out with his hands up and without comment.

"Stellen Sie sich der Front" (Face the front), Kate said. Her voice reflected the adrenalin flowing through her body.

Brad sensed a bearing in this man that didn't match that of a person in trouble. This man was not afraid—not good.

The man moved toward the front of the car as Brad bolted from the shrubs, making his way toward Kate. She put her arms down as she bolted to the other side of the Suburban to get in. It was a mistake. As Kate passed, the driver realized the ruse. He grabbed Kate going by while pulling a gun out from beneath his jacket. Grabbing her, the driver tried pinning her face down against the hood of the vehicle. To Brad's surprise, Kate managed to kick the inside of the man's knee, and he yelled out in pain.

Brad saw the gun and, approaching the man from behind, wrapped an arm around the man's neck and drew it tight as he reached around and grabbed the firearm's barrel to control the direction of fire away from Kate. With a firm grip on the barrel, he hit the back of the man's leg with his knee, causing it to bend, and at the same time, he made a primitive sound as he twisted both the neck hold and the hand that held the gun around and threw the man on the ground. The man was big, and Brad could hear him exhale as he hit the street with Brad landing on top of him. Upon impact, the man uttered the sound of someone not used to suffering but more used to inflicting pain. Brad's next worry was the man reaching for the gun, but the next thing he saw was Kate's foot coming down on the man's wrist, followed by the release of his grip. Brad grabbed the gun, raised it, and hit the man in the back of the head. Brad felt the man's consciousness release control of his muscles.

"Get in," Brad yelled, rising from the ground.

"On my way," Kate said, sprinting to the other side of the car and slamming the door behind her.

The engine was still running, and Brad could see the man lying close to the car on the ground just to his left. Steering around him, he hit the gas, bolting off down the street.

Kate said, "I guess they were covering all the exits after all."

Brad pressed harder on the accelerator, feeling the SUV's power quickly bringing the vehicle up to speed. He looked up in his rearview mirror, grateful not to see anyone following them.

"Are you all right?" he said.

"Yes, this is crazy. What's going on?"

"Someone wants us dead."

"That's impossible."

He looked at the gun in her hand and said, "How much proof do you need …?"

At that moment, Brad's head hit the side window hard as a vehicle struck them in the left rear fender at the next intersection. The car spun around counterclockwise and came to a halt facing the opposite direction. A man emerged from the driver's side and leveled a gun at their windshield. Brad grabbed Kate and pulled her and himself down below the dashboard as the windshield took the hit, a web of cracks emanating from the bullet's impact. Brad immediately realized the windshield was bullet-resistant and grabbed the gun Kate still had in her hand. Three more shots hit the glass. Brad opened the driver's door and ducked behind it as the door's window absorbed another shot. Brad brought the gun up between the split-A pillar, squeezed off two shots at center mass, and saw the man fall. The front passenger emerged and, using the hood of the vehicle as cover, was aiming just as Brad hit him squarely in the forehead. He slid off the hood onto the ground.

Kate screamed.

In a single motion, Brad was back in the car. He put it in reverse and slammed down the accelerator. Looking out the rear window, Brad drove backward to the next intersection. He then threw the wheel, starting a front-end spin, and hit the brakes, which started the car sliding in a circle. Brad put the car in neutral, and when the vehicle reversed itself to the road, put it in drive and slammed his foot down. The car lurched forward as he corrected his steering from the maneuver. In a second, they had reversed the Suburban's direction and were racing down the street away from the assailants.

Brad again looked behind them and continued down the street for a few blocks, then slowed down to normal speed and he turned another corner.

"What are you doing?!" Kate shouted. Brad's adrenalin and heart rate were off the charts as he focused on the rearview mirror, looking for anything indicating there was another car.

"Are you all right?" he asked in a heightened voice.

"Brad, why are we going slow?"

"Are you all right?" he asked again as he concentrated on looking through the fractured windshield and looking at intersections for any cars as they passed by.

"Yes, I'm fine," she said. "How about you?"

"Yeah, I'm going slow because we don't want to get pulled over or chased by the local police for something stupid like speeding." He turned in opposite directions at the following two blocks and then went straight in their escape.

"I wasn't born yesterday," he said.

"Sorry," Kate said.

They were both silent for a few minutes, and Brad finally said, "Who would want to wipe out the entire office? In fact, who would even know it's there?"

"I don't know," she said. "How did you know those were gunshots with silencers?"

"Would you believe television?" he asked with a half-smile. "Where did the Bruce Lee moves come from?" he asked.

"I promise to explain later," she said. "I don't think I'm the one with some explaining to do, but right now, we need to find a place to hide. How much gas do we have?"

Brad looked down, "A lot unless we are planning to drive to London. What we need is another car."

He reached into his coat and handed his cellphone to her. "Here," he said. "We need to get rid of this. Where's yours?"

She cracked the back of the phone open, removed the battery and memory stick, and threw it out the window.

"Mine is still in my purse. I left it behind on the conference table. They will have it by now and all the information it contains."

Brad was a little surprised she knew what to do with the phone and was still fascinated by the moves she had used on a guy twice her size. He decided there was a lot he didn't know about his friend, but was not surprised given her reluctance to talk about anything personal. He started to ask again, and she said, "Not now, Brad, but I think we need to find some time to level with each other. I promise I will explain it all if you will."

"There is nothing to explain. I was in the military, like a lot of guys, and was trying not to get killed."

"Brad Danner, you are such a horrible liar."

CHAPTER—14

IRGC MUNICH REVIEW

Maj. Gen. Khiabani was with his top advisors in the IRGC command center, waiting for information on the Munich operation. The center's construction ensured no eavesdropping would compromise their operation. Gen. Nabavi had been the last to enter the chamber.

Khiabani looked at the man as he took a seat at the table. "We have been waiting. What is the update?"

"Operations have been concluded with the team on their way out of the country. Apart from one female and one unknown, they eliminated all targets. We set the building on fire. It gutted the structure eliminating any trace of our being there."

Vahid's face revealed he was not happy. In a slow, deliberate delivery, he said, "Please tell me how we didn't get everyone?"

Everyone in the room, including Nabavi, recognized the body language and tone of Khiabani. It indicated great displeasure with his commanding officer.

Nabavi started, "We didn't have an exact count of the number inside, but counting the number of desks and workstations, the total count should have been eight, but there were only six targets. Agents found three purses but only two female targets. As we compared IDs to victims, we found the extra purse belonged to a Kate Adler. We are currently trying to track her down. We have her cellphone, but there doesn't seem to be anything but personal information on it, meaning nothing of value. The other employee is yet unidentified."

Khiabani slammed his hand flat on the table as he rose from his chair. "Did you check for employee records to identify the other target?"

"Yes, they must have been in a safe, which would have taken

too long to open before authorities arrived."

"This is unacceptable. You've failed. That even one person might know of our plans jeopardizes the success of the entire operation, let alone our exposure."

"Of course, my general."

None of this was lost on the others in the room. They joined with their general as soldiers would during national emergency times and trained to follow orders. However, a reckless pall had descended over the whole operation. It was unmistakable to all in attendance.

Khiabani was pacing the length of the room in thought. They don't understand what is at stake, he thought, what lies before their native land if they fail. He would have to get their attention before any further damage occurred.

"Gen. Nabavi, you are as a result of this relieved of your duties. There can be no mistakes. I will deal with you later. Gen. Lajani (Brig. Gen. Hamid Lajani, commander of special forces), you are now commanding Nabavi's forces." In quick, deliberate steps, he opened the command center door and yelled, "Where is the sergeant at arms?" The two guards on either side of the door became rigid as another guard rushed from a few feet away, coming to attention with a crisp salute.

"Yes, General, at your command."

Khiabani grabbed the guard by the uniform and dragged him inside the room. He pointed at Nabavi, yelling, "Arrest this man now."

Stunned, the guard hesitated just a second, trying to understand the impact such an action implied.

"Now," Khiabani shouted in the man's face.

Nabavi stepped forward, relieving the guard of an impossible situation, and proceeded out of the room.

Khiabani turned to his remaining staff. "We must proceed with our plans, avoid any further senseless errors, and hope that we have eliminated this loose end. Gen. Lajani, as the one responsible for the planning and execution of the next operation in our plan, I would like an update before you leave to attend to the Munich incompetence."

"Yes, sir," Lajani said.

In a tense atmosphere where members in the room avoided

looking at one another, he stood and started his presentation.

CHAPTER—15

ON THE RUN

For some time, Brad and Kate drove with a heightened awareness before pulling off the autobahn and into a large shopping center. Brad parked in the busiest part of the parking lot and said, "I think it's best if you stay here for a second. We are going to need another car."

"How are you going to do that?" she asked. "This is a shopping center, not an airport."

"Trust me this time," Brad said with a smile. He got out and walked to a dimly lit section of the lot where employees parked. He wandered through several cars and then disappeared.

Kate tried to keep track of him but didn't know where he was until the lights came alive on a dark Toyota Camry. It backed out of its parking place and stopped behind the wrecked SUV they had been driving since the escape.

Kate got out and opened the Camry's passenger door. As soon as she was in, she said, "Is black your favorite color for a car?"

"Not really," he said, "but basic black does not stand out in a stolen car alert like fire-engine red."

"We are going to have a little talk. I'm getting the feeling I never really knew you, Brad Danner, or whoever you are."

"Oh, please," he said. "Coming from the great sphinx, we hear the calls of inequity."

"What's that mean?"

"Buckle up, your majesty. There are laws in this country." He headed back to the autobahn. A short time later, they stopped off at a highway rest stop. The car park lit up as darkness approached. "I think we should stop and pick up several packaged sandwiches and some water."

"Go ahead; I need to find a coin phone," Kate said. "I'll be right back." She found the typical yellow German phone booth around the side of the building, and she pulled open the door with the iconic eight panes. She picked up the receiver and dialed a number she had remembered but had never had to use. Half a world away, at 4:35 p.m., a burner phone rang in Avery Stanton's jacket pocket. He reached in, knowing by the ring tone that it wasn't his personal or business phone. He kept an untraceable phone now in his briefcase, and if it was ringing, something was amiss.

Avery stood up, looked at his watch, and addressed those in his meeting. "Excuse me, gentlemen. I must take this."

He moved out of the room and into an adjacent empty office. "Katy, what's wrong?"

"Avery, thank you so much for the crisis phone idea. Someone just tried to kill us where I work, and I don't know why. But we are safe for now."

"We, who is the other person?" he said.

"Brad Danner, a friend and coworker. Do you know of a safe place to stay until I can figure out what is going on?"

"Where are you?"

"West of Munich on the E43, Friedrichshafen, I think. We are close to the Swiss border. We left everything behind; we don't have anything."

"Do you have transportation?"

"Yes, we stole a car."

"Who tried to kill you?"

"I don't know, but it was professional."

"Hold on a second," Avery said. He reached into his wallet and pulled out a thin memory stick. He inserted the SD card in the slot of the computer in the room. In seconds, the list was up. He put in the location and hit return, and an address appeared.

Avery came back on. "First, we need to get you safe. I have an address; tell me when you're ready."

"No, I will remember it."

"It's in Zurich, 1255 Haldenstrasse. The access code on the keypad is 1887. There is a woman there, and the password will be 'statefour.' Can you get there?"

"Yes, I'm sure we can. Thank you, Avery. All of this is so very confusing. They killed everyone."

"Did you say everyone else is dead? That's tragic and almost unbelievable," Avery said. "What do you need besides a place to stay?"

"I don't have a passport. I left without it, so I will need that and some euros to get clothes and stuff."

"I understand. A package will arrive at the Zurich location tomorrow by a man in a blue—not white—taxi. He will leave it at the door and walk away. He should not try to talk to anyone. If so, get out."

Kate was looking around outside the phone booth. "We need to get off the phone. It's almost a full minute."

"No, we are fine; mine is a burner phone with no name associated with it. Even if someone traced it, they wouldn't know it's you or me. You are on a coin phone, right?"

"Yes."

"Then we are okay."

"Good enough," Kate said. "We will head for the address in a few minutes."

"Kate," Stanton said.

"Yes?"

"No one should have known about your location. Something is very wrong, so be extra careful."

"Avery? How did you know exactly where I work? I have never told you."

"We can cover that later. Get to Zurich as quickly as you can, but don't get stopped by local police. Don't trust anyone."

Kate walked back to the car and leaned in through the window. "We need a paper map as we can't use the phone. I will be right back."

"Meet me behind the building," Brad said.

"Why?"

He gave her the "just do it" look, and she quietly said, "Okay, okay."

As Brad drove around to the back of the building, he tried to make sense of what was a scary night. People died; he almost died; Kate took out a guy twice her size. That was far afield from the person he knew.

He knew that a stolen car and a new set of plates were easy to trace if they occurred in the same location. But a stolen car and a new set of plates from a different location would require linking them together. That would take considerably longer. He secured the plates to the Toyota using a coin on the big screws and got back in the car.

A few minutes later, the car door opened and Kate got in. "What were you doing? Why drive over here?"

"We needed a different set of license plates to go with our new car. Who did you call?"

"A friend," she replied. "He is a friend of my father's. Or was a friend of my father's"

"Kate, I'm so …"

"Brad, I'm fine."

"That's the first time you've ever mentioned your family. I just thought it was off-limits."

"It normally is, but I don't think this is a normal situation."

As Brad pulled onto the autobahn, Kate unfolded the map.

* * *

Avery hung up the phone and walked over to his office, addressing his assistant. "Susan, can you contact Captain Wilson and get him and his crew ready. Have him file flight plans for Vianden for now. We will take off as soon as I arrive and he gets clearance. And could you please get my car here?" He reached into his pocket for a key and opened a drawer in the desk. He pulled out a rather sizeable portable phone.

CHAPTER—16

ZURICH SAFE HOUSE

Traveling at a leisurely speed, it was daylight when Kate and Brad came upon Zurich address. Instead of stopping right away, Brad drove by the house twice, looking for anything suspicious. Finally, he parked.

"I was expecting an embassy or something," Brad said.

"Good thinking," she said, "but this is better."

"I'll take your word for it."

They were walking down the side yard of the house when he asked, "Why are we going in the back?"

"Because the front didn't have a keypad lock," she said. "So, the back one must."

They ascended the stairs to the rear door. Kate put in the code and opened the door. The old two-story house was in fine shape, as was the residential neighborhood. They entered the kitchen and looked around. It had the distinct look of a grandmother's house, Kate thought. Looking up, she could see into the living room. Embroidered armrest covers and stacks of German celebrity magazines on a table in front of the couch added to her conclusion. A cabinet to one side of the kitchen held an extensive collection of Princess Di collectibles and fancy cups and saucers. Kate didn't hear anyone, but the place looked as if someone lived here full time, as sliced bread sat on a cutting board right next to her. Perhaps she should have knocked. She stepped forward into the living room and was met and startled by a senior woman ten feet away, holding a handgun with both hands, feet apart, and pointed at her head. They both immediately put their hands up.

"Don't be fooled," she said in German, "I can use this. What do you want?"

Kate replied in German, "I have a password that I would like to give you before you shoot."

"I don't have any passwords," the woman said.

"Statefour," Kate said. "I also had the keypad combination to get in, so it's no coincidence I have both. Perhaps we should not have walked right in. Did you get a message of any kind?"

The woman lowered the gun, "Your friend looks American."

Kate looked at Brad and said, "Yes, he is, and so am I."

The woman pointed the gun at the ceiling, set the safety, pressed the release, and the magazine dropped into her hand.

"Was anyone following you?" she asked in English.

"No," Kate replied.

"How do you know?" The woman pulled a cabinet drawer open and placed the pistol and magazine next to an ammunition box.

"Because we circled several times and pulled over twice. No duplicate cars and no pedestrians."

"Are you both okay?" the woman said, walking back toward the kitchen.

"Yes, we are. You're British," Kate continued in English.

"Yes, I am. You may think you're fine, but both of you look dreadfully in need of a cup of tea. Follow me. By the way, my name is Ethel Bannister."

"I'm …"

"Kate Adler," the woman said. Brad looked at Kate.

"This is Brad Danner. We both need a place to stay until we figure some things out."

Ethel put some cups and saucers on the table. "Me casa is your casa," she said with a smile.

Kate laughed. "Did you say that wrong on purpose?"

"Of course," she replied.

"What is this place?" Brad said.

Ethel looked at him. "A safe house, except you guys barged in here like it was the lobby of the Grand Hotel."

Kate looked out the windows toward the street. "Is anyone watching the house for us?"

"Yes, it's automatic when I got the message." Ethel poured three cups of tea, looking up at them both, saying, "Good timing, it was my first-morning cup. Might as well share it."

"How did you get the message?" Kate said.

"A note through the mail slot last night sometime," Ethel said.

"I don't know who drops them off. But you can be assured some competent people are on the lookout for bandits outside."

"That's colorful," Brad said.

"Well, thank you, young man. At this age, that's about all I can be."

Everyone smiled.

"Except for the gun thing," Brad said. He put his cup down, looked at Kate, and said, "I have been more than patient, and I think the smoke has cleared."

Kate looked at their host and said, "Mrs. Bannister, is there a place where Brad and I can talk for a bit? We have been through quite an ordeal and need to catch up."

"Of course, let me show you to your room or ... rooms?" she said, looking at Kate.

Kate looked at Brad, then back at Mrs. Bannister and, smiling, said, "Rooms."

Brad's head dropped in obvious disappointment, receiving a solid kick beneath the table from Kate.

A keen observer, Mrs. Bannister looked at Kate and said, "Boys will be boys, won't they?"

"Yes, Mrs. Bannister, especially this one."

After a glance at the rooms, as they had no luggage, Brad walked into Kate's and sat in the old but comfortable stuffed chair enveloped in a vivid floral fabric.

"I can't wait to hear what's coming," he said.

Kate sat on the bed, one foot hanging over, the other under her. "First, Brad, you are a very close friend, and I don't have many. I wish there were another word closer than a friend, but I want you to know I'm very grateful for that."

"Are we breaking up?" Brad said.

"No, it's just I haven't told you everything about myself."

Brad feigned a surprised look and said, "Really? Let's see, what was my first clue?"

"Right out of college, I was recruited by the CIA. They trawl colleges looking for students that fit specific profiles. They were looking for systems people with language skills for overseas service. I found out later one of my computer science professors put a bug in their ear."

Brad leaned forward, laughing, "Is that a joke?"

"No," she said. "I looked at what they had to offer and thought it would be an interesting way to start a career and would be great to have on a resume. They sent me to Virginia, Camp Peary, the location of the secret CIA training facility. That's classified, by the way; they call it the farm. They deny it's there, but the whole world knows, so it's stupid. I went through the training, which included all sorts of things, including how to protect yourself. Then I was posted to the US Embassy in Hanover. The short story is I performed some IT work combined with short stints in the field. It was nothing exciting like a shootout, but more like covering drops and escorting and interviewing defectors to see if they were serious or just trying to get money or, worse, becoming double agents. It was interesting but hardly challenging, so I decided to look for something else. I wanted to use what I learned in college. Several interviews later, I was accepted. I went through another security clearance and ended up assigned to Munich, where I met you."

Brad looked at her and said, "Aren't you lucky. So that's where all that kung fu stuff came from."

"It's not spooky spy stuff; they just do an outstanding job at teaching you how to protect yourself, pay attention to your surroundings, and how to evaluate options under pressure."

Brad put his hand up, stopping the conversation. "By the way, due to your cool head and our efforts, we got out of there. I will owe you always. Whom did you call while I was lifting the license plates? Which, now that I'm thinking about it, is a federal offense. So now, because of you, I'm being targeted by assassins in addition to being a fugitive from justice."

"You passed over the part about still being alive. Can I get to whom I called later? There is a good reason behind it."

"Sure, no problem, we can do that later. Thanks for letting me into your world a little. Now, what's next?"

There was a gentle knock on the bedroom door and Ethel said, "Can I come in?"

Brad got up, stepping back as he opened the door.

"My instructions are to give you this phone and this numerical key," Ethel said, handing them to Kate. "It's encrypted, so there is not to be a worry. Just follow the instructions on the screen."

Kate took the phone, saying, "Who told you to give it to me?"

Ethel smiled, "There is an awful lot of 'need to know' in my life, so let's say a little bird told me. You can use the phone in this room as it's audio- and frequency-safe, so feel free to talk."

Brad, standing next to the window, pulled back the curtain and rapped his knuckles against the glass. It made a bass sound due to the thickness and type of material.

"Didn't believe me, did you?" Ethel said, laughing and shaking her finger.

"I'm so sorry," Brad said, "my skepticism is just a natural reaction. I promise not to do it again if you don't turn me in."

"Consider it a narrow escape, my boy. We have taken your car, cleaned it thoroughly, changed the plates, and left it at the Hauptbahnhof. Is anyone hungry?"

"Very hungry," Brad said. "Can we eat before the call?" he said, looking at Kate.

"I think it's an excellent idea, so we don't pass out in the middle of the conversation."

"Good, just come downstairs when you're ready. After that, you both need to catch a few hours' sleep."

Brad said, "Yes, we have been up for quite a while."

"Then," she said, "after my sinkers hit bottom, I guarantee you will be asleep in no time."

CHAPTER—17

CARTEL OPERATIONS CENTER
Vianden Castle Luxembourg

Penn Hauer, director of operations, was responsible for executing kinetic assignments in the field. Under his command were the field forces stationed around the world that were generally considered the last resort. His responsibilities also included overseeing any information that would reveal anything to the public about the Cartel. He had been a special forces commander in his earlier days and had stayed fit although he was slightly larger. His greying hair, deep voice, and a world of experience gave credibility to whatever he had to say. Hauer had held the position for over eighteen years.

He walked into the operations center after a concerned call from Wilkerson. Hauer had been reading the POC Mom had generated and then looked at his watch. Addressing those in the room, agents who constantly monitored activities around the globe, he said, "Listen up, people, there is going to be another hijacking, but this time we could have thousands of innocent people dying. I need a boarding party in the Malacca Strait in two hours. We have a tight schedule here and will need everyone on their toes."

Rob called out, "Mom flagged the team at the Kuala Belait facility in Brunei; they're standing by."

"Good, tell them to prepare to fast-rope onto a tanker, then get them in the air toward the strait ASAP. We will send the team specific coordinates en route or call them back if necessary. Mike, start scrubbing a timeline and work backward to get me a delta time. Deborah, inventory what ballistic equipment we have at our disposal at the Kuala Belait base and merge that into Mike's timeline. Art, find out what shipping company owns Mom's target. Get them ready to notify their ship and crew of a boarding attempt, but not until we are sure we can pull this off.

"Okay, team, let's come up with a plan, and be the reason ten thousand people see tomorrow."

Off to the right, one of the agents said, "Boo-yah!"

Another said, "On it, boss."

"Dr. Wilkerson, I could use any information from your people that they think is relevant."

"I gave it to Lauren. Since she cannot do anything on the ship itself, she wants to flash all our people in the port to evacuate the area. I gave her the go-ahead."

"Great," Penn said. "Beth, can you locate Avery for me? Put him through to my internal cell. Has someone started the event log?"

Beth, behind him, said, "I started it retro to the POC notification."

"Excellent," he said.

"Mr. Hauer," Rob said. "Received confirmation that Group Alpha Team 4 is kitted up. Conveniently, a C-130 cargo plane contained a Black Hawk previously loaded for a training exercise. As a result, they can be wheels up in thirty minutes. They will be landing in Singapore, then transferring to the helo. The journey out puts them over the target in two hours and forty-five minutes."

Hauer looked at his watch again despite there being numerous time readouts around the room. "Rob? That's very close to Mom's estimate. Push for faster. I will have to notify the Singapore military for clearance to land an active force, unload and get the chopper on the way but not until we tighten this up."

"Mr. Hauer," Rob called out. "I have secured civilian landing rights to refuel for the flight home if nothing transpires."

"Good thinking."

Nancy walked up to Hauer and handed him a secure G9 phone. "Mr. Stanton is airborne, and en route to the facility, so we need this. You're cleared through to talk."

"Thanks, Nance. Avery, did you see the POC?"

"Yes, can we do anything?"

"It's very tight, but everyone is working on it.

Let's call our contact in the US and give them a heads up."

CHAPTER—18

CARTEL NOTIFICATION

Dr. Stephen Devroe was fast asleep when he heard the noise. Was it outside or inside? Was it a dream or—he looked at the big phone on his nightstand. He picked it up and followed the sequence until he hit 'talk.'

"Hello," he said.

"Dr. Devroe, our apologies for interrupting your night's sleep. I'm Security Agent 2854 with a message from operations control. They wish for me to inform you of an imminent event in the Malacca Strait. It will be picked up and reported by the world's intelligence agencies. This event is the result of defensive actions initiated by our group. It should be characterized in the media, not as another reason for concern but as the first step in eliminating the problem. Other Western powers were also anonymously informed. You are receiving this direct message because of our previous communication."

"Can we help?" Devroe asked.

"Not at this time. The response is well underway, and there was very little time for planning, let alone prompt communication. Of course, we will continue to be in touch. Good night, Doctor."

Devroe looked at the telephone, thinking, where did you go? He wasn't used to the clipped manner that this mysterious group seemed to employ. It was like dealing with a computer. Sitting on the side of the bed, he looked at the clock; it read 2:35. Grabbing the phone, he dialed the president's number.

Perez heard the phone ring and picked it up quickly.

"Sorry, it's Stephen; I just got a call from your friends."

"Our friends, I hope," Perez said.

"*Our* friends told me they had initiated a defensive action in the Malacca Strait. It's something big enough; everyone's going to

103

know about it."

The president frowned. "What's Darrell (White House press secretary) going to do with *that* at a press conference? He is going to *have* to give saying we don't know what happened or who did it but don't panic everything will be all right? What the hell is *that*?"

Devroe said, "Uh, let's not kill the messenger. You're the one who wanted me to be the contact."

"You're right. So, let's make sure our people get that info fast and get back to me. Then we will formulate what our next step will be at the briefing this morning.

"Sure thing, see you then," Devroe said, and he hung up the phone.

CHAPTER—19

LEAVING ZURICH

Brad and Kate sat in the kitchen after eating.

Brad said, "Mrs. Bannister, that was some great food. I can't thank you enough."

"You're quite welcome, young man. I don't get many guests and never any young and energetic like you two."

She looked at Kate and then turned back to Brad and said, "She's a cutie, isn't she?"

"Ethel," Kate said.

Brad looked over at Kate and said, "Yes, I would have to agree, but real ornery and plays hard to get."

"Well, well," Ethel said, smiling at Brad. "Girls will be girls, won't they?"

Kate stood up from the table, saying, "That's enough, you two, it's time to make the call."

In Kate's room, Brad watched as she entered in the characters. Finally, a colorful logo appeared; she hit talk.

Avery answered. "Kate, how are you doing?"

"Just fine," she said. "We made it to the house, and Mrs. Bannister is taking excellent care of us. Do you have any information on what this is all about?"

"We know very little at this point, but a well-educated guess would be Iran. They're up to something, but no one seems to know what at this point."

Kate thought for a second. "Avery, where I work, we uncovered an intrusion earlier that day. We were able to trace it back to a cyber cafe in Iran. Marc, my supervisor, was getting ready to send a flash message up the chain when whoever hit the place."

"Very interesting," Avery said. "We will go over that when we get together. I have sent a go package that should arrive today. Get some rest, and I will work to find out if it was just the station they were after or if it was you."

"Me, why me?" Kate said.

"Your safety is always my first concern, and it seems someone has put together a surprisingly detailed picture from information that's supposed to be a deep secret. I need you to stay right where you are unless Ethel tells you otherwise. Do not leave the house and stay out of sight. Give Ethel your sizes so she can get you some travel clothes and personal items. Does Brad have his passport?"

"Yes, he had it on him. Mine was in my purse, which I left behind."

He asked, "Were there other women in the room?"

"Yes."

"They will have photographed everyone matching to IDs and will see that you and perhaps Brad got away."

"Avery, what is the State Department saying? It was an NSA site. You can't go into another country and start shooting American citizens."

"It's too early," Avery said, "that will come in time. Meanwhile, we trust no one. Kate, are you going to stay there as I asked?"

"Yes, why?"

"Because you're Kate Adler, that's why, and you're not prone to do the expected and often do the opposite."

"Avery Stanton, I'm not that unreliable, and you know it."

"I didn't say unreliable; I was referring to unpredictable. Let Ethel get the package delivered to the door, as it's her neighborhood. I'm sending a car for you tomorrow morning. The driver will come to the house and identify himself with a small micro flash memory stick. Let Ethel handle the verification. She will plug the stick into the G9 phone, and it will bring up his picture and self-connect to a network. The verification process will request a fingerprint pressed onto the screen. That will bring up another picture of him stored in the database. The two pictures must be an identical match."

"Avery, how did you know about the safe house? Actually, whose safe house is it?"

"A minor detail, the important thing is, for the moment, you're no longer in danger. I'm trying to get there as soon as I can and will see you tomorrow as we also have other things to discuss."

"Avery, where are we going? Where is the car going to take us? What do we do when we get there?"

"You are going to a safe place, a very safe place. The driver will take you to a small airport where a helicopter will transport you to the final destination. Going to the airport, you may notice a car behind you, but it is one of ours. The trip will take about two hours. An escort will take you to an underground entrance."

"One of ours, what does that mean? What then?"

"You will go through a security check like the driver. There are two flash cards with the package, one for each of you. After the preliminaries, you will meet a delightful woman named Kira Vestrova. She will take care of you both until I arrive. Have dinner and get some rest as some changes are coming into your life."

"Changes, like what?"

"Get some sleep. I'm on my way, and we will discuss all of it when I arrive. You will know everything."

CHAPTER—20

OPERATION SKYBORN

The *IRGC Yunes* was the newest Kilo-class submarine in the Revolutionary Guard's Navy. It sat at a depth of nine meters, traveling south at four knots in the Strait of Malacca, a body of water located between the island of Sumatra and the Malaysian peninsula. The strait was barely forty miles wide at some points. At the end of the peninsula sat the Republic of Singapore, a global commerce, financial, and transportation hub strategically placed connecting the Pacific Ocean with the Indian Ocean. One-third of the world's oil and one-half of the world's natural gas passes through the area, making it one of the critical choke points of global surface-based commerce.

As the sub silently glided through the channel, Captain Hamid Mahmud peered through the periscope sweeping the immediate area.

"We are still clear," he said. "The *Serena* is still on course." He nodded to a seaman, who retracted the scope. He called out to his first in command, "Make your depth twelve meters."

The first officer gave the command, "Plainsman, make your depth twelve meters and report."

"Twelve meters, aye."

"We still have fifty-five minutes before deployment."

Captain Mahmud turned to his first officer and said, "Commander, you have the bridge. I will be in the deployment hold."

"Aye, Captain, the first officer has the bridge."

Captain Mahmud descended the stairs on his way to the pride of the Iranian submarine fleet. The boat was the first to be outfitted with a special middle section with an ocean interface to allow deployment of divers, special operations forces, and storage for small inflatable surface transports. Mahmud had told the *Yunes* crew they were on a historical blue water mission to demonstrate the Iranian Navy could operate thousands of miles from the home base. This mission would prove that no one was beyond the reach of the Islamic Republic of Iran. They would return home as heroes to their families. It was a cover for the operation that was about to take place.

In the interface compartment, Lieutenant Ghasemi was directing his men preparing for their mission.

The captain entered the space, looked at the team's faces, and said, "Lieutenant Ghasemi, how is it coming?"

Everyone came to attention. Ghasemi held his salute. "At ease, everybody."

"Fine, Captain, preparations are complete and on our third equipment check."

"Have you had any personnel down here snooping around or asking questions? Do you have any reason to believe there is a breach in our security?"

"None, Captain. We have stayed in our quarters with a secure door as directed since starting to deploy our equipment."

"And your team?"

"They're soldiers of the revolution. They will follow orders and keep their silence. They're good men," the lieutenant said.

"I'm sure that's true. We are about thirty minutes away. As planned, I will bring us close to the surface but still submerged and send you the egress signal. When you and your men are clear, the sub will then dive to maximum depth. When you return, signal us when you are directly overhead. The whole operation should take under two hours. I'm on my way to the bridge. Call if you need anything."

Captain Mahmud knew there would be no rescue. Those higher than he had decided to modify the team's detonation equipment to go off twenty minutes earlier than the timers would read out. The team would still be on board. They would disintegrate in the vapor cloud explosion destroying the ship and at least a mile of the surrounding docks and storage facilities. It would take years to rebuild the port. The devastation would disrupt a large portion of all commerce dependent on Singapore for bunkering, transiting, and repairs.

Capt. Nadeem Petropoulou of the LNG tanker *D.S. Serena* made a tight course correction and started down the Malacca Straits run at six knots under clear skies and twenty-mile visibility. Turning to the helmsman, he said, "Okay, now, right down the center of the channel markers. I want no mistakes."

He brought his binoculars up to his face and scanned the waterway.

"How long before the harbor pilot comes on board?" he asked his first officer.

"We received a message that he is twenty to twenty-five minutes out," the officer said.

The *D.S. Serena* was an LNG tanker transporting 143,000 cubic meters of liquefied natural gas at -160 degrees centigrade in four spherical tanks. The top halves of them were visible above the deck of the ship.

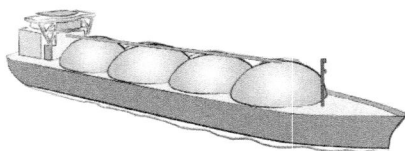

D.S. Serena

"Captain, there is a message coming in from the home office. It's a hard-copy transmission."

A message from them is highly unusual, the captain thought. "Read it," he said.

"Capt. Nadeem Petropoulos of the *D.S. Serena* tanker urgent message. Slow to three knots, expect airborne boarding party numbering four. Provide full cooperation to an agent in charge. Repeat. Full cooperation. Message your understanding of same."

"What the hell? Did it say boarding party? What in God's name does that mean? Reply our confirmation," the captain said.

"Message and reply in the log, sir."

"Captain," the lookout on the port side of the ship said, "I have an inbound helicopter five miles out."

The captain went to the engine room intercom, "Give me three knots steady, reverse to obtain."

Captain Mahmud on the *Yunes* selected the compartment and pressed the button on the com. "Lieutenant Ghasemi, this is the captain; start your deployment."

"Aye, Captain." He looked at his men as they checked their diving masks. Each gave a thumbs-up, and the lieutenant threw the switch. Doors opened, allowing the ocean to flood the room built for divers exiting the sub at medium depths.

Through the doors, the RHIB (rigid hull inflatable boat) was deployed and inflated, rising to the surface, and helping carry the attached heavy bags of equipment up through the darkened waters. Divers then advanced to the surface to pull the gear up onto the raft. The lieutenant closed the sub's hatch from the outside of the sub and was the last to the surface. With equipment and divers aboard, they started the electric outboard engine and proceeded at top speed to their objective.

The RHIB was low in the water; the men and equipment were all colored a muted grey-green to blend in with the coastal waters. They would be approaching without detection. The navigator looked at his compass and brought up his glasses, locating the *D.S. Serena* three thousand meters ahead. They were headed on a course to intercept the ship in about twenty minutes. A veteran of the war with Iraq, the lieutenant looked at his men, pleased all had gone to plan.

Captain Mahmud aboard the sub said to his first officer, "Make your depth twenty meters, course 320, all ahead standard."

"Aye, sir."

Colonel Langer, former SAS commando, was commander of Alpha Team 4 and leading his boarding unit on the approaching helicopter. He and his team sat on the floor of the copter on their way to the *Serena*. The doors were open, and their legs hung over the side as the ocean waves flew beneath them. The air ripped through the spacious cabin as the pilot maintained a course to intercept. Each man had an assignment and was equipped to execute quickly and effectively. They were all members of the loosely termed Circuit, a collection of retired Special Operations veterans from around the world. It was a natural place to seek employment, given their training and experience after serving their countries. His team and many others had signed up with a secretive group that did not seem to have an identity. They deployed for this group from several bases around the world. They were small in number but always had the best equipment with great pay and benefits. They were the envy of their counterparts who served in other private security companies.

"Thirty seconds, Colonel," the pilot said over the aircraft's communicating system.

Langer reached down to his belt and pressed button "B" on his transmitter, connecting him back to the Cartel's Operations Center. "Senior Blue, Senior Blue, this is Alpha Team 4. Over."

Back in the Cartel's Operations Center, Penn Hauer replied, "This is Senior Blue, over."

"Roger, Senior Blue, radio check, over."

"Roger. Five by five, over."

"LZ in sight, thirty seconds to boarding."

"Copy that, over."

"Alpha Team 4, out."

Langer hit the "A" button to return to the intercom and team communication.

Bodies started to move within the tight confines. Langer would be the first down the rappel rope, followed by three others of his unit. Langer spoke into his headset.

"Do you see anything, Mr. Barker?" the helicopter captain asked the copilot who was scanning the sea with his glasses.

"No, sir, the sea is clear, and as far as I can tell, there is no small watercraft in sight. The *Serena* is dead ahead."

"Keep me informed until we rope down."

The aircraft's intercom came on again. "Colonel, ten seconds to stationary hover," the pilot said.

Below him, Langer saw the ship come into view. Ropes dropped out each side as the colonel yelled, "Go go go." The pilot hovered over the bow, one of the few flat open deck spaces not taken up by the large, circular LNG tanks embedded into the ship. Each man clipped his descender into the rope and slid down quickly with his equipment. As each landed on the tanker's deck, they dropped to one knee rifles ready, and waited.

"All on board," Langer called up to the pilot.

The ropes were cut, landing in the water as the aircraft veered off. On Langer's command, the team ran aft, headed for the wheelhouse double time.

"Captain," said a lookout on the *Serena*, "we have people roping down onto the ship from a helicopter."

"What the hell is going on? Is this a movie or something?"

"They're coming our way on both sides of the ship. They have guns."

The captain could see right away; it was a situation that could get out of hand.

"Everybody, just stay calm," he said. Opening the hatch, he went out to the bridge wing, looking down at the deck five stories below, and could see the men approaching. He put his hands up in the act of peace, letting whoever was boarding his ship know they were not going to resist. It all happened so fast; he didn't have time to get his crew to safety. Uniforms were ascending the deckhouse stairs rapidly. Soon a tall, well-built man with a commanding presence stood in front of the captain.

Langer looked at the man, saying, "Are you the captain?"

"Yes, I'm Captain Nadeem Petropoulos," the captain said.

Langer pulled a small picture from his uniform pocket and looked at the man before him.

"Excellent," Langer said as he reached out with his hand and said, "My name is Colonel White, and we have reason to believe you are in danger. We are here to assist your ship and your crew. Can we expect your cooperation?"

"White?" Nadeem said. "Well, Colonel White, I'm glad to make your acquaintance. Who are you, and just what danger are you going to save us from?"

"We intend to keep you from being boarded by anonymous agents who wish to blow up your ship. And who we are is not important if we do our job, don't you agree?"

"I'm not sure," the captain said

"For safety, could you get your deck crew inside and away from outside bulkheads? We don't have much time."

"Into the safe rooms?" the captain asked.

"No, that won't be necessary. You will need to stay here on the bridge as the material authority. Also, have your men in the engine room stay in place, as we might need maneuvering capability. Mr. Black here will take over at the helm and radar. Mr. Green will be aft getting set up."

Mr. Black noted the heading and speed. Next, he addressed the

113

ship's radar. The shipping lane was marked on the screen picturing all the vessels in the area. Each tagged with identification information provided by the port indicating they had reason to be where they were, as none was flagged red.

"I have a green screen," Mr. Black said. Another of Langer's men in the wheelhouse provided a live video feed to the Operations Control Room, supplementing the real-time audio.

Langer stepped outside, pushed the transceiver, and, pulling in his headset's microphone, said, "Senior Blue, Senior Blue. This is Alpha Team 4, over."

"This is Senior Blue, over."

"Roger, Senior Blue, landing completed per plan. Proceeding Phase Two."

"Roger, Alpha Team 4, over."

"Alpha Team 4, out."

Langer went back inside and addressed his navigator. "We need to look for anything small and moving fast."

"Well, how about this," Mr. Black said. He pointed at a blip just appearing on the edge of the screen coming up from astern. Langer talked into the team's com system to three of his men outside waiting for his orders.

"Mr. Green, we have identified the approaching target. Remember, contact and ignition must be at least a thousand meters out, or we are all going to miss dinner."

"Copy that, one thousand meters."

Green's two shooters readied their equipment and set themselves up. There was one primary and one backup shooter. The M47 Dragon shoulder-fired missile fit the range requirement and, being wire-guided, could stay fixed on a moving target even from the moving deck of a ship.

Langer waited a few seconds and said to Mr. Green, "Have you acquired visual confirmation of the target yet?"

"Yes, sir," was his reply as he held the small craft in his binoculars.

Langer said, "The radar scope has it three thousand meters out."

"Copy that." Mr. Green said to his men. "We are close; get your screens up and ready."

"Good to go," said one.

"Ready here," said the other.

The colonel waited and then said, "Two thousand meters out—fire at your ready."

"Roger that."

* * *

The inflatable raft was riding hard at its current speed. The leader had his binoculars up and fixed on the ship they were chasing. The wet diving suits protected from the water, but the jolts were taking their toll. Usually, their approach was stealthy with little noise or anything visual to notify anyone they were in the area. This mission came about so quickly they didn't have time to train for this type of approach. He brought the glasses up again, keeping the target in sight. During loading the boat, securing equipment, and getting underway, they had missed the six minutes it took for Langer to get his team aboard.

"Continue as planned," he said.

At the ship's stern, the first shooter was on one knee with the Dragon's business end hovering between the top and middle railing. He was staring at the LCD screen containing a video feed of the approaching boat centered by crosshairs on the screen and range information.

With his cheek against the tube, the first shooter said, "Preparing to fire." Looking at the distance countdown on the screen, he yelled, "clear," and the rocket was on its way. Staying still after the shot, he followed the missile's trajectory in the screen, keeping the crosshairs on the quickly approaching target. The rocket by itself would have obliterated the small craft. However, since the small raft also contained 128 pounds of C4 explosives, the explosion was twenty times larger. The pressure wave tossed all three men in the Dragon team against the pump-housing terminal.

The backup shooter rolled himself up to a sitting position and grabbed his colleague so he could see his lips. He yelled, "Damn, couldn't you have hit it farther out?" He could barely hear what he had said, but the first shooter got his point.

The first shooter then pulled his buddy close and yelled into his ear. "I timed it to make absolutely sure I would hit it. We would all be dead if it were *your* shot." He then slapped him on his knit cap to make a point before helping him up. All three proceeded to pick up debris from the recoil and check around the area for anything that would prove they had been there and headed forward.

"It was a port side egress, right?"

"What? Oh, yes," he pointed out to sea, "it's on its way."

"Mr. Green, what is your status?" Langer said.

"All good here, Colonel, wrapping up."

"Nice job."

"Mr. Black, how are we doing with our extraction?"

"The Mark V is two minutes out at forty-five knots."

Langer turned to Capt. Petropoulos, who was in a bit of shock. "That explosion was larger than any of us planned, but it worked out. Our understanding was a foreign agent intended to blow up your ship in the Singapore harbor. It would have been a disaster of the first order."

"How did you know?" the captain asked. "Who do you represent, Mr. White or whoever you are? You just blew up some people. I guess I want to thank you for that, but still on whose authority?"

"Are you married, Captain?"

"Yes, I am."

"Kids?"

"Yes, but what does ...?"

"Everything, Captain, you get to call them tonight. Who cares about authority when compared to that? Port security will be here in full strength in about twenty minutes. Make sure you tell them how big the explosion was."

"You're British," the captain said.

"Yes, I am, but this was not a British operation. In truth, Mr. Black over there is from Colombia, but that's all I can give you."

"Colonel, they're coming up alongside," Mr. Black said. They started rappelling down to the Mark V. The skipper of the special operations craft tracked the larger vessel at the same speed.

Langer reached out, shaking the captain's hand. "Nice doing business with you."

Going down the stairs and out of earshot, Mr. Black said, "Colombian, really?"

"Sure, it was as good as any. Well, now that I have given it some thought, Chinese wouldn't have worked."

* * *

Minutes earlier aboard the *Yunes*, the boat's sonar operator jumped straight up from a sitting position, yelling as he desperately grasped at his headphones and ripped them off his head. He stood for a second, trying to regain his balance as his inner ear, overwhelmed, tried to compensate. His sophisticated equipment, meant to detect minute sounds in the water and amplify them, was working perfectly. It recreated the sound of the small assault craft blowing up directly into the middle of his head.

When expecting a prominent sound, the machine could be manually set to shunt any unusual sound above a certain decibel level. He had planned to set it in another twenty minutes, so he could still monitor traffic in the immediate area until the last minute. The officer in charge went over to the sonar station, sat him down, and scanned the readout cascading down the screen.

"Captain, there has been an explosion," the officer said.

"Can you give me anything else?"

"All the other traffic is normal except a new boat in the water turning over forty knots."

"Which direction is it headed?" the captain asked.

There was a pause, and the officer said, "It's hard to tell, but I know for sure it's not headed in our direction."

The captain thought for a moment. His options were limited without being discovered, which wasn't an option. Captain Hamid Mahmud knew the operation was compromised. Either the team prematurely set the timers, or someone intercepted the team.

Hamid barked, "Quartermaster, sounding."

"Twenty-five meters, Captain."

Mahmud shouted, "Officer of the deck, rig for dive, make your depth twenty meters."

"Aye, sir, bow planes down five degrees."

Mahmud gave another order. "Quartermaster, report availability of thirty meters depth."

"Aye, sir."

The *Yunes*, already at ten meters, silently drifted down to her maximum depth at this part of the strait. Mahmud wasn't sure what happened up there. He couldn't eliminate the possibility of military

117

ships searching for his position. He walked over to the sonar console where the officer had assumed the duties of the operator.

"Keep a heightened alert until we are clear of the strait."

"Yes, sir."

Mahmud would wait until he was in open water before coming up to message depth and sending a status of the operation. There are going to be some agitated people at the IRGC operations center, he thought. He would face an inquiry as to the operation's failure, and he would have few answers.

"Helm right fifteen degrees, set course three two zero."

"Aye, sir."

CHAPTER—21

PRESIDENT'S BRIEFING

Martin Perez, President of the United States
Dr. Stephen Devroe, Director of National Intelligence (DNI)
Dennis Corwen, Secretary of Defense
Paul Miller, Director of Central Intelligence Agency (CIA)
Royce Wakefield, Secretary of State

The president's daily briefing team assembled in the Oval Office. Devroe started by saying, "Mr. President, we had an incident in the Malacca Strait last night of some importance. We are still trying to put the pieces together, but our station chief in Singapore reports it concerns the *D.S. Serena*, an LNG tanker that was just outside the port of Singapore. An airborne assault team boarded the ship by rappelling from a Black Hawk helicopter onto the deck. They spoke English and took over the ship. According to the captain, two men stationed themselves at the stern and fired on a fast-approaching rigid inflatable, manned by several men. Firing at the inflatable caused an enormous explosion in the water."

"Who were the men in the inflatable?" the president asked.

"We don't know at this time. However, the tactics of the boarding team and accuracy of the fire team would certainly indicate a military operation with good field surveillance, preparation, and damn good equipment. It seems reasonable to assume, given the size of the explosion, the attackers were not there for a picnic."

Perez turned to Devroe, "Did our systems pick up anything prior to all of this?"

"Nothing," Devroe said. "I pinged everyone and got zero. We are going back over everything in the last forty-eight hours to see if we missed something."

Miller (CIA) said, "The captain was very clear about what occurred. He indicated the leader said the boat's men were terrorists planning to capture the tanker, sail it into the harbor, and blow it up. When the team fired their weapons, it appeared to ignite the explosives the raft carried to blow up the tanker."

The president threw a knowing look at Devroe. The president knew he wasn't entirely truthful when he said, "Paul, don't we have anything on who this boarding team was?"

"That's the big problem," Miller replied. "The captain doesn't know exactly. He did say the leader indicated they were not from the US, and he had a British accent. The leader also said one of the men was from Colombia. The Captain reports the assault team left his ship for shore in a Special Operations boat. They then went radio silent. We think they landed somewhere other than Singapore or Malaysia. We are trying to find out where now."

"Were they wearing any uniforms indicating who they were, any patches, rank insignia?" Devroe asked.

Paul Miller looked at his papers, and after turning a page, he read, "This is from the station chief's report: 'Capt. Nadeem Petropoulos served six years in the Greek Navy and was very knowledgeable regarding tactics and equipment. The assault team wore standard camouflage uniforms without any rank or identification markings. It seems they were a highly disciplined, very professional team with substantial resources. Helicopters brought them in, and Special Operations boats took them away. The captain indicated they strongly suggested he follow their instructions, but he never lost control of his ship."

Devroe had a note of exasperation in his voice. "Jesus, that type of equipment had to come from somewhere."

The president asked the room, "Could it be Singapore or Malaysian special forces? If the answer is yes, we still need to answer the question of how they picked this up and we didn't?"

Miller answered, "The Singapore military could have handled it had they known, but the report states they denied any involvement, and they're opening an investigation. The attack was an existential threat to their country. If the port goes, they're completely out of business. If it was them, they were out of uniform, but neither country admits to having any of their military personnel involved in any operation regarding the tanker."

"Mr. President," Devroe said, "the next news cycle is going to report on the attempted attack, and it will not be good news even though they avoided a catastrophe. It will be an additional event on top of the hijackings. It shows whoever is doing this has a global reach. Darrell (White House press secretary) will need a briefing so he isn't blindsided in the press room. He will need direction on a response as there will be other stories out there."

Perez looked at those before him. "I'm open to any suggestions. The bottom line is we don't know who the attackers were, so we don't know who saved the ship."

Royce said, "We could always go with 'investigations are underway.' It will buy us some time. It all comes down to what Wall Street will think of it."

Devroe looked at Perez and thought of his conversation the previous night with the agent. "Can we say it's all under wraps and hint that it is the beginning of activity to bring this craziness to a halt?"

Dennis (SOD) threw a curious look at the DNI. "How can you say something like that?"

"Because it's true. Didn't someone just avert a disaster that fits the past pattern of hijackings? The only problem is it wasn't us, and we don't know who. Can't we have Darrell say specifically what happened and finish with that's the extent of our statement at this time? 'We will keep you informed of any new developments of the efforts underway to curb these disruptions.' It leaves the impression something is going on, which it is, and gives the markets some hope. Meanwhile, we get to work and try to find out more."

The president said, "I want to go with that. Stephen, can you get to Darrell and give him exactly what you just outlined. I know it's not your job, but you're the one with the idea."

"Dennis, something's been bothering me," Devroe said. "How do you get a small boat loaded with explosives that far from shore ready to board a tanker without being detected?"

"We checked all surrounding traffic," he said. "They all had reason to be there and were on a prescribed schedule. However, it's not hard to figure it out. The team had to disembark from a submarine. The inflatable doesn't have the range to come from somewhere else, even from shore. If it surfaced, we should be able to retrieve satellite surveillance, at least proving the point. And if there is no evidence of a sub in the area, then they disembarked submerged. That's a problem because it's a capability the Iranians don't have."

Devroe said, "Or we *think* they don't have. I think we need to account for all the Iranian subs at the time of the attack. Keep track until they're all accounted for, even if it takes weeks. One of them coming straight back from Singapore should take a calculated amount of time. It just gets us closer to figuring this out."

Dennis cleared his throat. "Mr. President, we have a nuclear sub patrol in the area that no one on earth knows is there."

The president looked at his secretary of defense. "Are you suggesting we sink it?"

"No, sir, merely stating there is an option."

The president's voice rose an octave. "Dennis, I know that's your job. We don't even know who it is. What if we make a mistake? It's an unforgivable political error. There will be no firing on anybody until I give the order. Is this clear to the room?" he asked.

Everyone mumbled, with Dennis being the good soldier, saying "Yes, Mr. President."

Dennis added, "Well, short of that, we could have our sub try and locate and track any contacts that meet the time and location for returning home."

"That's a good idea; I will approve that, but no shooting."

"Thank you, Mr. President."

Everyone stood and filed out of the room.

Devroe lagged, and when they were alone, he said, "Mr. President, I thought they had a subtler hand."

The president shook his head, "So did I, but I'm not sure what their options were, given the time frame. All I know is the people of this country, and a few more, owe them a debt of gratitude. If that tanker had blown up and taken the country of Singapore with it, we could be looking at something ten times worse. We need to get in front of this and fast. I'm open to suggestions."

"I think you need to address the nation. People want to hear you're in charge, and everything is going to be all right."

"You're asking me to lie about the 'all right' part?"

"You need to buy time for us to uncover something actionable. It's the only thing I can think of right now anyway."

"I'm not going to make an address and lie to the American people regardless of the reason. When are you going to hear back from the Cartel?"

Devroe shook his head. "Last time I spoke to them, they were pretty busy with the tanker. My contact indicated as soon as they were able to meet, they hoped to come up with a longer-term plan."

The president shook his head. "I hate this relying on them. I feel like I'm suspended in air, unable to do anything. I like Dennis's idea of tracking any sub in the area and seeing if we can take roll call and account for all their subs. Listen, start being a pain in the ass, and get our 'unequaled' intelligence agencies to do their job." He looked at Devroe. "But no false information to meet my frustration."

CHAPTER—22

CHATEAU de VIANDEN

Brad was looking out his window as they approached a small private airport. The car Avery sent was not just a car but a nicely outfitted limousine that lumbered around any corner like a block of concrete. As soon as they started on the trip, it was quickly apparent that Karsten, the driver, had been instructed to stay off anything resembling an autobahn. Brad calculated the vehicle would survive an exploding IED directly below his seat, and all he would need were a few aspirins.

He looked over to the other side of the expansive bench seat to see Kate, asleep with her head on a pillow pushed up against the door. They had been in the car for under an hour, but the rocking must have overcome her. He moved the rest of his body, knowing that he must have also taken advantage of the silence and the hypnotic motion of the car to steal a nap. Kate moved, stretching her feet out, pushing against Brad's legs. He didn't move them. It was a stupid adolescent decision, one of many he made when it came to Kate Adler. His hand touched her shoulder. When she turned to look at him, her genuine, touching smile created a reaction inside him he had felt many times before. She put her hand on his arm and quietly asked, "How are you doing?"

"I'm doing fine. Did you fall asleep?"

"Oh, yes, of that, I'm sure," she said, gathering her hair back a

124

couple of times into a ponytail before letting it fall.

Brad petted the door sill like a dog and said, "Did you know we are on our way in a car that passes for a tank to jump on a helicopter to some unknown destination? Then we are to meet a 'very nice lady' who is a stranger, to hear some mysterious things this Avery has to tell you?"

"Stop complaining; it's better than being dead."

"There you go again; you've got me there. Where do you think we are going, secret hideout or something?"

"Honestly, Brad, I have no idea. I think we have to face the fact that someone wanted the entire office dead, and that included you and me. They didn't finish the job, so that means we are still a target. We will need to solve this before we can live normal lives again. I, for one, don't like people shooting at me."

"I hate being dead even worse," he said.

The car stopped, and they got out. A man from the trailing black SUV helped them step up into the helicopter. Kate and Brad were strapped in and donned the headphones. The man checked everything and tapped the shoulder of the pilot.

From the air, they could see the green countryside pass below, the quiet small towns and villages that make up most of Europe dotting the hills and valleys. It was a peaceful trip except for the engine noise and vibrations. After a while, Brad spoke into the headset. "Are you thirsty?" he said, holding up a bottle of water.

Kate put a hand on his shoulder and said, "No, thank you. It sure is loud. Have you ever been in a helicopter?"

"I'm not sure; anyway, it's classified."

"You're such a putz," she said, grabbing back the bottle.

Sometime later, over their headphones, they heard: "We are approaching Vianden just inside the Luxembourg border. I will make one pass around and then land. It's worth seeing."

Below them appeared a massive fortified stone castle sitting on the highest hill in the area. On all sides, thick forest surrounded it for a thousand feet or so. The small town with eighteen thousand people sat right on the Our river. The castle's vertical stone walls rose from the hillside. They were very thick and capped with arrow loops and a wall walk used by soldiers of old. The spires from the interior courtyards rose up but not to any recognizable style. It was beautiful and certainly looked very formidable. The town's main street, the Grand-Rue, was an attraction by itself with its cobblestoned course and centuries-old buildings lining both sides of the historic downtown lane.

Brad looked at Kate and said. "What do you think?"

"What's to think," she said. "Avery said it would be safe."

"A prison is safe," Brad said. They slowed to a hover and slowly came down on the landing pad just outside the massive walls. Two men stood just off the pad with their backs to the thrusting wind caused by the rotors. When the helicopter doors opened, a man walked them to a protected alcove at the foot of the wall. At the back, it was closed off by an ornate iron gate. In the nook was a small guard shack.

"Good afternoon," the guard said in German.

"English," one of the men from the landing pad said.

"I'm sorry. May I have your identification cards?" the guard said in English. They both presented the flash cards, and after nodding with a smile, he went back to a small shack inside the room.

"What is this place?" Kate asked one of the other guards.

"Dieses ist ein Schloss," he said.

"Well, that was informative," Kate said, looking at Brad.

"Yes, thank you. We already picked up it was a castle," Brad said.

The first guard looked up from a phone similar to the one Kate had used at the safe house, apparently pleased with the result, and returned their cards. One of the men reached in front of Kate to slide back the gate. As he did so, his suit jacket opened, and Kate saw a shoulder holster with the strap over the gun holding it in place. She didn't say anything. Lights bathed the drab concrete in the short hall as an oversized, ornate wooden door opened directly in front of them. In stark contrast to everything in the immediate area, there stood a vividly attractive middle-aged woman of medium build in a long, silk, red dress that she held at the side with her hand. Her smooth, shiny hair fell on her shoulders, reflecting the soft light emanating from behind her. Brad was quick to notice the light partially silhouetting her body and stopped walking.

"Really?" Kate said as she pushed him forward.

"Hello," she said, extending her hand to Kate. "My name is Kira Vestrova. I'm a business associate of Avery's, and I would like to welcome you to Vianden Castle."

"Thank you," Kate said. "This is my friend and associate, Brad."

Brad reached for Kira's extended hand, encountering a gentle softness. He held it just long enough before reluctantly letting it free.

"Welcome to you both," Kira said. They walked into a good-sized foyer with slate floors and a type of shield on one wall. Kira pulled back the protective screen of the cage lift and motioned for them to enter.

Vestrova pushed a button and said in her Russian accent, "We are very relieved as you've now arrived. I trust your trip was as comfortable as was possible. There were certain restrictions placed on your travel, limiting our being able to utilize truly first-class accommodations. We hope to make it up to you presently."

Kate looked at a transfixed Brad with amusement and great sympathy as he listened to Kira's words formed in smooth, effortless sentences with her hands moving in subtle accompaniment as she spoke. She had to be very aware of the effect she projected, Kate thought.

They moved out of the lift, again following Ms. Vestrova. Kate had to understand Brad's distraction as, certainly in her late forties, Ms. Vestrova was a classic beauty who, Kate guessed, probably modeled at some time in her life, acquiring the posture and rhythmic motion currently holding Brad hostage. Brad looked at Kate with a guilty grin holding his face rigid. Kate smiled back, shaking her head. "Mrs. Banister was right; boys will be boys."

They ended up in a beautiful space with fourteen-foot coffered ceilings and large leaded-glass windows at one end with an intricate design framing the clear glass at the center. Ms. Vestrova had tea on the table centered between two large sofas, all in front of an oversized but not ostentatious fireplace. Kate sat down next to Kira, and Brad was on the opposite side. The place was very comfortable with crocheted afghans folded over the arms of the sofas and armchairs. Wooden tables on each end of the couches supported bronze-based table lamps with translucent parchment shades that tinted the walls with an amber glow. The space was surprisingly warmer than one would expect inside a castle.

"Thank you for your patience with the security regime,"

Vestrova said. "The necessity of absolute security is a result of your recent experiences and, of course, our activities at the Castle. You will understand as soon as Avery fills you in on the details."

Kira reached over, gently placing her hand on Kate's, and said, "I cannot tell you the profound sadness I felt upon hearing of your father's passing. I have known him for a very long time and the sorrow, while not to be compared with that of a child losing a parent, was very deep indeed."

"Thank you," Kate said, struck by Kira's offer of sympathy; it was very thoughtful and kind.

Kira removed her hand. Kate had received many offers of condolences; nevertheless, this time, the soft, sincere manner somehow let loose the emotion that she had held at bay.

A woman appeared and began to serve the tea. Ms. Vestrova waited with her hands folded in her lap until she had finished.

"Thank you, Hedda," she said.

Kira turned toward Kate to inquire as to how she wanted her tea. Seeing Kate's reddened eyes and the rose color rising within her cheeks, she said, "Oh dear, I have upset you, and it couldn't have been further from my intentions. I do so apologize for my lack of thoughtfulness." She leaned over, picked up a cloth napkin from the tray offering it to Kate.

"Kate?" Brad said, seeing the same effects of emotion in her.

"Thank you," Kate said to Kira. Kate brought the napkin to her eyes and, addressing them both, said, "I won't apologize as I'm allowed to express sadness." She tried to say it in a lighthearted tone. "It seems recent events have kept me so occupied that I haven't allowed myself to think about the drastic change that takes place when your last parent dies. Lost forever is the ability to say 'I love you' ever again. To thank him for bringing me into this life, but there is something else: Whatever I did, right or wrong, I knew my father would protect me, would take my side, and would be there in a storm. When that certainty leaves, it leaves a hollow space, filled with the knowledge you are truly on your own. It's a little harder to deal with than I thought."

Brad made note that she had just shared more of her feelings and life than in all the time he had known her. It was a moment he wouldn't forget; it confirmed what his heart had been telling him.

Kira patiently waited before speaking. "Age is a wonderful

teacher; the young, being just that, have yet to encounter its wonderfully relevant lessons. One thing I have learned is just being able to think about the situation in the way you just described is very healthy, uncommon, and contributes greatly in dealing with the inevitable tragedies in life."

"Kate?" Brad said. "Can I do anything? I will do anything."

"No," Kate said. "I thank you both. I think delving into some of the answers as to why we are here will help distract me. Could we address some of the mysteries?"

"Of course," Kira said. "How about we start with where you are."

"Yes," Kate said. "All we know is that Avery said he was sending us to a place for protection."

"And," Brad said, "it certainly looks like this fits the bill."

"Yes, it's called Vianden Castle, and we are in Luxembourg," Kira said. One of her hands left the saucer she held. Her arm drifted from right to left as she continued. "It was built during the eleventh to the fourteenth centuries. Unfortunately, it has gone through several owners with various agendas and available resources before falling into a ruinous state by 1977. The final owner, the Grand Duke Jean, ruler of Luxembourg's constitutional monarchy, decided the renovation was an excessive burden on his struggling economy. The king, having other castles, was so anxious to rid himself of the burden; he accepted an offer from our organization that included the land being declared an independent sovereign state, much like Monaco or the Vatican. So as far as the outside world is concerned, we are our own country."

"What is it used for?" Brad asked.

"It's an office of Morton-Roth, a maritime management company."

"I know that name," Kate said. "That's one of my father's companies, but I never paid any attention."

"Yes, that's true," Kira smiled. "The high level of security is one of the reasons Mr. Stanton selected this location as your destination."

"That makes sense," Kate said.

Brad nervously shifted his position on the couch, "Ah, Ms. Vestrova, I don't want to be rude but …"

"Please, Mr. Danner, you must call me Kira," she said, leaning back as she lifted the cup from the saucer and brought it to her lips.

"Yes, of course," Brad said, captivated at her performing the act in slow motion. As a result, he lost his train of thought and failed to continue his question.

Kate gave Brad a hopeless look before saying, "What my colleague is trying to ask is, what happens next?"

"Of course, I'm not in a position to address the next steps in any plans. However, Mr. Stanton is due to arrive within the hour whereupon you may cover any issues or questions. I can't hope to imagine the kinds of stress you both have experienced since that terrible incident. What I can do is have Jimmy get you situated in your rooms so you can freshen up. He is at your disposal for anything. He will notify you when Mr. Stanton arrives as he left instructions you were to meet upon his arrival."

Kate leaned forward, placing her teacup on the tray. As she retreated into the sofa, she offered, "Ms. – I mean, Kira, I'm curious, if I may, what was the very comforting tone in Avery's voice when he said, 'You will meet a very delightful Ms. Vestrova'?"

Ms. Vestrova looked genuinely surprised. "Delightful, he said? Well, Mr. Stanton is the consummate gentleman, so the expression does not surprise me in the least. We have known each other for a very long time."

"That's strange," Kate said slowly. "Avery is all but a second father, and he never shared having so close a friend."

"Colleague," Kira corrected, "business colleague. However, if you know Mr. Stanton, which you do, you know it is not hard to come under the protective circle he extends to those he considers family

CHAPTER—23

KATE MEETS REALITY

An hour after the discussion with Kira and being shown to their rooms, Avery knocked on Kate's door. She opened it and immediately gave him the kind of hug that left no mistake about how she felt.

"Avery, thank you so much for helping us out. Even with some field experience, I was getting a little scared not knowing what could be happening."

"Well, you are all right, and that's all that matters," Avery said. "We have some significant and, frankly, very secret matters to discuss, and I want all of your attention."

Avery stepped back, allowing Kate to close her door, and they walked down the hall.

"I hope we are going to get into the incident at the station."

"It will be that and much more," he said.

"Avery, I want Brad to attend; he was, after all, almost killed. He deserves an explanation or some participation in resolving this."

"How well do you know Brad? How close are you both?"

"I never really thought about how close we are, but I would say he is my … best friend. We also really work well together. I'm not sure exactly what he did at the station, however, because of the classified nature of the information."

"Kate, we are going to cover some very personal information," Avery said. "How much do you want him to know about your personal life?"

"That's an excellent point, but, in some ways, I wouldn't have a life if it weren't for him. That and we are very close; therefore, yes, I'm willing to share that information."

They stopped in front of the door to Brad's room and knocked. Brad opened the door with a smile on his face. "This is one special place," he said. "I have never seen such stonework. Even as high as we are, the walls are still incredibly thick."

Kate looked at Avery. "Brad, let me introduce Avery Stanton, a close friend and my father's most trusted business partner. We are going to be discussing some rather private things, and I would like to have you there."

"No problem, Kate," Brad said. "You know that."

"However, there is one important condition. You must agree not to disclose anything you hear to anyone. I mean, really close to the vest, like keep your mouth shut forever. I won't go into NDAs or anything, but it's essential. I need your promise."

Brad's head went back as he took in the words. "That's interesting, and I didn't see that coming, but, sure, I will promise anything if I'm going to finally find out the secrets you keep in that twenty-ton bank vault in your head."

She gave him a look, "Brad, this is serious."

Defensively, he said, "Okay, then, I agree."

They all entered the same room they had occupied earlier in the afternoon. Despite the very high ceilings, it was a comfortable space, and Kate went to the same spot on the couch. She unconsciously ran her hand across its woven surface before Avery started talking.

"Can I get you anything, a drink, some tea?" Avery asked.

"No, thank you," she said. "Where's Brad?"

"Right here," he said, appearing with a quick step. "Are you extending the drink offer?"

"Brad Danner, I wouldn't be here if it wasn't for you. If it weren't for your lack of coffee-making skills, this would be a very different kind of day. Also, you were the getaway driver in a stolen car."

Brad laughed and said to Avery, "Well, do you still want to do this? It appears I'm a bad influence."

"What would you like?" Avery said.

"Nothing, and thank you."

Avery looked at Kate, and she said, " Avery, what is this place? Why are we—and perhaps more interesting—why are you here?"

"Believe me, that's a conversation that's weighed on me for some time. First," Avery said, tell me what happened at the station?"

Brad looked at Kate, and she nodded for him to start. "There had been some activity during the day regarding an Iranian break-in into the system, and we gathered into the conference room for our usual six o'clock meeting to review the results. While we were waiting, Kate and I went to make some coffee in another room. That's when we heard the shooting. We were not in the room, and that's why we got away."

"We managed to get out a side door," Kate said. "We planned to hijack a random passerby but soon found he was anything but a passerby. A fight ensued, and it was quickly obvious he knew how to defend himself. Finally, we—well, specifically Brad—got him under control. I was lucky enough to loosen his grip on a gun, then Brad stole it and used it to knock him out. We made it into the car and took off."

She looked at Brad, and he continued. "Then driving away, another vehicle hit us in the rear, turning us around. People got out and started shooting at us. We managed to …"

"We?" Kate said.

"Okay, *I* was able to take care of the problem using the gun I still had."

"So," Kate said, "that's our side. What do we know about who did this?"

"We have been working on that and have a good feeling for the players," Avery said. "There is a meeting in progress addressing just that problem. They're sifting through intelligence, trying to piece together a picture of the problem before we can establish the full parameters of our response."

"Who is 'they' and what do you mean 'our response'?" Kate asked. "You mean, where we hide?"

"No, I mean our response."

Kate's throat tightened, and the altered effect in her speech was evident as she said, "Hold it. Response to whom? Do we know who attacked the station? I want to give them a big piece of my mind, right between the eyes. Those were my friends; somebody just decided they wanted them to disappear." She waved her hand in the air. "This will not go away quietly."

"Just settle down and stop acting like your father," Avery said.

"I'm not acting," she said, vigorously crossing her arms and legs, all the while intrigued and startled by the strength in Avery's voice.

"Kate," Avery said, "first, you weren't working at an NSA station. I will explain, but it must come later. I promise to address that whole issue before we finish, but first are issues we need to address regarding you, your father, the Adler Group, and, to some extent, myself. You've been avoiding these, but the time has come. No escaping. I will lock the door if I have to."

"Avery, what's with the drama? I have never been shy about my avoiding the internal affairs of the company."

Avery ignored Kate's comment and began. "Some time ago, when your father knew his health was failing, I gladly accepted the responsibility to step in and manage his companies. He also asked me to do everything in my power to look after you with an emphasis on your security. I accepted that responsibility."

Kate's body language had become attentive. She said, perhaps a little too loudly, "Wait a minute. Just how long has that been going on?"

Again, Avery did not answer her question. "Through hundreds of business deals, there were some who were bound to be unhappy. In business, sometimes, someone wins, and someone loses. Such is the nature of business, and your father was concerned about any negative issues drifting into your life. It's a common thought among those with considerable influence and attractive resources. So, yes," Avery said, "fulfilling your father's wishes, we have kept abreast of your life but, again, mostly for your safety. Well-selected people in the CIA knew who you were while you were there. Their only assignment was to notify us if you were in danger. It was a workplace thing. No one was concerned about your private life."

"Why didn't you tell me? Why didn't someone tell me?" Kate asked.

Avery paused. "I think there is an obvious answer to that. Also, we had someone in the Munich office."

"What?" Kate said. "You had someone spying on me? Who?"

"Not spying, making sure you were all right. Again, it's what your father wanted."

Kate, in a commanding tone, again asked, "Who?"

Brad leaned forward and broke his silence. "Kate," he said sheepishly, "that would be me."

Kate stared at Brad for several seconds without any comment.

Brad knew the look. "I'm sorry, Kate; it started as a job and turned into where we are now—wherever that is."

Kate pointed a finger directly at Brad and, like a teacher talking to a student, said, "You and I will talk later."

"No problem," Brad said. "Don't hate me."

Avery's voice lifted. "Don't place all this on Brad; *you* expressed a desire to live your own life. Did we like you becoming a systems analyst? Yes. Did we like you going into the CIA? No. You've always been aware of your father's desire that you would eventually find his business as fulfilling for you as it was for him."

Kate was still trying to determine what she thought of Brad and said, "Avery, we have had this discussion and ..."

"Actually," Avery forcefully interrupted, "we have never had *exactly* this discussion. The instructions were not to overtly influence your decisions, but try to facilitate where you wanted to go with your father's wishes considered. Of course, we did not count on your deciding to separate yourself completely from the company. Your leaving the CIA and looking for something else was also not foreseen, but was fortuitous."

"What does that mean?"

Avery again ignored her and continued. "However, when we were in New York, you were to come to a critical board meeting. We were to vote on a standing motion transferring my proxy over to the rightful owner. That would be you. Somehow you got out of the city, leaving me to face an unhappy group of important people."

"Look," Kate said, "I'm sorry, but I hate that room. The whole idea of a huge corporation goes against what I stand for. There is nothing more impersonal than a faceless corporation."

"I have a feeling that, in the next few minutes, you might

change your mind, or at the least see things in a different light."

Kate looked over at Brad; he was pretending not to be paying attention. "Well," she paused, "after the other night, anything is possible."

Avery leaned forward. "Kate, your father's influence reached out on a global scale."

"I know; I have lived with that almost my entire life."

"*No*, actually, you haven't."

The comment took her by surprise. Again, she was not used to any abruptness from Avery, regardless of the situation. The man was simply unflappable, encased in his calm, authoritative manner, but beyond that, there was always a deferential air regarding Kate. Nonetheless, she countered with, "I think you are going to have to explain that."

"The keyword is scale, and it's on a level that you are completely unaware. Therefore, to provide some perspective, first, I need to bring you up to date on Adler industries. Only then can you fully understand the second half of this conversation and what lies before you. After that, there are the issues of the moment."

Avery took a deep breath. "Kate, throughout your life you were aware of your special financial status."

"Yes, I have been, but I have never taken advantage of it. I didn't need the money, and I still don't."

Avery put his hand up as she spoke to stop further comment. Something new had entered their relationship in a few brief moments, and it was a confusing turn. She looked at him, wondering what was coming next.

Avery placed a folder in front of her on the table.

"Here is a balance sheet for your review. I know you understand it even if you deny it. Nevertheless, let me summarize for the sake of brevity. Due to the private, not public, status of the individual Adler companies, and the fact they do not financially report, as a whole, the financial community does not know much about the company. There are over seventy interlocked companies in multiple market segments. Several do secret work for the US government, especially those projects that require plausible deniability. Last year's revenue was seventy-two billion in US dollars with a profit of $12 billion. Those sales came primarily from electronics, shipping, and finance. The current market capitalization of the Adler Group is $143 billion. You can compare that to privately owned Walmart at $249 billion, and it sits on a cash reserve of $53 billion. Of that amount, ninety percent is overseas and not repatriated. It is in the top twenty largest privately held companies in the US"

Kate had no response to Avery's figures. Avery was right; she had judiciously avoided precisely this kind of information, but he was also right about her not having any idea of the magnitude of the situation.

"Now, to offer some perspective before informing you of what's ahead," Avery said. "In the world, there have always been different organizations and partnerships that have existed to promote their agenda. As Lenin put it, they were organized and influenced by the sector of society with the money and power to dictate policy and direction. Those families and individuals who reside at the apex of culture exert a profound influence in the world. The Medicis of each age, if you will. Most of these entities prefer, for understandable reasons, to remain out of the public eye and surround themselves in secrecy."

To Kate, this was out of left field. She thought, Did we just change from talking about the company to secret organizations? She decided to wait for the explanation.

Avery continued. "Nineteen seventy-six saw the creation of an ultra-secret organization like no other. As an organization, it has no name. However, it has become known in certain circles as the Cartel. Its members include the European and North American political elite, present and former heads of state, and dominant personalities from global corporations and financial institutions. They have pledged their wealth and influence to promote stability in the global economy as a more effective means of enriching the lives of a greater number of individuals."

"That's a big goal," Kate said. "How do they go about doing that?"

"The Cartel monitors anything or anyone that causes a geopolitical problem that threatens to disrupt the world's financial stability. Often this requires unique solutions not available to conventional nation-states like the US or European Union. The Munich station was part of that monitoring effort and run by the Cartel."

Kate, taken entirely off guard, didn't have to say a word as her look said it all.

"I know," Avery said. "This is a complete surprise. You didn't want anything to do with the company. Still, your quitting the CIA and looking for a job allowed us to place you in a trusted strategic position, specifically matching your skillset. The office where you were working was not an NSA facility, but designed to look like one. That's why we established a layer of secrecy so tight no one was ever allowed to contact an NSA office directly nor anyone in any government. It was a way to maintain cover for everyone who worked there.

"When an event or action appears on the organization's radar, the Cartel can take direct and effective action. Not being bound by international treaties or the rule of international law, we can sometimes create and participate in situations mainstream nations cannot. The Cartel, in most instances, can influence outcomes in a non-violent manner, but there are exceptions. In those cases, they have at hand a robust capability."

"Well," Kate said to Avery. She was still back at being deceived at the station. "You knew about this, right? You knew about my working at the station?"

"Of course. You were accepted after you interviewed and proved you had the skills. Even if we *were* involved in the decision, you couldn't just sit there. You had to have the skills, so it worked out to both our advantages."

Avery stopped, providing time for Kate to absorb the information.

"Avery," she said, "I'm not happy finding out I have not been living my own life."

"Of course, you were. Didn't you feel like you were? Didn't you feel like you were contributing? Whatever you accomplished, and I know that was a lot, you did yourself. We had nothing to do with it."

Clearly wrong-footed, Kate was not happy. She nervously turned the bracelet on her wrist. Kate decided, at the moment, moving onto the organization avoided a very emotional subject. "That leaves the question of how do you promote the ideals of an organization without any power? Violent power, that is."

Avery took the lead and continued. "Historically, the Cartel's commerce tools are a combination of silent trade blockades of countries or companies by restricting the docking of shipping at key ports, using inspections, schedule mishaps, insurance cancellations, mechanical malfunctions, sabotage on many levels. As to financing tools, bad actors are targeted and influenced through longstanding contacts in the world's banking system, some of whom are members. When needed, punitive interest rates can be applied or transactions delayed. Often, just the threat of disrupting a small percentage of shipping or material results in a behavior change."

Kate, still irritated, challenged Avery. "I can't believe you can influence enough trade from the thousand ships a country sends out in a year to make a difference."

"Believe me, it is possible. Think about it. In a good year, an economy only grows two to three percent. We only need to reverse that to negative one percent to severely affect an economy, especially if there is doubt about the origin or duration of the effect. The unknown is the multiplier and always more of a threat than the known. A five percent effect would be catastrophic, causing social unrest with people in the streets. The tools at hand, at first glance, do not appear to be compelling, but when used in concert, they're extremely effective. Amschel Rothschild once said, 'Give me control of a nation's money, and I care not who makes its laws.'"

Kate had a quizzical look on her face. Having listened to Avery's presentation, she was having problems trying to understand how the Adler Group's assets intersected with this Cartel organization. "Avery, this is fascinating, but you indicated this had something to do with my father."

"It does." He slowly stood up and stepped to the fireplace, feeling the heat through his gray wool slacks. Kate took note of the deliberate pause in the conversation. Avery put his hand on the mantel and studied the flames as he knew what followed would change Kate's life forever. An angular glance in her direction provided him with a living picture of the little girl whose early life had consisted of walking and talking constantly and of loving her father completely. There couldn't be another relationship like it in the world. Her father had worshiped her. He saw in his little girl the millions who could benefit from his efforts to make the next world a better place for everyone to pursue their dreams. Those in the Cartel shared this vision, but he was the original and brightest light in their room.

Avery's voice shifted from business formal to fatherly informal. "Katy, with the passing of your father, you've become, by default, not choice, head of a multi-billion-dollar conglomerate that gainfully employs hundreds of thousands of people all over the world. The assets set in the transfer make you one of the richest people in the world."

Kate's eyes went wide. She sat up and started with, "Wait a minute, I thought you …"

Avery again put up his hand, interrupting her. "Katy, I'm not done. Your father is the founder of the Cartel and, its bylaws specify that you inherit the power of that throne."

Kate's head pulled back. "Hold on here. What?" she said rather loudly. "What does that mean?"

"It means you are one of the most powerful people in the world—a millennial Medici."

"No. No, it can't be. I didn't ask for this."

"No, you didn't. Nevertheless, it's true. You've repeatedly stated you wanted your life to make a difference on this planet. Now the greatest tool you could imagine to affect change lies at your feet. It was your father's wish to ease you into his world by convincing you to participate, in some manner, within the companies. Nevertheless, you chose your path. With change comes opportunity and, in this case, an exponential chance to change the lives of millions by furthering your father's work. Katy, you will be voted in as current chairman of the group unless you reject it, and I'm asking, will you help us continue your father's legacy?"

"If powerful men make up the organization, how could Father wield enough power to dictate that I'm the one to assume control?"

"Well, first I must point out, they're not all men. Second, the Adler Group and the Cartel are, at several legal levels, connected. The company reported only to him and now solely reports to you. In addition, your father was the Cartel's most significant contributor in annual donations from its members.

"The private nature of the Adler companies placed them above most regulations imposed on other public organizations and allowed for a more opaque existence. This private nature gives the

140

Cartel wider freedom. You will find it under 'Special Projects' in the budget report in front of you. Every member knew of the succession arrangement. They joined the organization for what it stood for and the influence your father had in their careers."

Avery paused. "I must offer my apology; due to the current situation and the need for action, I didn't have any other choice than to be uncomfortably blunt. Ingeniously, you've avoided every other opportunity, including New York, for me to present this more acceptably."

Kate looked around the room mindlessly while reminding herself to breathe. It was as if an earthquake had thrown her to the floor, and the shaking continued. She felt the contradictory sensations of power and confinement simultaneously. Was the private part of her life, the wall she judiciously retained as a therapy against reality, just ripped from her existence? She got up almost in a daze and walked over to the large windows that nearly approached the ceiling. She stood there for a moment, looking outside onto a great courtyard of well-laid stone. What appeared was a familiar scene for her in dreams and times alone. Translucent images of children dancing around a Maypole, oblivious to the world they were to inherit. Then an ominous, amorphous figure swooped in, circling, and chasing the children away. She felt the emotion rising within as she experienced for the first time the ability to influence the scene playing out just beyond the glass. Everyone in the room waited.

Avery could see the impact on Kate as she slowly walked to the windows. "Kate, I'm genuinely relieved that this has finally seen the light of day. Again, I regret the abrupt manner in the presentation. It was simply a situation that had lingered, and you needed to have explained."

"I know that all my life, I have had an agenda separate from my father's. It's come as quite a surprise that our goals were remarkably similar but kept a secret," said Kate. "I could have been closer to my father had I embraced it while he was alive."

Avery looked up. "My dear Kate, I must take issue with that. We have tried to get you involved, but because of the nature of the effort, to read you in, it had to be all or nothing. Your choices made it nothing, *your* choices, not anyone else's."

"Avery, I fully agree; there will be no argument there."

"Besides," he said, "I don't see how you could have been closer. It was an extraordinary relationship that I was able to observe through the years."

"It's going to take a while for me to absorb everything, but I can say there will be no more running. Amazingly, such an immense change in my life was one step away from a simple conversation." She took a big breath. "If my participation is what the organization needs, I'm willing, but I will need a tremendous amount of help."

Avery walked over to the couch facing Kate and sat down as if the weight of the world sat with him. He was silent for a moment and then, without looking at Kate, said, "This moment has been coming for some time. I cannot express the level of gratitude that will be forthcoming from the Cartel's membership. We have discussed your ability to take the reins, and most agreed you would be the person. It might take some time, and a few members have some questions, but there was no doubt, because of the lineage and your personality and capabilities, you had to be the one to take the group forward."

CHAPTER—24

KATE AND BRAD MAKE NICE

Kate had listened to Avery lay out her new reality. It was an Avery addressing her with a directness she had never seen. Given the weight of the situation and her past behavior, it was justified, but still unexpected.

"Avery, I'm so very sorry to have made your life so complicated and hard. As you said, I didn't know the whole picture."

"No apologies are necessary as I was only following what your father wanted. As to Brad, I need to take responsibility for bringing him into your life. It was the most prudent thing to do at the time, and, frankly, I still think it's a good idea. You need not blame him for any betrayal you might feel."

Kate looked at Brad, who had a very non-committal look on his face.

"Avery, are we through for right now?" Kate asked.

"Yes."

"Can I have a little time with Brad? We need to have a conversation, and I want to do it now, not later." She looked directly at Brad and, with a light sarcastic note, said, "One has a right to know if one is scheduled for execution at dawn's early light."

"Whoa," Brad said.

"No problem," Avery said. "I need a few minutes to check on the availability of the members for the next meeting. Let me know when you're ready." He pointed to a phone and said, "Just ask for me on the phone." He got up and started out of the room and, without turning, added, "Good luck Brad, I can't save you."

As Avery walked out of the room, Brad said, "Hold on here, Avery, you're my boss."

Avery had the door handle in his hand and said matter-of-factly, "Not anymore, my friend."

"That means you're mine," Kate said with a sly smile. "So am I to understand all this time you've been on assignment?"

"In a manner of speaking, I guess that's true," Brad said.

"What does that mean?"

"I don't know, Kate. At first, it was obvious. My instructions were to keep an eye on you at work. I was to report big stuff, like if you were in trouble or if anyone was bothering you or if you disappeared. It did not extend to your personal life. They knew not covering you outside the office carried a level of risk, but my instructions were clear. Besides, you never shared anything personal. Therefore, it wasn't that hard. When we first met, you were very likable, we worked well together, and I think we became genuine friends. However, that came separately and later. You were very pleasant company, and I never saw it conflicting with the assignment. Who would?" What he didn't say was he had fallen in love. It wasn't something he had planned. When is it ever planned? He was pretty sure she knew his true feelings and wouldn't let him through her defenses. He was okay with that for now, he thought. But it could all go away in the next few minutes.

"So, when they hit the office?" Kate asked.

"It was my responsibly to get you out of there safely."

"Did you know what was happening?"

"No, I was saving my own skin at the same time. Kate, I never knew who you were until today. As far as I was concerned, we both worked at an NSA substation. I didn't know about the Cartel or its agenda. I was hired to perform a task and felt I did a good job."

"What was the mysterious super-secretive job you had at the office?"

"The top-secret thing was a cover supporting why I was in the office. However, I did my share of work. I pursued computer-systems design in college, but it was boring. I wanted action, so I played that knowledge down and enlisted. I went through the training, then they found me out, and I ended up in surveillance and intelligence support through one tour in Afghanistan. Being sequestered in a dark room and chunking code was the closest I got to action. Therefore, I understand what Mom does, and the military training qualified me for the assignment. I answered an ad, Avery called back, and it's as simple as that."

"So, you were a bodyguard to someone you didn't know. You then pretended to become friends to make the job easier without telling me," Kate said.

"Well, yes, I was a bodyguard, but I wasn't allowed to tell you who I was. Other than that, I wasn't pretending anything, and it is what it became. I value what we have or had, and there isn't any better way to say it. I want to be your friend, Kate. However, it would be nice if I also had a job."

"Where do we go from here?" Kate said.

"That's in your hands, it seems," he said.

"Brad, I want to clarify something. I genuinely like you as a friend. I wish there was another word. Yes, we work well together as there is a similar thinking process. However, you seem to see things I don't making for better solutions. Also, I trusted you, at least until today, but I see that wasn't entirely your fault. Nevertheless, I see a scenario where we could continue to work together, but it obviously will have completely new ground rules. Could you see yourself, in effect, working for me in the capacity of an advisor without portfolio?"

"What does that mean?"

"I don't know; it means whatever it means. We will have to see. Be by my side and contribute when you can."

"Like make your coffee?" he said with a smile.

"Brad Danner, you can be so stupid sometimes. Let's just see where this goes. Meanwhile, you will be privileged to all the information, so you will have to sign your life away. I'm not thinking of an assistant, but more like a vice president with standing and limited authority. A second set of eyes. What do you say?"

"Kate, I would be delighted. It's an offer I can't refuse. Can I still guard your body?" he said, now with a devious smile.

Her laugh came out despite an effort to suppress it. "Please stay out of my private life. The protection part continues, as before. It's somewhat comforting. Is that all right?"

"Yes, that's all right, Kate, no worries. Are we fine?"

"Yes," she said, and they stood up. Kate came over, gave Brad a brief hug, and whispered into his ear, "Just remember I can still fire your ass."

"And I can still quit," he said.

CHAPTER—25

IRGC MEETING LNG RESULTS

Again, the generals gathered in the IRGC command center. Most of them had already learned of the failed attack on the Singapore facilities and knew someone had to tell Khiabani. To a man, they were aware of the unanswered question of how someone could have known about the Singapore effort and possess the wherewithal to sabotage the operation in real-time. It would have to be a world power, and none of them were talking.

Khiabani looked up from some papers he was reading as everyone waited. He signed the last sheet and handed it to the attendant standing at his side. After waiting for the attendant to leave the room, he finally said, "Let's go over the LNG attack. Admiral Rahmani, what is the news?"

The admiral stood, looking around the room at his fellow soldiers. "All elements of deployment in this very complicated plan went as designed," he said. "The submarine arrived on time and offloaded the special forces team undetected and waited for their return."

Sitting forward, Khiabani looked at Rahmani, saying, "Something is wrong. What is it?"

"The team started toward the tanker and experienced an unexpected explosion."

Exasperated, Khiabani said, "What ... what kind of explosion? Was it the tanker?"

"We do not know at this time. It could have been the team's explosives prematurely detonating as they were on timers, or it could have been from another source."

Khiabani put his hands on the table and rose from his chair. "Did they at least blow up the tanker?" he said, with a now-familiar volume and tone. "I want to know; did they destroy the tanker?" he yelled.

"No, general, at this time, it does not appear the explosion was the tanker."

"So, Admiral Rahmani, by the grace of Allah, it will appear so at a later time perhaps?"

Rahmani was a little confused at the comment and didn't immediately answer.

"It's a simple question, general. Was the mission a success or failure?"

Rahmani looked around the table. "Information is still coming in. Having detected the premature explosion, the submarine captain proceeded to vacate the area to avoid any chance of detection. When clear of the area, he reported the explosion and his actions. We are still trying to determine what occurred, and I cannot answer the question at this time."

"Lucky for you," Khiabani said. "You have three hours."

"Sir," Rahmani said.

"Three hours, admiral, to find out exactly what happened. You are dismissed. I suggest you make the most of your time."

Rahmani gathered his papers and left the room.

Khiabani looked at the remaining members of his staff. "We have accomplished a great deal in our time together, but it will mean nothing if we don't accomplish the goals set out in the plan. I find it necessary to remind you of the importance this plan has to your survival and our nation.

"Each of you is responsible for a piece of the plan, and I would advise you upon leaving this room to recheck every detail of your part of the endeavor. We failed to contain the breach in our security with Munich's operation; we failed at eliminating Singapore's port facility. We *cannot* afford to have any further disruptions in our plans. The markets are reacting as we anticipated, and within a short time, we should see the West's financial systems enter a critical phase. Despite the failure of the Singapore operation, it will have made its point and add to the volatility the markets are experiencing."

"And what about Gen. Nabavi?" one of the senior generals asked.

Khiabani met the question with a cold stare. "He is no concern of yours. You are all dismissed."

148

* * * *

Brig. Gen. Lajani ducked his head as he entered his car. His attendant closed the door and sat in the front with the driver.

"Back to my office," Lajani said, "but don't take the normal way."

"Yes, sir," the driver said.

Hamid Lajani could see the signs. This operation was falling apart, not due to the plan but to the man in charge of the project. Nabavi was the fall guy, a ruthless example to impress the rest of the group. If Khiabani trusted the people who served him, an example would not be needed. A well-intentioned effort to restore the nation to its rightful place in the world had turned into a personal agenda to further Khiabani's position within the ruling elite, and all but Khiabani were expendable.

Regardless of success or failure, they would be held accountable for crimes against the nation. It would be their word against Khiabani's. Lajani knew not to talk to any of the others involved for fear one was a handpicked agent meant to feed information back to Khiabani. He would never have thought this way before the last meeting. He had worked with his fellow generals for years. They were a competent group who trusted one another and worked well through the many crises that had faced the nation.

"Stop here," he directed the driver.

"Sir? We are still far from the office."

He pointed. "Go to that house, and see if anyone is home."

"Yes, sir," the attendant said without further hesitation.

He knocked on the door several times, and finally, someone answered. He looked back at the general as he was getting out of the car.

"Stay outside," the general said.

The general addressed the man at the door. "I need to use your phone. Do you have one?"

"Yes," the man replied but could not hide his confusion at the request.

"Take me to it. You and your family will stand outside."

The man walked to the phone and pointed to it sitting on a table. He then gathered his family and proceeded outside to the courtyard in front of the small house.

It wasn't perfect, Lajani thought, but if they were monitoring his house phone, the logs would contain only contact points and not transcripts. He didn't want to have the record include a call from his office to his house right after that last meeting. Lajani picked up the phone and called the home number of the family's closest friend, a neighbor across the street, another indirect call that would not be connected back to him. He was going to ask her to get his wife next door, but as it turned out, she was there.

"Reyhan, it's Hamid," he said. His wife was surprised due to the unusual call to their neighbor and because they never spoke during the day.

"Reyhan, I want you to go into another room to talk privately." Again, he waited.

"Okay, I'm in another room. Hamid, what is going on?"

"Listen carefully: I want you and the children to go visit your brother today. Take only a few day's clothes and use the dollar off-shore account for expenses. Do not withdraw any of our local money."

"My brother in Paris? Hamid, what is wrong?"

"I will explain later. The family might be in danger, and this is what I want. Do you understand?"

"No, how can we be in danger? Your standing in the military. Hamid, is everything all right?"

"I don't know right now; I'm being cautious. Tell both neighbors you are visiting family unexpectedly due to your brother's illness. Do not use any phones. Purchase the ticket at the airport, not online. I will contact you in Paris in a few days. Do not talk to anyone about this. Give your brother any excuse you want. Do you understand?"

"Not really. Hamid, what is wrong? You must tell me."

"I can't. It's too sensitive."

"Hamid, you are sending me out of the country with your children. I have a right to know."

"An attack on the port of Singapore didn't go as planned, and Khiabani has lost all perspective. They arrested Nabavi. That's all I can say, and it's already too much. You must go now."

"As you wish," she said.

"I love you, Reyhan. Everything will be all right."

CHAPTER—26

THE FIRST CARTEL MEETING

Inside the secure Luxembourg Castle Vianden, an extraordinarily wealthy and influential group of distinguished members gathered inside the drawing-room. Surrounding them was Brazilian walnut, Cuir de Cordoue tapestries, and two sizable paintings by German artist Albrecht Durer from the fourteenth century. Theirs was a group like no other, comprised of bankers, politicians, businesspeople, and directors of large companies. Those who gathered possessed wealth and influence through various means that, when assembled as a single entity, resulted in a powerful shadow force, a power through which agendas could be driven anywhere in the world, altering the fate of nations. Those who experienced unexplained events from this unseen hand referred to it vaguely as the Cartel.

To the limits of each individual, they pledged their wealth to the Cartel in achieving its goals and not to the general philanthropic organizations chosen by others of their ilk.

The Cartel had its informal origins back in the Eisenhower administration and its concerns about the instability surrounding the spread of communism and its threat to capitalism. The chairman of the steering committee is the Cartel's highest position. Kate's father became the first chairman in 1976 and held that office until his recent death. Under his leadership, the Cartel soon

151

realized that influencing shipping and commerce as a tool was quickly supplemented by finance and technology. At that time, Kate's father's companies comprised one of the great conglomerates participating in those segments, and he was, by a substantial margin, the Cartel's biggest donor.

Its combination of unique resources, contacts at the highest levels, and answering only to themselves allowed the Cartel to act in a manner unavailable to small sovereign organizations. They were, in fact, a stateless, super-secret superpower.

Matthew Corbett, acting chairman of the steering committee, tapped the gavel and said, "Gentlemen, the meeting will come to order. First, on behalf of the group, I would like to thank each one of you present and those participating electronically for taking the time to attend this meeting on such short notice. These are unusual times. But first, I move to dispense with any minute's corrections and recognize Mr. Weldon Stovall." A voice down the table offered a second. The motion passed, and the chair recognized Mr. Stovall.

Stovall, chairman of one of Europe's biggest banking houses, rose from his seat. "Thank you, Mr. Chairman. We all have a hollow space in our hearts with the passing of Mr. Helmut Adler. His contribution to this organization is without equal. One might say he *was* the organization. His total dedication to the principles upon which this organization stands was beyond equal. Without his financial support during the dark days of this decade, we might not exist to deal with the situation before us today. His organizational skills have provided an unequaled field network. On a personal note, there is not one of us today who does not owe this man their gratitude on a personal or business basis. I have a daughter attending Stanford today due to his efforts. Of course, it was not without some concessions on my part."

Everyone laughed at the known fact that Helmut Adler was always looking for a deal or quid pro quo. "We each have our memories of this great man, and as one of his many friends, I propose a moment of silence in memory of this extraordinary individual."

After the appropriate amount of time, Corbett said, "Thank you, Mr. Stovall. I believe what lies before us is a period that will test our ability to fulfill Chairman Adler's vision of stability in this

152

group's leadership and our response to what is a growing problem in the field. I refer to the succession issue and the unprecedented loss of our people in an ambush at the Munich facility. I defer my time to Mr. Penn Hauer, director of operations, who will bring us up to date on what we have been able to put together."

Hauer, solidly built beneath his custom suit, sported a Marine haircut. It didn't take any imagination to envision him in fatigues, firing whatever weapon was in his hands.

"As we all know," Hauer began, "the effort to keep any facet of our agency a profound secret to the entire world exceeds even the maximum typically deployed to other organizations. Hence, the mere fact that someone knew of the Munich facility, let alone that it was part of our system, is of great concern. That someone managed to assassinate six of our personnel places this incident at another level. There were two survivors, a Mr. Bradley Danner, and Helmut's daughter, Kate Adler. They managed to escape unharmed. Efforts are underway by the Geneva9 Services team to uncover any piece of evidence that will lead us to those responsible, but logic leads us to Iran.

"We have been in unofficial contact with both the US and GCHQ (Government Communication Headquarters) in the UK. Neither can offer any proof of the group responsible. Both have offered their qualified assistance, which is all that's possible under the circumstances.

"We are working on the theory there is a connection between the attack and the hijackings. We know that the only way they could have executed such an elaborate plan was to have assets in place. The efforts to disrupt the Hormuz channel's shipping lanes have also been very sophisticated and well-executed.

"Using the G9 asset, we penetrated the Iranian network using the internet provider that serviced the Iranian Revolutionary Guard Corps, looking for anything tying them to the Gulf attacks. It was a dead-end, which was surprising and discouraging as they were the primary suspect. Later, Iran somehow placed a trace on that incoming signal to their network. The Geneva9 asset back traced the source to a cybercafe in a town outside of Tehran.

"The detection was troubling as the IP spoofing used by Mom would have generated a series of possible alternate locations. We believe the discovery of the site had more to do with feet on the ground than anything. In other words, they got lucky.

"At the end of the day's work, the employees were all in a meeting. A normal daily occurrence; however, this time, it was to have a deadly result. The attackers have to be aware that they did not eliminate everyone, and the search is on."

Stovall spoke up. "Hijacking ships has to be only part of whatever they're up to as upping the price of oil in such a volatile manner is a tactical, not a strategic objective. The Iranians are risking far too much in the form of Western trade retaliation to increase the price of their limited oil exports."

"I agree," Hauer said. "At this time, their overall objective is not fully understood. I yield to Paul Samson (director of finance). I understand he wants to address, from a financial perspective, the effects of the Iranian actions."

"Thanks, Penn," Paul said. "This is the working understanding we have regarding Iranian activities. As Penn indicated, there is a dedicated effort to disrupt the world's shipping, particularly oil tankers, at choke points worldwide.

"The markets depend on stability, and any instability will drive them down. The markets are particularly susceptible to the transfer of petroleum products. Any instability and uncertainty cause the world's markets to react negatively, with a substantial loss of stockholder value. Large institutions are in equities, but so are many individuals who have their money in those institutions. This loss in an individual's portfolio would lead to weakened consumer spending, company layoffs, and increased unemployment. This weakened spending is on top of a loss of faith in the global reserve currency when companies and individuals globally start to pull out dollars. This cascades into a run on the banks and a loss of faith in the monitory system. If they successfully execute this plan, with their participation an open secret but without proof, the West must take their demands more seriously."

Paul sat down.

"Thanks, Paul," Corbett said. "I would say that was pretty concise. Penn, do you want to continue with the Singapore incident?"

"Yes," he said, standing once again. "We diverted late Monday's efforts towards investigating the Gulf hijackings to a more immediate matter. We received a POC with an 87 percent probability estimate from the Geneva system defining an LNG tanker attack near the Port of Singapore. Due to the communications blackout over open and even private channels, the two previous hijackings did not generate a POC. This estimate came about due to G9's Convergence Searchability, which compares and merges related events. The threat estimate outlined the possibility of exploding the tanker after it docked, creating devastation for miles in all directions. The explosion, of course, would have caused further panic due to the strategic location of the Singapore facilities. Direct action is never desirable; however, given the extreme time frame and within the committee's parameters, we initiated a counter operation consisting of four of our personnel.

"A full debriefing report is being prepared. However, in summary, we were able to airlift an MH-6 helicopter and a Mark V Special Operations craft to the area. Our men rappelled down to the tanker from the Black Hawk before the enemy boarded the vessel and were able to remove the threat. A small boat exploded in the water that first-line intelligence agencies will detect. Other than the antagonists, there were no casualties, and we maintained complete anonymity on our side. We exfiltrated the team out of the country to a nearby cooperating vessel in international waters. Our aircraft all returned safely. Unfortunately, there was no evidence the Iranian's initiated the attack."

One of the members asked, "Then how do we know it was them?"

"Again, it's circumstantial; the Iranians have not acknowledged the explosion in any way. It's unusual because it's a missed opportunity to take a shot at the West, but there has been nothing but silence."

"Penn, may I ask how we were able to assemble that equipment profile in such a short time?"

"Our facility in Kuala Belait in Brunei covers Southeast Asia. The equipment came out of our inventory at the base. The boarding team was already there training for a possible North Korean operation. As I said, the timing was tight, so we were very fortunate they were close. We put them in the air to meet the deadline without a complete plan. They received their instructions en route. Receiving orders during transit isn't uncommon, and they're trained for it."

Another member asked, "Have we decided on a plan of action to address the overall problem?"

Mr. Hauer replied, "No, there is not a specific plan in place at this time, and I'm sure you want to know why. Singapore was a significant distraction, but we are rapidly moving toward a plan in hopes of presenting it at the next meeting. We are working closely with Ms. Maleeva and the Geneva Services team." Penn smiled widely. "She is at Morton-Roth right now but has things well in hand and moving."

Everyone exchanged knowing glances and smiles at their individual encounters with the formidable director. The bottom line with her was that you better always have your act together or don't waste her time.

"We are coming up with options. There might also be a security leak on their side. It's something we are constantly monitoring. We are aiming for the next meeting to discuss those findings as well as the appointment of the new chairman—or chairperson or, I guess, chair." He smiled at the slip. "That's going to take some time getting used to."

Mr. Gerrit Brouwer, chairman of Cittel Oil PLC, stood. "Mr. Chairman," he said.

"The chair recognizes Mr. Brouwer."

"First, I would like to thank the whole team for coming together and solving some very sticky problems. You are to be commended, Mr. Hauer, for the professionalism of your team. Right now, we could be looking at video on every news outlet showing carnage and mayhem. To prevent these kinds of incidents is why we're here."

Hauer nodded in recognition of the acknowledgment.

Brouwer continued. "Regarding the succession, I must bring to the group's attention that this is a vulnerable time in our organization with the passing of the current chairman, the loss of our people, and Iran trying to disrupt the world. Wouldn't it be advisable to settle the transition issue quickly, so we have firm and continuous leadership through this trying time? In addition, some of us have some reservations as to the preparedness of Ms. Adler to step into a very complicated position with significant ramifications."

Mr. Corbett nodded his head. "I believe Mr. Brouwer has a point. Mr. Stanton is addressing this issue and is currently meeting with Ms. Adler, bringing her up to date on the group's organizational aspects. Mr. Brouwer, I believe I speak for all of us in stating the impending change in leadership has some of us concerned as to the ability of Ms. Adler to step right into managing an international enterprise of this size and sophistication.

"Mr. Stanton, our current acting chairman, has called for another meeting later this evening. He will be addressing this issue, and we shall, as a majority, bring ourselves to an acceptable position. The meeting time is in flux, so please stay within the residence. Cocktails shall be served as you wait, and for those who wish to stay, after the second meeting, dinner shall be served."

Corbett said, "The chair recognizes Mr. Jonathan Thorn."

"Thank you," Mr. Thorn said, standing. "Many of us have had conversations on delaying the North Korean issue until after we have addressed the Iranian incidents." He turned to Mr. Corbett and said: "Thank you, Mr. Chairman."

"I move the motion for approval," Mr. Becker said from down the table.

Corbett said, "The motion moves to approval. Those in favor vote aye, those opposed vote no."

Each member present and some online entered their vote with the tally appearing on a wall screen.

Corbett tapped the mallet, "The motion passes and will be adopted. Concerning the Iranian issue, we will proceed in an open-forum fashion at the discretion of the chair."

Mr. Westbrook, former assistant secretary of defense in the Carson administration, spoke. "With Iran already on sanctions, this naturally limits our traditional options. With a breach such as this, we need action immediately. Also, Mr. Hauer, what is the US position on this?"

"I think the short answer is nowhere. The administration does not have any evidence that would allow them to move on the Iranians. We have been in contact with the White House, giving them what we can, but the key is developing a plan. As I said, we hope to have something shortly." Corbett looked around the table and said, "Without further business, we will adjourn until the next meeting."

CHAPTER—27

KATE MAKES A DECISION

Kate had let Avery know she and Brad were done coming to an understanding and wanted to move on as quickly as possible. Brad was getting a brandy when Avery stepped into the room.

Avery looked at Brad and said with feigned surprise, "You're still alive?"

"No thanks to you, I might add."

Kate started. "Brad and I have come to an understanding. As I said before, there is a debt of gratitude to be paid. It's also a fact that I value his opinion, so in somewhat of a vague position, he will be helping me. I want him to participate in whatever I might be doing."

"Of course, I will make arrangements right away. So, I take it Brad will be here after dawn tomorrow?"

"It's a short leash, but yes."

Brad said, "I think the two of you don't appreciate talent even when it's standing right in front of you—which it is."

"Kate," Avery said, "I must ask, before taking care of the arrangements, is Brad's a permanent position?"

He then turned to look at Brad with a straight face.

"I don't know," she said, "as he will be on probation for the next three years."

"Okay, you guys have had your fun," Brad said.

"Yes, we have," Kate said, "now I need to get serious. Avery, I'm overwhelmed with what I have learned in the last few hours. Now realizing I'm head of my father's estate and then the surprise of the Cartel, it's difficult to absorb that much information, let alone create a clear perspective. However, one thing didn't get answered when we spoke: Why were you the person to have this conversation with me? I guess I'm asking, just how involved are you in this Cartel?"

"Very involved as I have been temporary chairman for two years but became a member years ago when your father presented the opportunity."

"You're currently head of the Cartel?"

"Yes, I'm chairman of the Steering Committee, that's until they officially vote you in. Your father and I have done some wonderful things using the Cartel as a tool for positive change."

"Then why can't you continue being head of the committee?"

"I could, Kate. There's the little issue of it being your father's express wishes that you head the Cartel. Everyone is aware of this and are, for the most part, in line with this thinking."

"Most?"

"There are some, and one in particular, who are not comfortable with your age and experience but haven't met you. However, Kate, you must understand, the Cartel is an organization that's a player on the world stage. Its members contribute billions a year that they could give to charity as their contemporaries do. They must constantly explain away why they haven't followed suit because everything we do is beyond secret. The leadership of the organization is an important issue for the members. They're well-intentioned, I can assure you. They're looking to you to give them a sense you can take the reins, especially given the state of the world this morning."

Kate listened attentively, taking it all in. Her life was infinitely simpler just a day ago. "So what happens next?"

"That meeting upstairs I spoke of was a Cartel meeting; that couldn't wait. They're dealing with the events of the last forty-eight hours. Holding the Adler Group proxy, I should be chairing that meeting. However, our discussion was infinitely more important. There will be another meeting tonight of the Steering Committee that we both will attend or all three of us. On the agenda are several items, including your induction as chair and the Munich tragedy."

"So I guess you need to bring me up on what we know?"

"At this point, we believe the Iranians are purposely creating chaos within the world's markets, but we are not sure why. Or more specifically the IRGC or, I mean …"

"I know what it means," Kate said.

"They're doing it by staging attacks affecting world trade and disrupting the financial markets. It's exactly that kind of thing the Cartel addresses. The political leadership of Iran has shown a certain willingness to move into the Western world, so their behavior is at the least confusing."

"Let me get this straight," Kate said, "we have a country that's trying to curry favor with the West and just decided to destroy the Western financial system?"

"As I said, we don't yet know what their end game is."

"Okay, I'm with you so far, but what can the Cartel, uh, *we* do about it?"

"The answer to that question is being worked out right now by a Mr. Hauer and his associates. It requires addressing asymmetrical problems with new solutions. The US, for instance, has its hands tied because it cannot prove who the perpetrator is. By the time they get to a legal footing, everything could be beyond repair. That's where the Cartel comes in. The Cartel's huge advantage lies in its not being constrained by the normal rules of the world."

"I understand the logic of all that; however, why would the general world condone an organization that works outside the law in pursuing their personal agenda? Wouldn't they just shut us down?"

"The answer is no one would allow us to exist unless it also complemented their agenda. If our agendas were juxtaposed, or the power we possess used in the wrong manner, the picture would change instantly. We perform a deniable service that's in concert with their strategic goals. As to shutting us down, technically, we don't exist. Even the local police cannot set foot on the grounds because we are like the Vatican within Luxembourg."

Kate looked up, "So no one can control what we do. That power could end up in the wrong hands."

"Yes, and it is up to us to maintain the ideals that your father instilled in this organization. It's as much an inspirational effort as a managerial one. You have before you an unbelievable opportunity to control this power in pursuing a positive agenda."

"Why do you or the others think I'm qualified to be head of an organization of which I know nothing? If these people are so smart, then one of them must be infinitely more qualified than I am. Take you, for instance."

"King Tut was pharaoh at thirteen. Do you think he ruled by himself? Do you think he made line decisions or balanced the budget? No, he was the symbol, the very essence, of a civilization. He was the one with the heritage that united the country. Constantly surrounded by advisors experienced in areas he was not. We need you to accept leadership, with help from some competent people, and fulfill your own goal to make a difference."

"Have you been polling the voting members?"

"Yes," Avery said.

"Is that allowed?"

"Unofficial and casual conversations usually precede any critical decision. Before the next meeting and vote, I understand the G9 asset has recently provided a critical piece of information."

"Okay," Kate said. "We know they're up to something big. We penetrated their network, and they, in turn, somehow discovered the location of our Munich operation. They hit it because they think we may have uncovered their plans."

"That's about it," Avery said.

"You said, after our discussion, there is another meeting scheduled. Where is everyone who will attend?"

"They're standing by, waiting to be called."

"So at the meeting, we will address my election and any response we might consider regarding the Iranians. Does that sound reasonable?"

Avery noticed the change in her voice. Kate was assuming some authority already. It would take some time, and she would undoubtedly make some mistakes, but she was on her way. It fit right into the part of a strong personality that resisted what she didn't want but wholly-owned what she did. The switch had flipped in her mind.

Avery allowed himself a sizeable internal smile that slipped to some degree to the outside as Kate noticed and said, "Avery, do you have anything to add? Because there is more than one way to approach this. You're the steady hand, and now is the time to explore all options."

Avery waved no, saying, "I have no problem with anything. We are finally on the way to meeting this problem, and it's a relief to see it underway."

CHAPTER—28

SECOND CARTEL MEETING

Avery and Kate walked down the hall to the group that had gathered. Avery stopped in front of two massive doors into the conference room.

He turned to Kate and said, "Hold here just one second." He opened the door, stepped into the room, and immediately received everyone's attention.

"Gentlemen, to those of you who have not met her, may I introduce Ms. Katerina Adler." Avery looked back and motioned for her to come into the room. The group rose as one, and she entered to a formal round of genteel applause. The members all gathered around her, providing welcoming comments. Out of the crowd, one man stepped forward and extended his hand.

"Hello, Ms. Adler; my name is Kenneth Harper. Your father and I were very close."

Kate looked at the man in front of her, unable to contain her surprised expression.

"President Harper," Kate said, "needless to say, I'm surprised to see you here."

"I think it's safe to say there will be more surprises coming into your life. Welcome aboard."

Avery led Kate to an empty chair next to Corbett.

Corbett put a hand on Avery's shoulder and spoke close to his ear. "Do you want to transfer acting authority to you?"

"No," Avery said. "You keep running the meeting."

With everyone in place, Corbett took the seat at the head of the table and said, "Ms. Adler, as a group, we wish to extend our deep condolences. We are so sorry for your loss of your father. Your father will be forever remembered by anyone who came into his circle. Certainly for the integrity with which he ran his businesses, but also living a life based on a strict set of principles.

Kate knew something like this would be said and was afraid she would fall apart in front of those who needed to see her strong, but it didn't happen.

Kate took a deep breath she hoped would not be noticed. "I want to thank all of you for welcoming me into this important effort. I look forward to meeting each of you individually."

Corbett opened by saying, "The first of two items on the agenda is the succession discussion before voting. Mr. Anton Guerard (former minister of finance in French President Navarre's administration), I believe you had some comments you wanted to present."

Everyone turned to the large flat screen on the wall as he was attending the meeting remotely. At the bottom of the screen were the four-square inset images of those connected through a G9 connection. Guerard's picture expanded to fill the screen.

"Yes, thank you, Mr. Chairman." Guerard looked into the camera and, with a thick French accent, continued. "Ms. Adler, members, we are all aware of the position Helmut held in the company and the unique contributions he made to this organization. We are also aware of the succession plan we agreed to years ago. There is, however, a concern that should be addressed regarding Ms. Adler's ability to, with limited knowledge and experience, step into a position of such importance and gravity. Given our current situation, can she familiarize herself with the levers of power that are available to the chairman of the Steering Committee to solve the critical problems that lie before us?

"Ms. Adler," he said, addressing her directly, "this issue is not whether you can eventually learn what's required to run the organization, but can you do this from, what is the phrase, a dead start. I should like to point out that the liability of a wrong decision is just too significant to leave to chance. I respectfully present this issue for discussion before the installation vote of Ms. Adler as chairman."

Guerard hit the button, indicating he had given up the floor.

Avery stood up. "Mr. Chairman."

"The chair recognizes Mr. Stanton."

"The concerns of Mr. Guerard in these trying times, where we must act quickly, accurately, and with resolve, are valid. The hesitation some or one of you may be experiencing is due to not knowing the character of Ms. Adler as well as I."

Kate listened to Avery start to talk about her and defend her position. It was a natural reaction based on their relationship. The problem was that the other members also knew this. His credibility, his inability not to be influenced, was in question. She decided to act.

She put a hand on Avery's arm. "Let me," she said quietly.

Avery nodded and sat down. Kate stood up and looked at Corbett.

"The chair recognizes Ms. Adler," he said.

Kate looked around the room at those gathered. She was in an atmosphere that she had been born into but never actually experienced. She started with, "Mr. Guerard, gentlemen, though I have not had much time, I have given serious thought to the issues that are being raised and take no offense at the direct nature of your concerns. My father decided my place in this organization well before I was even aware of the group's existence. I have a very good education that provides a solid base upon which I view the world. My time in the CIA and, without my knowledge, working for the Cartel, has extended that base. I have been trained to connect the dots and to observe and discern patterns. I believe this would serve as a good foundation in conflict resolution, a mainstay of the Cartel. My discussions with Avery regarding this organization have, to be frank, left me in awe of what you've accomplished.

"Nevertheless, understanding is one thing. There is no way for me to manage efficiently, let alone immediately, an unfamiliar organization. Thus, I would expect and accept a great deal of help from all corners as we move forward. I have committed to Avery that I will not step away from this challenge and will make all of you comfortable that the group will receive the stewardship it deserves. However, a step must be taken requiring a certain amount of faith in my untested ability. You will not know if I'm up to the task until I'm elected chair of this organization."

"Chairman Corbett, may I?" a voice said.

Corbett looked at Kate, and she nodded but did not sit down. Mr. Bothard, from the London-based bond house of Bothard and Bates, stood. "I would like to remind everyone that we have known and accepted for some time Helmut's wish for Ms. Adler if she was so inclined. I just heard her say she will not step away from the challenge. I find this whole discussion curious at best, unnecessary at the least." He sat down.

"Thank you, Mr. Bothard," Kate said. "Yes, I would like to accept the position. However, I want to dispense with any issue of inevitability. I would like to make a succession vote necessary because I want to move forward with a mandate from the membership and not the rubber stamp of a document. Tonight, there is no ordained CSC. The vote should be up or down. Either you feel I'm worthy of the job, or we should take another path. I think it's critically important to this organization that you want not my father's daughter but *me*."

Avery moved uncomfortably in his seat.

"Well said," someone mumbled.

President Harper said, "Mr. Guerard, I would like to hear your thoughts on the change to a succession vote. Is that acceptable?"

Everyone waited for Mr. Guerard to respond. He replied, "My friends, what I just heard was a comforting demonstration of maturity. The first of many, I'm sure. I believe it's time to take the vote."

Avery leaned over to Corbett and whispered, "Ask for any objections to a vote."

Corbett addressed those gathered. "On the subject of a vote to install Ms. Adler as chair of the Steering Committee, do I hear any objections?" After a quick scan of the faces in the room and on screens, he said, "Then let us vote, yay for installation of Ms. Adler as chair of the Steering Committee and nay to decline."

Everyone again turned to the screen at the end of the room to see the immediate results. Avery purposely held the smile showing the pride he had in Kate.

Corbett tapped the mallet and stated, "The membership by a

unanimous vote approves the installation of Ms. Adler as chair of the Steering Committee. As a result of this vote, I relinquish the chair in favor of Kate Adler."

"Hear, hear!" a few said to applause.

Kate moved to the head of the table where she stood and looked at the room and its occupants.

"I'm humbled," she said. "I wish to thank all of you for the demonstration of support. With recent events, we have encountered a bit of, as Sir Bothard would say, a sticky wicket." Laughter followed around the table.

"It is imperative that we move as one to solve these problems without any doubt in anyone's mind as to the competency of the management team. I know at least some of you still have reservations, although you've graciously given me your support. To that end, as my first order of business, I move to make a change in the management structure, ensuring a high level of continuity. I appoint, with his acceptance, Avery Stanton to the new position of executive chairman with authority over all departments, wherein his word will be final except upon receiving written or validated verbal instructions from me to the contrary. Mr. Stanton, would you be willing to accept this position?"

Avery, genuinely impressed with the show of corporate intrigue and now in full smile, said, "Yes, of course, it would be an honor."

Kate said, "It was my intention all along to proceed with this appointment; however, it was imperative that you first accept me into the fold, as it were, before revealing my plans."

She continued, "Also, any action approved by me can be modified or halted by a two-thirds vote of all members of this committee, but only when I'm present to defend the issue in question. I must be present physically or remotely. I will sign the following changes into the minutes as soon as they're available before moving to a more formal document. The new arrangement will move our organization's governing structure to resemble more of a democracy than the former benevolent dictatorship. I believe it will serve us well in the years to come. May I ask who approved the Singapore operation?"

"I did," Avery said, "as per my position at the time."

"Well, then, with the changes outlined, I feel everyone should be comfortable with our decisions under this new arrangement."

The measure was met with vigorous applause, with Harper standing, thereby asking for the floor. Kate said, "The chair recognized Mr. Harper."

"Ms. Adler, I believe I speak for the committee, if not the entire membership when I say we are most impressed with your decisions, and we look forward to working with you."

Again, applause filled the room.

"Thank you, President Harper," Kate said. "Without wasting a minute, we must address the second objective stopping the Iranians and their actions. Avery has informed me that Dr. John Wilkerson of the security committee is prepared to present their findings. We will move from formal to open discussion. Dr. Wilkerson, you have the floor."

"Earlier today, the G9 asset monitored a call on an unsecured line placed by an Iranian Brig. Gen. Lajani to his wife. The conversation was flagged due to the keywords Singapore, attack, Khiabani, and Reyhand, his wife's name. Considerable effort went into validating the conversation as it went from an unknown origin and terminated at another unknown house for reasons we do not understand. We believe it is the smoking gun implicating Iran in at least the Singapore incident. It's the first open communication we have been able to track regarding the Iranians. Other than this, there has been complete silence on all possible communication channels. The facts dictate they're also involved in the hijackings as the coincidence factor is too significant to ignore. The pertinent portion of the transcript was, and I quote:

There was an attack on Singapore's port that didn't go as planned, and Khiabani has lost all perspective. He had Nabavi arrested. That's all I can say, and it's already too much. You must go now.

"The call was Lajani telling his family to leave the country immediately and secretly as he felt they could be in danger. What else does this tell us? We know the IRGC is behind the Singapore raid. We can deduce the IRGC is behind the hijackings and that there is a least some turmoil in the IRGC leadership. We are not aware if the rest of the Iranian leadership is participating or even aware of the effort. We also do not know their primary objective.

169

So, there is a lot of work to be done."

"Can't we assume they're going after the West's economy?" one of the members offered.

"I cannot ever use the word 'assume.' As to their primary objective, disrupting the economy could be a piece of a larger, more comprehensive plan. We don't have the data to support moving it from an assumption to a deduction."

What Kate heard was music to her ears. She immediately knew that Dr. Wilkerson was the right man in the right job. He dealt in facts, not fiction.

Kate said, "So at least the IRGC is involved, the clergy may not be. It's obvious we start with the IRGC and get them to stop."

"That, Ms. Adler," Wilkerson said, "is where the committee is in agreement. I would like to turn over that portion to Mr. Penn Hauer."

Hauer stood. "In the hours since the last meeting, we have a much clearer picture of what lies before us. Given the time frame we are dealing with, we find that direct communication with the IRGC is the most expeditious way to start the resolution process."

Kate said, "That's, of course, assuming," she cast a glance at Dr. Wilkerson, having used *the* word, "they want resolution. My guess is they don't, as they're too far in. The transcript of the phone call sounds like their lives are on the line, and the only thing that will stop the momentum is an equal and opposite force."

Hauer said, "We agree the situation has degraded into something beyond polite conversation. Also, given the timeline before us, sovereign financial and trade sanctions are not available."

Kate said, "So what I'm hearing is that we must talk to the IRGC and present something that will force them to cease and desist."

"Again, we agree. First, there is the issue of a meeting which will require an invitation Maj. Gen. Khiabani can't refuse, and then applying a force he must recognize as too great to ignore."

Kate looked at the security head and said, "Penn, this is where my needing a great deal of help from all corners comes in?"

"Of course," Hauer said, "and Ms. Adler, you shall receive it. We routinely work on pre-establishing pressure points for possible use involving important personalities around the world. We are confident we can present an invitation to a meeting with a compelling reason that he attends.

"Next," Hauer said, "is the issue of the application of force."

Kate had a quizzical look on her face. "Whatever transpires, it must be immediate. The issue is with what."

Penn said, "Given the penetration of the Geneva9 asset, we have a wide range of options, such as directly manipulating various elements within the country."

"What kind of elements?" Kate said.

"The power grid, all forms of communication such as phones, television, and the Internet. We can send blanket messages to groups or individuals or even turn off traffic lights. The list is endless."

"Can you turn off the power in certain areas?"

"Yes, we can specifically manipulate certain areas."

Kate thought for a minute. "Okay, tell me if this is crazy; I talk to Khiabani and …"

Avery waved his hand. "Hold it; nobody said you were going to be in this Khiabani meeting. That's what the security committee is for, and besides, it's too dangerous. We generally use third parties to maintain the anonymity of the group."

"If I may," Brad spoke up, "having an interest in your safety, I also don't think it's a good idea for you to be there."

"This is way too important to leave to a third party," Kate said. "Besides, it's a diplomatic conversation, not a wrestling match, and I'm sure the security will be tight on both sides. Otherwise, it's not going to happen at all. Damn it; those were our friends in the Munich office; I am participating in making their lives matter. Besides, I have an idea on how to handle that."

It was a forceful answer, precisely the kind everyone wanted to hear. The Adler girl was indeed of her father, and it was a comforting thing to see.

"Again," she continued, "I talk to Khiabani and layout what we want. He will refuse, saying, who are you? And there is no reason to take us seriously, except somehow Penn got him to this meeting. At that point, I want to tell him to call someone to verify the electrical power to a particular grid has been cut. That will get his attention. If the mullahs aren't involved, it will look like just a glitch in the system, but Khiabani will know it was us. Then I tell

171

him something else is going to happen, and Penn makes it happen. That should move us to a serious conversation, and we dictate terms."

Avery said, "Penn, give her some options under this scenario."

"The obvious," Penn said, "would be a glitch at the Bakhtaran power dam. It's the largest dam in Iran, and a construction company controlled by the IRGC is responsible for its maintenance. We could interrupt the power, and it would be a huge issue, especially as the reason wouldn't be readily apparent."

"Penn," Kate said, "is there a way it can occur while I'm talking to him, giving it an aura of something that couldn't possibly happen, except at our will?"

"Yes, we could wire you so that we monitor your conversation, and at the right moment, I, or Lauren, who controls cyber-influence, could activate the pre-programmed event. It would appear you were using magic."

"Wonderful. That's what we want instead of bombs. What else can we do?"

"The next on the list would be the Natanz nuclear facility, which is under the IRGC purview. We could cut the power there also."

Harper chimed in, saying, "Cutting the power at the Natanz site says more than you can simply cut off the power. Given their experience with the Stuxnet virus, their imagination will run wild trying to envision what other capabilities might be up your sleeve. It's a compelling message, and I doubt you would need anything else."

Kate was in the flow of the meeting and found it was more logical than grand leadership ability. However, given the last few hours, she was beginning to feel the walls closing in on her. Kate was doing her best to fight the feeling. Coming back, she said, "I agree, but just the same, I would like to have a third. Anything else we can do?"

Paul Samson from finance interrupted, "In studying the Iranian national budget, I ran across something of interest. The supreme leader has many palaces that consume enormous amounts of money, but one seems to play an important part. The Golestan Palace sits right next to an airport."

"Excuse me," Secretary Monroe said, "during my days at State, we knew that that's where he went during the uprising in 2009. If his regime fell, he intended to fly out of there to Syria and live off his billions stashed away. Playing with that would perhaps be getting closer to the supreme leader than he would like. If their Supreme Leader Ali is already involved, it will hit him at his escape point."

"What a wonderful idea, Secretary Monroe," Avery said.

"I agree," Kate said. "Paul, could you also fill me in on some of the things you found about the money our dear supreme leader spends out of the coffers?"

"Sure," Paul said. "I have a lot of material."

"And Penn, we will need detailed plans to go over as well as your choice of some site you think will work. Okay," Kate said. "We can start in the morning going over your recommendations."

Everyone seemed to agree, and she stood up to address all the members present. "Again, I appreciate your trust in my being capable of handling the Cartel's business. All of us on staff will prove you were correct in your choice. Now, I declare the meeting adjourned, as I know some of you must return to your responsibilities. To those who can stay, I understand dinner is available."

CHAPTER—29

AFTER THE CARTEL MEETING

After the group dinner with the other members, Brad and Kate walked back to their rooms. They got to Kate's door and, as she unlocked it, she said, "Can you come in and talk?"

Brad paused for a second as Kate walked inside; she looked back and said, "Really, Brad? Do we have a problem?"

"No, not at all," he said.

"Then get your ass in here. If I ask nicely, can you fix me a drink while I get out of these shoes?"

"Probably not," Brad said.

"That's what I figured," she said, walking into the bedroom. She closed the door and, moments later, emerged in an oversized robe and bare feet. She walked over to a large Reynold's tufted chair and fell into it with a big, *un*ladylike sigh.

Brad handed her a drink. He backed up to the chair opposite her, saying, "Kate, I always thought you were good. However, today I must hand it to you. You were brilliant."

"Nice try."

"I'm sorry, I don't care if you believe me, but it's the truth. You went from napping this morning in the car to head of the Cartel. It was something out of a novel. Your head must be spinning with all the information. On top of that, it's just not normal information. Suddenly, you have the weight of the world on your shoulders, and you handled it like a champion. Sorry, lady, like it or not, I'm impressed."

"In some ways, I knew it was coming, with Dad's businesses and all. It was learning about the Cartel that took me completely by surprise, and it might be the most important. That's the part that interests me most. That's why I wanted you involved."

She lifted her head from the back of the chair and looked at him. "Brad, I need your counsel and help. Not necessarily forming any battle plans, but keeping everything in perspective. You're the one person from my former life who offers the stability that is not available anywhere else, and, unfortunately for you, it's too late to back out."

"You mean your former life when you were just another pretty girl in the office worried about rent? Besides, who said I wanted to back out?"

"You're pushing it, my boy, but at some point, you will, and when that day comes, I hope we are still friends. I have a question. Pay attention as this is your first test in your new job. I'm not sure how to deal with facing all those people and being in charge."

"As I said, I thought you were doing just fine."

"Not really. I'm a woman in charge, and, by its nature, it is a tricky business. Everyone wants me to be strong, but any woman who comes on strong is considered a bitch. I'm not sure how to act strongly without alienating everyone. It's a balance lost on me right now. I never cared what anyone thought, but now I think it's important."

"That's an interesting issue." He thought for a second and said, "So you saved the toughest one for the first question?"

She didn't respond.

"When I was in the service and stuck in that tent, my commanding officer was a woman about my age. Rumor had it she was on the fast track to a star. There was every reason for all of us to resent her position as we were supposedly the best and brightest and knew more about our jobs than she did. She was good at her assigned duties; however, what stood out was her management style. She didn't care about taking credit for anything. Perfectly willing to let anyone higher up know who came up with a great idea. Also, when two of her people presented conflicting advice, she would listen, ask questions, and then say something like, 'I believe this time the situation requires this tactic, but good work, both of you.' She made the decision, again, without ever getting herself involved. It was all about the problem. I can tell you, all of us wanted to make her a hero whenever possible. It dawned on me one day why she was on the fast track. The people who worked for her put her there."

Kate listened with her eyes closed. Brad finished, and she remained still, lying back, resting.

"Are you asleep? Did you hear what I said?"

"Of course, I did; I was the one who asked the question."

He chuckled. "Could have fooled me."

"That is a great analogy. You have passed your first test."

Brad said, "By the way, did you notice how relieved Avery was when he told you about the Cartel?"

Kate laughed. "I have treated that man so horribly, and he doesn't deserve it at all. He is a wonderful person who is also very capable, a rare mixture. What do you think about Avery and Ms. Vestrova?"

"What about her?" Brad said.

"They're a couple well past the dating stage. Avery had never said anything about her, ever. They were rarely apart this evening. When they were apart, you were next to her like glue."

"Glue? I got her a drink once, and she asked me to sit down for a chat."

"Come on, Brad, you were drooling all over her like a little puppy. It's okay, you know, but don't deny it."

"Drooling? If that's what you call appreciating a classy woman of breeding, then I'm guilty. It was pure chance I sat next to her at dinner."

"And pure chance she found you interesting? You two were in the corner long enough to have written a book."

"I'm sorry, I'm a charming guy. Moreover, she is fascinating. Also, I have to say, you clean up nice. I mean earlier, not the robe and all."

She ignored the comment and took another drink. "Do you think we can pull this off?"

"Given what I saw today and the history of the organization, I think *you* can. Anyway, we will know tomorrow after all the planning meetings."

"I want you in all of the meetings. Bring up anything you want, but keep in mind they have been doing this much longer than we have. It's often the outside set of eyes that catch the obvious."

Kate rested her head on the chair back again while balancing her empty glass on the arm. She sat silently still for a few minutes.

Brad got up and took the glass from her hand.

She opened her eyes.

"I can find my way out, Sunshine. See you in the morning."

"Brad?"

He was at the door and turned.

"Thanks," she said. "You're the greatest."

CHAPTER—30

KATE NEEDS A BREAK

Kate listened as Brad shut the door. Things were quiet, and, in the silence and dim light, she looked at the walls thinking about the day. Thought after thought and visions of faces crept into her thinking as she felt a familiar feeling, a sickness really. The room she sat in turned into a four-sided space that began to get smaller and darker. Her eyes opened wide, but it didn't help. Her breathing quickened, and she could hear her heart beating. Tightness started to move across her chest, and she grabbed the arms of the chair and quickly stood up to regain control. Slightly dizzy, she went to the bathroom, washed her face with a wet cloth, and supported herself, gripping both sides of the sink. She looked into the mirror. Time for some personal air, she thought.

She reached for the phone. "Jimmy, can you get me a car in thirty minutes? Oh, and I don't want anyone to know about it. Can you do that?"

"Ms. Adler, I have been advised that it is not prudent for you to be outside the chateau."

"Am I a prisoner?"

"Heavens no, Ms. Adler, that's not …"

"Then I will meet you where we entered earlier today. Is that a good place? I have an identification card to get back in, so there shouldn't be any problem. Just make sure the chauffeur is more than a driver, right?"

"Ah, yes, Ms. Adler, he is definitely more than a chauffeur. Okay, as you wish."

Kate knew Jimmy didn't like the idea, but she needed to escape into her other world and temporarily leave behind the mountain of changes having taken place in her life in such a short time. The persona she had to portray didn't fit quite as well as it appeared, and it would be a while before it did. Thankfully, she had Brad and Avery.

Jimmy was in the garage, standing with the driver as she stepped out of the same door Kira had been standing in when she welcomed them to the castle.

Jimmy stepped forward, his hands behind his back, and said, "Ms. Adler, I would like to vigorously stress the unusual nature of your leaving the security of the grounds."

"Jimmy, nothing untoward will occur because of you helping me. As of today, you report to me anyway. Who is my driver?"

"Ms. Adler, let me introduce Mr. Willerby; he will be driving you this evening."

Kate said, "What is your first name?"

"Andrew," he said.

"Andrew, do you know how to contact the castle in an emergency?"

"Yes, madame, of course."

She turned to Jimmy, "Are we okay now? I'm not a foolish type, but I'm very independent and need this time to myself."

"Yes, madame, I shall wait for your return … shall we say, anxiously."

"Very good. Andrew, let's get on with it."

Jimmy opened the door of the Bentley, and Andrew went around to the driver's side.

Security checked their identification as they left, and Andrew proceeded down the winding lane that would take them off the castle grounds.

"Where would you like me to take you this evening, Ms. Adler?"

Kate tapped her fingers on the armrest and said, "I know this is a small town, but I want to go to a decent place where I can get a drink and hopefully be alone. What's the best place in town?"

"That would be the Auberge Aal Veinen. It's a restaurant with a lounge and a very nice clientele."

"Good, let's go there."

Kate could still feel the invisible enclosure, and she cracked the window for a bit of fresh air. She took a deep breath. The invisible compression that had started to form in the room seemed to dissipate as they rode through the quaint little town. In no time, Andrew pulled up to the entrance of an exceptionally old building, and two young men came out dressed in formal wear. One stood by the entrance door, and the other opened her door. Kate stepped out under the tightly drawn canopy, saying, "Thank you, and Mr. Willerby will take care of you."

"Madame, do you wish me to stay?" Andrew said, handing the boy a tip.

"Yes," she said, noting he didn't use her name for security reasons. It was a small thing until it became big. They were, from top to bottom, a group of very well-mannered people. They would be very out of place in the States.

The other man opened the entrance door for her.

"Cocktails?" she said when she was inside. The man led her to a wide opening, and turning, extended a hand and said, "Please, madame."

She proceeded inside and spent a few seconds admiring the room before her. It was perfect, she thought. The soft, low lighting and beautiful earthy colors were Old World warm. Small pendant lights hung over the customers seated at the L-shaped bar, and gentle indirect lighting from under the bar top washed down to the floor. The bar, located in the same room as the dining tables, suited her just fine. A mixture of conversations from the various groups enjoying dinner filled the room. A collection of paintings hung on a rough wall of straw stucco, separated by revealed dark beams.

She moved to a seat where she could enjoy the room and its pleasant atmosphere. The youngish bartender, in black slacks and white shirt, came over, placing a napkin down.

"Puis-Je vous aider?"

"Yes, you can," she said in English.

He smiled and said, "Of course, what would you like?"

She thought for a moment before saying, "Surprise me."

Amused, he said, "Vodka, gin or wine?"

"Vodka," she said.

"Straight or flavored?"

"Straight."

"Now see, that wasn't too hard?" he said.

"You're from the US," she said. "Midwest."

He stopped as he was walking away and said. "Well, the lady

knows her stuff. I'm from Chicago."

"Chicago?" she said. "It's not like you *can't* come here, but Vianden? What's your name?"

"Phil. My uncle owns the place, and I'm here for six months trying to find myself after college."

"Can I help?"

'Help?"

"Yes," she said. "Without a doubt, I can say you're right here."

He laughed loudly and then caught himself being in a somewhat subdued room. "You're going to get me fired."

"I thought your uncle owned the place?"

"He does, and he is a nice man, but he is a businessman first and a member of the family second, if you know what I mean? He has taught me a lot since I have been here. I'll be back in a second with your drink."

Kate loved the place right away. She felt special in one of her favorite dresses and pulled her compact out to glance at her makeup. All is fine, Kate thought. She checked her money and closed her clutch, putting it aside.

Back he came, placing a drink on the bar top. "Vodka martini, dry with a twist, shaken. Will that please the lady?"

She took a small sip and said, "Consider the lady pleased."

"How long have you been here?" she asked.

"Three months and I'm completely fascinated with the difference in European culture compared to what we have in the States." Phil nodded toward the entrance of the room and said, "Gastwirt" (restaurant proprietor).

She smiled at the reference and saw a tall, well-built, neat, and elegant man walk into the room. He was dressed immaculately in a chalk-striped, double-breasted, five-thousand-dollar suit. A large Arrow collar framed the knot of his tie, and the Dunaway fold of his pocket square spoke legions about his unconventional view of life. His hair was very European, abundant, and slicked back in a racy manner that matched the moneyed appearance he wished to project. His bearing was unmistakable as he entered the room. A waiter handed him a drink and, as he brought it to his lips, he inserted his other hand halfway into the left pocket of his jacket and surveyed the dining room before him.

Kate was fascinated; he looked like a tall James Bond aged

181

about fifty, right out of central casting. He greeted several tables with his quick laugh putting everyone at ease. Graciously listening to each person as they spoke before casting an eye over the room and moving on to the following table. The next time he scanned the room, he stopped at Kate sitting alone. She watched him change direction, start walking over, adjust his cufflinks, and pull his pure white shirt out from his coat sleeve.

Amused, Kate looked at him as he approached. Here comes trouble, she thought.

His last few steps included looking intently at his quest.

"American?" he asked.

"Red, white and blue," she said. "Oh, I guess that could also be French," she conceded.

Standing next to her, he reached down for her hand and brought it close to his face. Without actually kissing her hand, he looked up and said, "Enchanted."

Kate thought it a tender, reserved gesture except when delivered by a boulevardier with apparent intentions.

"If I had known such a beautiful woman was to be in my establishment tonight, I would have closed down so we could have it just for ourselves."

She slowly withdrew her hand, saying, "Just a little on the heavy side. Why don't we start over with what's my sign?"

"I'm so sorry, did I offend you? This was not my intention; I can assure you. However," he continued with a wink, "I was not lying."

Men, she thought. "So, my bartender said you own this quite comfortable little piece of the world?"

"Yes, it is mine, and my father's before me, and my grandfather's before that. I'm very fortunate. However, so are you, look at you. How long are you in Vianden?"

"I leave early tomorrow morning," she said.

"How unfortunate. Were you here on business?"

Kate slowly picked up her glass and raised it, saying, "To your fine establishment. It's truly lovely."

"Oh, I thank you, but I have been so rude. Phil," he said to the bartender, motioning toward Kate, "she is not to pay for anything." He turned back, "There, we have set things straight."

"Well, such generosity, you must now tell me your name," she said. "My name is Jane."

"Federico Damiano D'Argenio," he stood up straight and said, "à votre service" (at your service).

Kate provided a quaint smile and said, "Cela ne fonctionne vraiment que pour les femmes qui ne parlent pas français" (that only really works on women who don't speak French).

Laughing hardily, he extended his arm, picked up her drink, and said, "Please, let me get the lady a proper table befitting her classical nurturing and streak of independence."

"Well, thank you," she said, grabbing his arm. "You're so kind."

He pulled the reserved card off a round table in a corner and pulled a chair out for her. He moved to the other side and, while looking at Phil, pointed at her glass, then to himself.

Kate rotated her martini glass around by the stem and said, "Federico?"

"Yes, you have a question? Do you need something?"

"No, thank you. As I said, I'm an American."

"Of course, I knew this right away. A lovely American, I might say."

"We are rather blunt. Do you know 'blunt'?"

"Yes, of course. Why do you say this?"

"Because you are a player, a ladies' man, a charming and handsome one but a first-class player. So I'm warning you, don't mess with me; this isn't going anywhere."

"Jane," he said, sitting back in his chair with an incredulous look on his face. "What do you mean by saying that?"

"Damiano D'Argenio, you know damn well what I mean, but that's enough of that. So what's an Italian family doing settling in Luxembourg?"

"It seems my grandfather didn't like the Italian government at the time and decided to move his family here. It's been a good life."

"Are you married?" she asked.

"Sadly, no, marriage and I have never found a way to be happy. It is supposed to make life brighter. It has never done that for me."

"Somehow, I don't find that surprising. However, I wish that you find what works best in your life."

"That's a very nice and touching thing to say," he said. "I wish

183

to find a woman that emotionally takes me to places where neither of us has ever been. Meanwhile, I will have to enjoy the company of the many wonderful roses that fill life's garden."

"Roses?"

"Yes, women are exactly like roses, each one beautiful, and no two are the same."

Kate looked at him. "Federico, you mean that, don't you?"

He looked at her with a quizzical expression and wondered why she would say that. "Of course, what else could be more enjoyable than finding a woman with a gentle hand, who knows how to properly wear a floor-length dress, gliding on luscious high heels to a rhythm that makes your heart stop?"

"Wow, that's quite a description. You are a hopeless romantic. Have you ever found this gentle hand?"

"No, but these dreams are not necessary when confronted with a woman who draws your interest. To have dinner and find out what matters in her life, what keeps her content."

"Federico, are we talking sex here?"

He placed a hand over his heart. "Have I mentioned intimacy? When a man truly loves women, I'm talking about one who loves and appreciates every individual petal of the rose, this pursuit is never necessary. When a woman discovers your interest is sincere, all the defenses recede into pleasant conversation. If intimacy is appropriate and never sought, it is never a problem. Who would want to share a time that is, but for the body and not the soul?"

Kate raised her glass in a toast, "I have to say you are one interesting man."

"We spoke of what works best. What works for you, Jane? What makes you happy as I also see you are single?"

"Up until recently, I thought it was very apparent what made me happy, but now I'm not so sure."

"You've had a ..." he paused for a word, "disruption?"

"More like a surprise. I had this one life, and now it looks like I'm going to live another."

"I sense disappointment; this cannot be good for the future."

"Not really; there just hasn't been enough time for it to feel comfortable."

"Well," he said, raising his glass. "I wish you find what works best for your life."

"You are charming, Federico, and I have to say I misjudged you because you are different."

"No, you are different. Remember, no two the same."

"Can I ask you something?"

"But of course."

"If you woke up tomorrow morning and found yourself totally poor or perhaps totally rich, how would you handle it?"

"That's easy. It would all depend on what I decided was a good life. Poor has its advantages, as does being rich. What you think is good for you will answer your question."

"Federico, the philosopher," she said.

"Tell me, Jane," he said, leaning forward and smiling a knowing smile, " I ask what would work for you, as I think you need to answer this question?"

"I used to think it was poor, but it's an existence that affects a tiny circle. Wealth could effect change in a substantial way if one's goal were to create change." Kate looked at the man across from her as he silently let the moment speak for itself.

"You don't know this, Federico, but this short but pleasant conversation provided exactly what I wanted when I walked in the door. A chance to have my mind taken to another place, and meeting you has certainly accomplished this. For that, I must thank you."

"Is it possible we can enjoy your company the next time you are in town?"

"I think that would be nice. Now I must go." She stood up, and he walked her to the door and stood outside as she entered the car. She powered down the window and said, "I wish you the best of luck in your rose garden."

"Thank you, madam," he said with his hand over his heart and bowing forward, "but luck has nothing to do with it."

CHAPTER—31

KHIABANI PLANNING MEETING

Kate had set a loose time for the meeting the next morning. They knew the staff would be working through the night, forming a plan. Avery, Kate, and Brad sat in the conference room. Avery had walked in the door reading some report and was now at the table flipping pages and making notes dressed in a very Seville dark blue suit. He was always formally attired, adding to his already bigger-than-life stature in the organization.

Brad wondered how quickly Kate would attain the same respect; making the jump from Founder's Princess to full-blown Queen of the Kingdom was a huge step. He knew she was capable, but this was an old organization dominated over the years by just two powerful men. He stood at the credenza, holding the saucer supporting his latest refill. Brad looked at her sitting at the end of the conference table. There was something about Kate that rose above her outer beauty, something that acted as gravity adhering him to her orbit. He couldn't move forward or backward and couldn't break away, although he had very briefly considered the option. Holding her cup deep in thought, he watched her put her fingers into the handle and wrap her hand around the outside. She continued staring at the table. It was a familiar sight, and he left her alone.

Two minutes later, the staff entered the room and took their place. There were Penn Hauer and two assistants, along with two others.

Kate said, "All of you look tired, and I want you to know we appreciate the work you've put in and are very anxious to hear your plans."

"It's what we do," Penn said in his low, assuring voice. "There isn't time to invent layers of options, so we have to get right to the point."

"Still, all of your efforts are appreciated. What did you come up with?"

"First," Avery said, "I would like to introduce you to Elena Maleeva; she is director of Geneva Services and has been at Morton-Roth this week. She came in last night. She's known as Mom's Mom. Here is an organization chart to help get a feel for the players."

He handed Kate a diagram.

"It's nice to meet you, Ms. Maleeva," Kate said, grabbing the chart from Avery.

Elena just offered an enigmatic half-smile as acknowledgment before saying, "And I would like to introduce Lauren Sorrel, directing the G9 asset in the real world, and I believe you know Dr. Wilkerson."

Otherwise, she sat with her hands on her folders.

Kate noticed the lack of response and continued. "Given the results of the Steering Committee meeting, I have had little time to absorb the operational details of the organization. A briefing on the G9 asset as well as the management and reporting structure would be helpful. Can we quickly take some time to go over this before planning our next moves?"

Penn looked at Elena and said, "This is your part of the country."

Ms. Maleeva was thirty-three and, before she had spoken a word, Kate had noticed confidence and poise in her natural manner. Also, she saw a slight perception of resentment. It could be, as a woman, she didn't appreciate Kate's position, thus setting them up to be rivals. Elena was slight of frame, with long, straight, dark blonde hair parted down the middle and pulled back in a loose ponytail that came down slightly on the sides. She wore a dark grey, knee-length skirt and an off-white, simply cut blouse with a shirt collar. All of it said: business.

"Would you like me to stand?" she asked.

"Elena, it's your choice. The meeting is very informal," Kate said.

Elena remained seated. When she quickly spoke, her English was perfect with a sharp Eastern European accent. Brad's eyebrows went up at the sound of her voice, and Kate discreetly looked over to see him staring at Elena, with a most pleasant look on his face.

Elena started right into her presentation. "Geneva9 is a one-of-a-kind worldwide data, communications, and surveillance system. It was a secret so dark and buried that the NSA organization, let alone the US government and its closest allies, were not aware of its existence. The project started in 1995 within the Adler Electronics Company. It was the ninth revision, and during its constant development cycle, it cost over a billion US dollars. Your father directly supervised the secret development of the G9. He was meticulous in dividing it up into separate modules and sending it to separate teams. Only the compiling team, here at Vianden, knew its ultimate composition and purpose. It has unparalleled access to real-world local surveillance feeds and media broadcasts and a unique ability to penetrate networks.

"The G9 system excels where others have not due to three characteristics. Unlike the NSA, it does not attempt to acquire and decrypt all the data available in the world. While we obtain massive amounts of data, we are much more targeted and thus more efficient within a defined set of parameters.

"The second reason is the number of massive data centers restrict most other surveillance efforts. Geneva9 is not a computer in the typical sense of the word, but a decentralized software program like the BitTorrent or peer-to-peer file-sharing systems. It operates on computing assets connected to the Internet. By inserting a harmless application, it utilizes only the excess computing power across both the open and dark sides of the Internet. The dark side of the Internet is estimated to be 500 times bigger than the surface web accessible by search engines like Google. The peer-to-peer system results in a vast reservoir of unprecedented power to execute its list of assignments.

"The third reason is, when combining this raw computing power with an artificial intelligence-based operating system, it's able to resolve encryption protocols at an unprecedented rate—the increased rate of speed results in unmatched access to almost all protected networks. G9 can masquerade as any routable IPv4 or IPv6 host, appearing to be anywhere and anyone on the Internet. It also has a significant off-net capability. It surreptitiously plants eavesdropping devices on computers and telecom systems and industrial controls accessing the control-system layer. This level of access is unique and unknown to users, consumers, professionals, or governments. The Geneva9 asset connects the dots, but humans make the decisions."

Elena rose, walked over to the whiteboard, and picked up a marker pen.

Kate looked over again, and Brad was looking at Elena's finely defined rear end moving as she wrote on the board.

Elena reached up and drew three boxes, and as she filled them in, she continued. "The Geneva Services team is divided into three parts: Intelligence and Analysis, Maintenance and Security, and Real-World Interaction. Ms. Adler, you were part of the MS group in Munich under Marc Henderson, a dear friend. We kept that function out of the Vianden facility as you were not aware of your work's true nature. In fact, you were unaware of the organization. We devised an NSA cover, and," she said looking at Kate, "some of the coded product that came out of that facility was simply elegant."

Kate studied Elena as she calmly addressed Kate's previous outside status. No one had previously discussed the subject. Did she mean it in a negative slight, or was it just a product of Elena's practical personality?

Elena circled the I&A box on the board and said, "This department receives and filters the data collected from around the world and is run by Dr. Wilkerson. G9 isn't just a passive bulk-data collection program; it prioritizes data categories to store for later collating and specific inquiries. With the operating system's AI nature, we can create classifiers, which pull aside any information within the set parameters for analysis. The classifiers would include keywords, weather, documents, news feeds, public and private statements, or the timing of any issue that's related to the subject of interest."

Wilkerson had his hand on the table and just raised a finger for recognition. Elena responded. "John?"

"It was here," John said, "that the system generated the POC or Pattern of Concern allowing us to intercept the LNG tanker. The operating system's AI nature brought together the reassignment of an IRGC special forces team to the submarine base two days before it departed. All communications to the submarine before it set sail, the off-schedule departure of the submarine, the capabilities of that specific sub, and the range and possible assignment came together in the alert. This information was all based on the classifier profile."

Brad interrupted. "John, why didn't we get a POC on the hijackings?"

"A question we asked ourselves," John said. "To collate information, you need data. There was a complete lack of any signet or electronic trail in that case. We scrubbed the entire IRGC network and found nothing. Placing a few already trained men on a boat is a lot easier to hide than a submarine. Otherwise, they were virtually perfect up to the Internet cafe's incident and the open-air intercept of Gen. Lajani calling his family. The search provided a definite Iranian connection. With that defined as 'true,' the association libraries within the classifiers had a field day."

Brad nodded, saying, "Well, that certainly answers that."

Avery said, "That's good, John, but it doesn't answer how they discovered the location of the Munich office."

"We don't have an explanation for that yet, but suspect it took a great deal of old-fashion boots on the ground detective work. We have simulations running, and that should come up with an answer."

Elena patiently waited for Wilkerson to finish, then turned back to the board and continued. "Thanks, John, nice summary. So finally, yet importantly, is RWI. Lauren Sorrel's section deals with directing the G9 asset for Real-World Interaction. It seems liberal society has a problem calling things what they are. I call it Offensive Operations because that's exactly what it is, and it makes sweet little Lauren over there," she waved her marker toward her, "the scariest person in the room."

Lauren, dressed in pastels, looked very young and shy. At five-foot-four, she was less than a commanding figure and, in a word, tiny. She lowered her head and acted as if she were embarrassed at being called out.

Elena then tapped the box labeled RWI with the marker and said, "G9 utilizes the increased use of the Internet of Things to reach out and touch people and systems in the real world. We can do things like take over control boards at electrical power stations, turn off public transportation, and software-driven mechanical hardware like industrial control systems. We create libraries of penetrated companies, governments, and institutions for future use. For instance, we have access to a staggering number of banks, port authorities, gunrunners, and drug and military organizations for whenever they're needed."

Elena dropped her arms to her side and looked at Kate. "I know that's brief, and there is a lot more detail, but I would suppose you would like to get into that later."

At the Offensive Operations comment, Kate decided immediately that Elena was a complete straight shooter and any perceived agenda was a misread on her part.

"Elena, that was excellent," Kate said. "I had no idea the reach Mom had when I was working on her. I now feel infinitely more comfortable and informed."

Addressing the group, Kate continued. "So, let's get into the recommendations for dealing with the IRGC."

Penn spoke up as Elena sat down. "We decided a direct face-to-face meeting would impress upon Khiabani both the urgency of his changing and our ability to apply leverage. Both of those are required to give him justification to abandon his plans. We suggest an invitation delivering a message implying we know more about his plans than he realizes.

"Our demonstrations will include shutting down parts of the Iranian power grid and suspending the bank accounts of Khiabani and the IRGC leadership. Also, G9 accessed the grades of Khiabani's son and left behind what will appear as a crude hack to manipulate his grades. The appearance of guilt will be used as a lever getting his son to deliver an invitation directly to his father. The invitation will leave Ali no room but to attend a meeting we will have arranged in a public venue. Ms. Adler, you had expressed a desire to meet personally with Khiabani. We will suggest in the invitation that three from each side attend. I presume you, Mr. Stanton, and one of our agents will be there."

"Penn," Kate said, "I said yesterday that I wanted to be the one to talk directly to Khiabani. Today, I want to know what you and your people think. Did you discuss this?"

Penn was a little surprised at the question and said, "Yes, we did discuss exactly that. We recognized the direct meeting's whole purpose was to deliver a message with information not easily explained in a letter. We felt the conviction you demonstrated yesterday would emphasize any words you will deliver."

Brad was still concerned about Kate's safety, especially after Munich. "If that's the case," Brad said, "what kind of security posture are you proposing?"

"We decided on two security vehicles in front and back of our limo for transportation to and from the airport," Penn said. "With the route decided at the last minute."

Brad still wasn't satisfied. "Who is in the detail, and how heavily are they armed?"

"It's the European equivalent of the team that executed the LNG attack. They're all former special forces."

"Are they ours?" Brad asked.

"Completely. We formed the team two years ago. While the individuals have changed over time, they're a highly-trained unit equipped with everything they need for special operations.

"Kate?" Avery said. "Are you sure you won't reconsider? Penn's feelings aside, with your conviction to address this yourself, you must see this is not entirely without risk."

"Kate," Brad interjected, "I have to say I'm with Avery here. Khiabani is a wild card. It leaves a big hole in exactly knowing what's going to happen."

Kate paused and took a few moments to think. "I appreciate the input from you both, but I think this situation needs Penn's solution."

Brad looked at Kate with a knowing smile. She had indeed listened during their talk.

"Well," Avery said, "my field days are over, and I won't be attending the meeting, but I will be on the plane. If you're going to insist on going, then I insist Brad be the second person from our side."

Kate glanced at Avery, realizing this was the change taking place. He was stepping back and defining his level of participation.

"I have no problem with that," she said. "So, what else is there?"

"We will be listening to everything you say during the meeting," Penn continued. "During your conversation, we will be putting in motion the set of demonstrations Elena and Lauren have cooked up. That way, they will flow into the conversation at your pace. When you ask him to call his people to confirm the demonstration, it will have occurred moments before the call is connected. It will add to his bewilderment and will confirm your leverage. We will, however, need a favor from the Americans."

"What is that?" Kate asked.

"We would like them to assemble a group of ships right off Iran's coast. We like it as a demonstration as it conveys a powerful message. We will, of course, call it coincidence, but Khiabani will know better. It will confuse him as to who we are."

"Excellent," Kate said. "Avery? Brad?"

"I still don't like it," Avery said.

"I know," she said, "but I think the plan is as good as it can be. All of you have done a nice job. When do we take off?"

Penn said, "0900 tomorrow morning. It will give us plenty of time to avoid any unforeseen holdups, ensuring we make the meeting at noon. The invitation can," he looked at his watch, "take place within the hour. That also gives Khiabani plenty of time to make his decision and fly into Vienna."

Kate said, "Any comments for or against?"

Brad and Avery both shook their heads but without any visible enthusiasm.

"Extend the invitation," Kate said to Penn.

Penn looked at one of his assistants, and she got up and left the room to start the process. "The security team left early this morning with all the vehicles and equipment. We would have recalled them if we didn't approve this plan. They will arrive at the private corporate terminal and go through their equipment checks and travel routes. We have laid out a floor plan to give you a sense of where you will be at the meeting."

Still not entirely comfortable with all the details, Brad said, "Have you taken into account escape routes if everything goes south?"

"Yes. The room has two exits that lead into concrete basement passageways used by the hotel staff. Each makes a turn, eliminating any straight shot down the hall when escaping. They both lead directly to a public street. We will hear everything that's going on; if an escape is needed, we will be at the street exit before you are. Of course, the formal entry and exit will be from your limo to the front door of the hotel. So you can review it beforehand, we have prepared the list of the demonstrations and a general direction of the conversation, which should be very short."

"Very well done," Kate said. "This is the kind of professional assistance I was hoping to get when I took this job. That leaves a final element being someone calling the Americans and requesting their cooperation. That seems a rather large favor. How do we plan on doing that?"

Hauer said, "One of our agents, who has been in contact with the Americans, said they would cooperate as far as they can, but again, cannot take any direct action."

"Well, our request seems to fall into that category."

"I agree," Penn said. "We will take care of the request and notify you immediately if there is a change in plans."

Kate thought for a second. "Also, can we prepare a brief for the Steering Committee? I promised them I would keep them informed, and I intend to follow through. If that's it, you people will need to go. Thanks again for everything."

Everyone got up and was milling around the room, conversing in small groups, when Kate noticed Brad had moved over to Elena and started a conversation. He was telling her how impressed he was with her work. She seemed to be listening and appreciative, nodding her head and smiling. Brad's body language spoke volumes as they walked out of the room.

Avery interrupted her observations. "Kate, I want you to reconsider being directly involved. I just can't let this feeling go."

"I need to do this, Avery, for many reasons that are as obvious to you as they're to me."

"Still," he said, "I'm supposed to keep you out of harm's way."

"Avery, you can't have it both ways. You want me involved in this but want to monitor the extent? It's all or nothing, Avery; there's no middle ground. You're the one who wanted me to step up. It's your call."

"Old commitments die hard," he said.

Kate looked up and saw that everyone else had left the room. "Avery, what would I do without you?" She gave him a big hug and stayed there awhile. "You're going to let me do this, right?" she said into the lapel of his suit coat.

"Do I have a say?" he said.

She looked up at him, smiling her well-practiced and frequently used little girl smile.

Avery shook his head, "I didn't think so."

CHAPTER—32

PENN CALLS DEVROE

Devroe heard the phone ring but sensed it was not normal. It was also not a reasonable time—five thirty in the morning. He searched for his phone to discover it was not ringing. However, something was still making an early morning racket. Through the fog, he sat up and tried to ascertain a direction. It was coming from inside his briefcase. It was the G9 phone. He rushed over, picked up the phone, and looked at the screen. "Please enter connection code," the screen read. Devroe looked at the card in his briefcase with the character sequence the president had eventually given him and touched it in. It took a second, then the screen read "voice – touch to connect."

He did and then put the phone to his ear.

Penn Hauer spoke into his headset. "Dr. Devroe, this is Agent 2062. Can you please place your finger on the square provided and hold it for one second?"

Devroe completed the instructions. What's with these people anyway? he thought. I'm the God-damned head of security of the most powerful nation on earth. He decided not to say any of that.

Penn looked at the screen in front of him, waiting for approval.

"Thank you, Doctor. I want to tell you this call is being recorded and is available only to our Steering Committee. I'm calling with an update and a request regarding the previously discussed issue. We have determined through a telecom intercept that the Iranian IRGC is responsible for the hijackings and the attempted bombing of the tanker in Singapore. We do not, as yet, know if the administration of Iran is involved or is even aware of who is responsible for the actions to date."

"Excuse me," Devroe interjected, "was that your operation that stopped the LNG explosion?"

"I'm not authorized to discuss any operational details that may or may not have occurred in the field."

"You're kidding me," Devroe said. "You can't say anything? Do you know who I am?"

"Yes, sir, born January 17, 1979, to Ellen and Andrew Devroe in Salem Oregon. You went to school at ..."

"Okay, it's the standard response, and I get it. You're not going to tell me anything." He was a little ticked at their highhandedness, or perhaps jealous at their efficiency. He had checked with his counterparts in the intelligence community only to find out none of his people were involved. Therefore, he was sure it was this organization. "Let's get to what you *can* talk about," he said.

"We have a strategic plan in place. We hope this will be enough to stop the IRGC aggression. It will take place at 1300 hours on Wednesday. They will, of course, deny any involvement, but our demand that they stop and the incentives for doing so will take place nevertheless. We believe your cooperation in providing a substantial and visible increase in naval vessels just outside their territorial waters, where the last hijacked tanker made port, would greatly help add pressure during the negotiations. Call it an exercise if you wish, although the Iranians will believe differently. It would only need to be in position a few hours preceding and behind the one p.m. meeting time. We would, of course, deny there is any connection and that US naval forces are free to distribute their ships as they see fit. However, they cannot ignore the coincidence. Holding off on any provocation by the Iranians would help us to keep this solution diplomatic."

"Nice bit of leverage without actually tipping any hands," Devroe said. "That will require the president's approval, but I don't see a problem. Count on the assistance unless you hear differently. They will certainly object to our being there. There is also the possibility they might try something like approaching with a swarm of their vessels. Rest assured, we will only react defensively and not escalate the situation."

"Excellent," Hauer said. "Although this is a diplomatic effort, it is a volatile situation. We don't expect them to just fade away at our demand, but we are hopeful there is enough leverage to have them change their mind eventually. We will bring you up to date as soon as our meeting is complete and what, if any, additional actions will be needed."

"Looks like you have the bases covered. Let us know if there is anything else we can do to help. I have a question. What's with the need for a large communication device? We have encrypted phones that are much easier to lug around, and I guarantee they're foolproof."

"I'm not an engineer, so I cannot speak to the design. I know they're highly secure anywhere in the world, using multiple methods of connection and encryption. I *can* say don't try to open the unit by taking the cover off, as it will create a high voltage spike through the electronics and fry everything to a crisp, electronically speaking."

"Amazing," Devroe said in a low tone, not believing it. "By the way, doesn't anyone on your side have a name?"

Devroe could tell the man had a smile when he said, "Yes, Dr. Devroe, you can call me Mr.," and he paused, "2062."

Devroe laughed and dropped the phone by his side for a second with an exasperated look at the ceiling. "Okay," he said, still chuckling. "I get it. I want to be clear: We appreciate this phone call and any assistance you can offer in getting this problem under control."

"On behalf of myself and the Steering Committee, you're welcome. We will talk soon."

CHAPTER—33

KHIABANI'S INVITATION

A lone man approached Fared Khiabani, a college student, descending the outside steps of his lecture hall at the prestigious University of Tehran, a school many considered the best in the country. Potential students must be connected in some way outside of the average population to be accepted.

The student looked like any student anywhere, carrying a backpack full of heavy books and wearing jeans and tennis shoes. Unlike some of the other young men coming out of the building, his hair was cut very short. He was troubled at the meeting he had just had with his headmaster. What was his father's reaction going to be when he found out? The accusations would disgrace the family. Would he believe his son's explanation that he didn't know?

At both the right and left corners of the building stood men, hands clasped in front, not pretending to be anything other than what they were—security guards for the student.

"Fared Khiabani," a lone man said as he approached Fared holding out an envelope. The guards started a slow approach. "Call them off, Fared; I will leave in a minute, I assure you."

Fared looked back to his guards and waved his hand for them to stop.

"What do you want? You've ten seconds, or the world will end for you," Fared said, wielding the authority of his family.

"You and only you must hand-deliver this envelope to your father and quickly. I cannot overstate the importance with regards to the safety of your family."

Fared looked up at the man, first with concern then confusion and then defiant anger. "You will not speak of my family if you wish to live. Besides, my father has many people who perform his wishes; he does not need me to bring him messages."

"This is true; he is an important man, and we have chosen you because it affects the safety of your mother, Sepideh, and sister, Nasrin."

Fared looked over to his security people before making a decision.

"Fared, if they interfere," the man said, "this message will never arrive in time, and the responsibility will be yours." He held the envelope higher. The boy took it, looking at the front, then the back.

"This is very important," the man said. "You must deliver it now only to your father, and you must not open it. How are your studies?"

Fared, caught off guard, answered vaguely, "Fine, except they think I'm cheating. I'm not a cheat. Besides, why would you care?"

"You are not a cheat; I know this," the man said.

"How can you know this?"

"If you do me this favor, I will speak to the headmaster to take care of that misunderstanding before your father finds out. Do we have a deal?"

Fared curiously looked directly at the man.

"It is only an envelope, Fared. However, with a critical message that he must only read. I have taken the liberty and ordered you a taxi," the man said, pointing to the waiting Peugeot. "He will take you there now."

"I have my own transportation," Fared said, pointing to the two Toyota SUVs parked across the street.

"As you wish," the man said. "Upon delivery, your school problems will disappear."

Fared turned to the security team and said, "Let this man go and come with me." He headed to his vehicles, and they all got in. Fared looked out the open window at his mysterious visitor as they drove away. Turning the envelope over again, he spoke to his driver. "Take me to my father's office."

* * *

The intercom on his desk came to life. "General, I know you are in an important meeting; however your son is here to see you. Can I send him in?"

Vahid pressed the intercom button and quietly said, "Of course." He looked at the others and got up from his chair, making his way to the door as his assistant opened it. Fared stood there, sans his backpack, which he had left in the SUV. "Fared, what are you doing here?" his father said. "Come in."

"Hello, Father. I'm only here to deliver this message. A man approached me at school and insisted I personally deliver this to you. He said it was crucial. He knew the names of Nasrin and Mother, so I did as he said. Other than that, I know nothing. If it is okay, I will go home and start my studies?"

"Of course," his father said. "Is everything alright? You sound different or something. You would let me know, yes?"

"Everything is fine, Father, and I will not make a habit of bothering you at your work. I will see you this evening at home." Fared turned and headed down the hall.

Vahid looked at the envelope as he walked back to his desk noting the lack of writing on either side. He opened the clasp and brought the letter up to read while lowering himself into his chair.

Maj. Gen. Vahid Khiabani
Chief Commander IRGC

We apologize for inconveniencing your son in delivering this letter. It was to ensure only you received the message and the paper letter assured no electronic signature. By way of introduction, we know your family's names and the location of your son to aid in delivering this letter. Also, you will find as of today, the mortgage on your mother's house is paid in full. We also know your daughter, Nasrin, is successfully studying art in Paris and wish her well. We are in your life and want you to know bad decisions come at a price.

We are requesting your presence at the Palais Coburg Residenz Vienna, Austria, this coming Thursday at 1300 to discuss privately your recent actions and their less than desirable objectives.

We are a nonaligned private organization that prevented your attack in the Singapore harbor and suffered at your hand in

Munich. We do not represent any nation and come addressing our agenda. As to security, if we intended to harm you, we would have suggested less public arrangements.

We have reserved a table for four, two from each party, a principal, and an aide in a private dining area under your name. The room will be empty except for a single table with the aides performing mutual security checks at the door. Your aide may complete a sweep of the room. Only one additional person from each side will stand outside, making sure we are not disturbed. When you are satisfied, call the concierge, and we will meet you at the door. Security cameras inside the building will monitor any unnecessary people in the facility. You will want to bring a secure cellphone to confirm specific details with your office during the meeting. Subverting this meeting in any way will only leave you with questions and our subsequent actions. As always, answers change the world.

We look forward to meeting with you.

Vahid could barely contain his emotions. Since childhood, Vahid had mastered the methods of the street. More than once, he had his revenge for the smallest of slights against his sisters. He had beaten senseless more than his share of adversaries.

Nevertheless, what he just read made the old methods return in an instant. The letter shook in his hands. No one on earth or in the heavens could threaten his family. He would strangle them with his own hands. Yet there it was. At his command was all the power he needed to start another world war should he wish, but none of it helped regarding this letter.

"Leave the room, all of you," he said. "Wait outside."

They quickly filed out, knowing the tone as one to be feared, but were perplexed as to why it appeared suddenly.

Vahid got up from his desk and looked at the pictures in ornate khatam frames on the wall. The letter still in his hands was crushed as he tried to regain his composure. He now had several problems. First was the threat to his family. Then, despite their careful actions, their plans had been compromised. Was it the network breach? Did the mullahs know? Who wrote the letter? The Munich operation didn't seal the leak. He needed to act fast to keep their plans on track. He needed something to counter whoever was behind this and fast.

Given the redundant secrecy and precautions, how could anyone have known about Singapore? They didn't even have personnel in the open until thirty minutes before they were to board, but someone knew they were there. The letter didn't provide any method of communication. In their opinion, with the mention of his family, not attending the meeting wasn't an option.

Who had the logistical capability to do this? The CIA, GCHQ, or the French, or all of them? One thing was for sure; he had certainly gotten the West's attention, which had been one of the objectives. Still, threatening his family was not their style. They all played within certain rules. Playing by those rules instilled a weakness quickly exploited by those treading on the outside edges of the Great Satan.

He hit the button on his intercom. "Tell them to get back in here."

They returned to the room, but the tone had changed. The reaction of the general left no doubt as to a change in intensity.

Still looking at the letter, Khiabani said, "There has been a serious breach in our efforts. Where or who it is, I do not know. I have received a letter addressed directly to me. Someone or some group wants to meet in a public place to discuss our intentions in twenty-two hours. Because we hit the NSA station in Munich, I would guess it's America, but they deny any association."

Vahid looked at the letter again. "Who are these people?" he said aloud but really to himself.

"But, sir, how would they know it was us, and how could they possibly know our intentions?"

"You tell me. Perhaps it was the security breach on our computers."

"But, sir, Captain Abasi said there was nothing on that network remotely connected to our actions. Nothing, I can assure you. The network containing our planning is completely isolated. It's not connected to the outside world or the Internet."

"Well, then perhaps someone in this room. How else can we explain it? Maybe even Nabavi who failed to carry out a critical assignment. We need to up the risk for the other side. We need to move up the timeline of the fifth incident. Where do we stand?"

"Sir, we are set to disburse false information directly to the news outlets regarding the inevitably of a market crash."

"Good," Khibani said. "Do it immediately."

CHAPTER—34

KATE AND BRAD DISAGREE

Sometime later, the day of the meeting with Khiabani, Brad knocked on Kate's door. "Kate, it's me."

She opened the door halfway and said, "Come in, hurry, I'm not dressed."

Brad stepped in and observed she was in a bathrobe. However, she was wearing two big fluffy bunny slippers, and her hair was wet.

Brad looked at her slippers and said, "Don't *you* look spiffy."

"Danner, if you even hint to anybody you saw those, I will punch your lights out."

"Feeling comfortable, are we?"

"Look, I let you in, but that doesn't give you the right to criticize. Did you come here to harass me, or do you have something substantial to go over?"

Brad looked at the stack of folders and briefing books piled on the table that served as a desk in the room. "I'm here as a friend."

It was a strange comment, and Kate recognized the conversation had just changed. "Can I get you anything?" she said.

"No, I have something to discuss."

"Does it have to do with little Elena today? You are a complete pushover for her accent because it's the same as Vestrova's."

He laughed. "No, it's not that, although you caught me as I'm intrigued. I want to talk about last night."

"What about last night? You left and called me sunshine. Really?"

"It's what happened after."

Kate was now unsure where this was going. "What about after?"

"I came back later to get my phone as it has my brother's number on it that I don't know by heart. You didn't answer, and one must assume you were not here. I called Jimmy, and he was very uncomfortable saying he didn't know where you were. Anything you want to tell me?"

Kate thought for a second. It was tricky as his question was out of concern, but bordered on entering into her private life. "Remember in Munich when you kept asking me out, and I said I had something going? Well, I had something going, but it was private. It's my other side."

"Other side?" he said.

"Yes, I need to get away to keep my sanity, and I go out alone to places and meet people who don't know who I am. I can be anyone I want to be and avoid the phony interest wealth brings. I have a good time and say goodbye. I have been doing it most of my life. The last time I did, it was in New York with my girlfriends."

"You meet people—men?"

"Yes, Brad, I'm single and straight and sometimes horny. We are getting into an uncomfortable area here. Where are we going with this?"

"So, you left the compound last night, went to a bar and met a man, and had drinks?"

"Yes, it sounds pretty normal to me. What's the problem? What's going on?"

"Under normal circumstances, I would agree, but given your new set of responsibilities, don't you think it's risky behavior?"

"What?"

"Don't you think going out with a stranger in the middle of the night is risky behavior?"

"No, I don't," she said. "As I said, they don't know who I am. I have agreed to be all these things people want me to be; I also get to have a life."

"How do you know they don't know it's you?"

"If this is a secret organization of the highest order, I doubt some faceless guy I meet and have drinks with is going to know anything. Besides, I can take care of myself. Andrew, a staff driver, drove me there. I met a most interesting gentleman; we had a drink, and Andrew drove me back. The time away was exactly what I needed."

"Look, Kate, you said to offer my opinion, and that's what I'm doing. Your actions could place the organization in a tough spot if someone decided to use you as a bargaining chip. This whole thing could come apart."

"Well, in this case, I wholeheartedly disagree with your opinion."

"Kate, if you become president of the United States, your time going to parks and reading a newspaper under a tree, watching little kids play with Frisbees is over. Security clears the park removing the kids, ruining many people's days in the sun. You have to face a new reality."

"It's not the same," she said. "Everyone knows it's the president, and no one is going to kidnap him."

"Exactly, he won't be kidnapped because he has an army around him to keep that from occurring. Don't you see?"

"No," she said. "I need that time if you want me sane."

Raising his hands in exasperation, he said, "Okay, you're the one in charge. I can only do so much. Besides, why don't you just go out with *me*? You know exactly who I am."

"You know, Brad, I wouldn't mind that at all, but it's not the same. You're not anonymous. Besides, we have discussed the 'no dating at work' rules. I have been very clear. Is that what this is about, you and me?"

"Did you sleep with him?"

"Brad Danner, that's none of your damn business. Brad, you're closer to me than anyone, but you just overstepped your bounds."

"I apologize," Brad said, "that just slipped out."

They stared at each other for a second before Brad stood up and headed for the door. "No, it's not about you and me, but I don't see any point in continuing this conversation."

Brad had the door open on his way out.

"Brad?" Kate said quickly.

He didn't turn around and said, "What?"
"I didn't."
"Rest up, Kate, we have a big day tomorrow."

CHAPTER—35

MEETING WITH KHIABANI

Brad and Kate walked up to the meeting room door where Khiabani and two other people were waiting.

Kate reached out, saying, "Hello, my name is Audrey Smith, and this is my colleague Mr. Frank Delling. We are with an NGO funded by the Carter Center in the US"

Vahid stepped forward and shook hands with them both. "I'm Vahid Khiabani," he said in English, "and my aide," he said without introducing him. "Please," the general said as he motioned to his security man.

The man patted Brad down and checked Kate's purse.

Kate said, "I understand we have a room set aside to meet. Is this correct?"

Vahid looked at her and said, "You set it up, and you don't know?"

Kate was ready. "We didn't set it up. An anonymous group contacted us to represent them in this conversation. They instructed us to deliver a message. They will contact us after the meeting to relay any communication back. We do this on occasion, representing governments wanting to be anonymous in negotiations. These are mostly regarding hostage payments and the like."

Khiabani took it in but wasn't sure he believed the whole story. Eventually, he decided it didn't matter. One of the aides opened the door, and they entered the ornate room with its abundance of gold leaf and crystal. The space served as an overflow from the hotel's restaurant next door. It was full of tables arranged to the sides, with one set up in the center. Brad made motions indicating who wanted to sit where and Khiabani answered by pulling out a chair and sitting down.

"I'm not here willingly," he started. "So, the quicker we can get this over with, the better."

Kate started. "Thank you for speaking English. A translator from the hotel was on standby but now will not be needed."

Khiabani, getting impatient, said, "I went to school at Durham University in the UK. Can we get on with it?"

"Of course. The entity we only know as the group has requested you cease and desist all operations regarding disrupting international shipping lanes."

"I'm not aware of what you speak."

"General, we are beyond that and have been assured this information is correct. They are asking you to stop the armed incidents at the world's chokepoints to disrupt the free flow of trade."

Khiabani dismissed the comment. "Let's get to why I'm here. Your 'group,' as you say, threatened my family, and that's something that will not stand."

"General, if we can reach an agreement regarding your efforts to date, I am sure that will disappear."

"I'm sorry, Ms. Smith, but there is nothing to be agreed upon."

Kate looked at him. "So, you deny any involvement?"

"Of course. So, let those mysterious people know and stop threatening my family. Now."

"Did you bring a cellphone to contact your office?"

"Yes," he said, not moving.

"General, if you check with your office, you will find the power plant that provides electricity to the distribution facility at Isfahan encountered an overload due to a series of circuit breaker malfunctions. The situation has started automated shutdown protocols, putting 135,000 people in the dark. I believe you've just over four hundred such plants in the country, including one at the Natanz nuclear facility. They tell me that they can be targeted one by one in a very short period of time."

Khiabani smiled. "Really?" he said. "This is, as you say, bush league and not worthy of the time and does not address the main issue." He looked over, and his aide rose and walked a few feet away. "If any harm were to come to my family, rest assured, I have the resources to hunt down your anonymous people and kill them if I have to." He looked back at his aide, who shook his head

210

negatively with the cellphone at his ear. "I see it's a bluff and an inferior one at that."

"Patience," Brad said. "Even today, communication takes time if for no other reason than people are involved."

"General?" the aide said, holding out the phone. Khiabani got up, went over, and put the phone to his ear. In a second, his arm was waving in the air, emphasizing a statement.

He came back to the table. "As I said, it is a bluff, and you are lying."

"It didn't sound like it. If you check again, this time with your office, you will find the power has failed there also."

"General," the aide, who was still at the back of the room, said quickly. Khiabani waved him to the table. He put the phone up to his ear without giving anything away.

He looked up at Kate and Brad. "You don't know what you are dealing with," he said with barely restrained anger.

"I'm truly sorry, General, but these are simple instructions that we are following. The next tranche of actions will be more personal. If you check with IRGC Finance Minister Drachma, he will also confirm the secret IRGC accounts held in Swiss banks have just been flagged for review, thus frozen. Also frozen are the personal accounts of you and your loyalists. These actions eliminate your escape plan of living out your days in Morocco, which does not have an extradition treaty with the US with a pile of cash."

He stood quickly and again retreated with his aide out of earshot. It was a few minutes before he returned. His face said it all: clenched teeth, taut skin, and eyes enlarged with anger. In a deliberately slow manner, he sat down, motioned to his aide to sit down. It was all to garner time to gather what composure he had left before speaking to the two before him.

"Ms. Smith, is your group trying to intimidate the head of the Iranian Revolutionary Guards and the sovereign country of Iran?"

"Intimidation? No, General—*it's a direct threat.*"

With one hand, Vahid quietly bent the spoon from one of the settings on the table. He could barely get out the words. "What do you want?"

"Stop playing with the world's economy. You can play all the political games you wish in Iran, but the free flow of trade and the world's financial stability is off-limits."

"And if we don't?" he said.

"Simple," Kate replied. "Measures will be taken restricting your all-important wheat importation program, the so-called bread of the masses. You were an exporting nation, supplying North Korea, but recent drought and mismanagement mean grain imports are now vital. Do you know how many revolutions were precipitated by the lack of bread on store shelves? Such a situation will bring your country to a halt, and quite possibly, the clerics will execute you and your team if they're not involved."

"You can't possibly do that," the general said. "The Western world will not stand for waging war on the civilian population. Starving people went out with siege warfare in the Middle Ages."

"Apparently not," Kate said. "Some of the old tools of war seem to have found modern uses. Those who are inconvenienced and scrambling for food are not a happy population. Nevertheless, it is far better than any number of deaths due to war. Therefore, yes, I'm told they can do that. Mr. Khiabani, they already have started. And when you realize it, who will you ask to stop starving your population? To whom will the U.N. Security Council direct its demands? It is my experience, this group essentially does not exist. Because of the group's secrecy, no entity or authority exists to which you can direct your actions. Mr. Khiabani, I'm only the messenger who is recounting events that have and will occur. It is my understanding you've employed the art of gray warfare in an admirable series of actions. It seems they have deployed the same tactic; it is now you who will have to deal with its frustrating inability to present a specific target to eliminate."

Brad addressed the aide and said, "Before this meeting, information arrived indicating a sizable US task force might be right outside your waters."

Without checking with his general, the aide got up, and with the line still open, spoke directly to his office.

"You are representing the Great Satan?"

"No," Kate replied. "I have been told that's not the case. However, in the end, it doesn't matter. You've lost power in Isfahan, your third-largest city, and at your headquarters. The next could easily involve Natanz, the site of your nuclear ambitions. Should you ignore the hardships of your fellow citizens in pursuit of a reckless agenda, the clergy is sure to become aware of your treason. With the information out, it sets up a situation where you must stage a coup to avoid execution by the state. Protecting the clerics and government was the very reason the IRGC existed after the revolution, a fact that becomes painfully inconvenient, don't you think?"

The aide returned and whispered in the general's ear, confirming the US deployment of ships.

"The ships," Khiabani roared, slamming a fist on the table. "This is something the US will regret."

"General, there is little you can do to alter the position you now find yourself in. The group's reach is beyond your comprehension. They have been described as the unseen hand with the power and influence to defeat your plans. It is now up to you which direction to take in this situation you've created."

Kate saw the anger grow in the man's eyes and the muscles in his face told the tale of defiance after being in almost ultimate power for nearly twenty-three years and being addressed as if a schoolboy did not set well. Seemingly stopped at every turn, and with no way out, his reaction was a violent one. Khiabani stood up and threw his chair behind him, creating a considerable amount of noise and distraction in the usual formal atmosphere of the Palais Coburg.

At the sound, two men dressed as waiters entered the room from one of the two entrances, dropping the trays and towels that had covered their firearms. Immediately, Brad reached over and grabbed Kate, toppling her over onto the floor. Khiabani had moved toward the two after throwing his chair. As Brad fell away from the table, he grabbed a gun from his ankle holster. Dropping to his side onto the floor, he locked his arm straight out with a Browning 357 pointed directly at Vahid's head.

Brad shouted, "Call off your boys, Vahid, or I guarantee the first person that dies today will be you."

Khiabani lifted his hands slightly while backing away. He turned to the waiters and nodded his head. They lowered their firearms.

"Guns on the floor, and then the men go behind the doors," Brad demanded as the two locked eyes.

Again, Vahid nodded.

"Mr. Delling," Khiabani said, "this is not the end. Messenger or not, you are involved with this farce and are not immune. Everyone is a puppet of the Great Satan, and you will find Iran cannot be bullied by a nation of heretics and blasphemers. Certainly not by a *woman* who talks with deep disrespect to a man. You talk as if you hold all the cards. You do not even know the game you are playing."

He turned and walked to one of the two back exits.

Brad spoke into the comm set, saying, "Khiabani is leaving via the south exit. Let him go."

Hauer responded from the van. "Are you sure, really sure?"

"Yes, he is the only one who can go back and stop the program."

Kate looked up at Brad from the floor. She didn't need to hear the other side of the conversation to understand the exchange.

She started to move and said, "That hurt."

"Oh, sorry," Brad said, standing up and offering her a hand. "I didn't mean to ignore you, but needed to take care of that first."

She reached out before getting to her feet. "Well, Brad Danner, you are just full of surprises."

"Yes, let's get out of here," he said. He spoke again into the comm set. "Penn, bring up the car and get some personnel to clear a path to the front discreetly. I will wait for your all clear."

"Roger that," Penn said.

Brad put the gun away and motioned for Kate to step behind him.

"Was that necessary?" Kate asked.

"Seemed like it to me. You did see the people come into the room with guns, didn't you? I thought you were just going to lean on him a little. You didn't have to kick his ass. Coming from a woman, it was just too much. He lost it, and it got a little edgy there."

"I don't care what the bastard thinks," Kate said. "He killed our friends and almost killed us. He deserves that and more."

"I agree. It's just that, as a woman, you don't need to be in the room when you yank his pants down in front of the world; there are safer ways."

"Safer, yes—more effective, I don't think so. I wanted Khiabani to hear the tone of voice, the certainty of what was to occur. That's why we are not doing this through a third party or via video. How about the 'it's a threat' line? I thought that was somewhat effective."

Brad glanced at their plainclothes men in the lobby as they walked through. He opened the door of the group's armored limo brought in on the plane and followed Kate into the back seat.

Closing the car door, he said, "Scottie, get us to the plane."

CHAPTER—36

KHIABANI STRIKES BACK

The two SUVs and the limo took off, turning right out of the hotel driveway onto Coburgbastei past the back of the Vienna Marriott and onto Weihburggasse. It was one of two exit routes chosen earlier, the call being made at the last minute as they got into the limo.

Kate said, "Thanks for the support in there."

"You keep forgetting I was also in there saving myself again. Is this going to be a habit?"

"I certainly hope not."

A motorcycle weaved its way down the same street as the motorcade. As the three vehicles came to a stop, the motorcyclist shot up from behind, slapping a magnetic charge against the limo's left rear panel. The driver then lowered himself on the bike and hit the accelerator.

In his haste, the rider failed to secure the charge to the vehicle. Brad heard the thump and saw the rider's excessive speed as he drove away and instinctively threw himself over Kate. The charge fell to the ground and detonated. The explosive force blew skyward rather than towards the inside of the limo.

Still, the explosion lifted the limo's left side off the ground, pushing it forward and to the left. The heavy vehicle crashed into a market stand and a private wall with a doorway. Automatic weapons fire began peppering the sedan, but was held back by the car's reinforcing armor and bulletproof glass. The Cartel's vans pulled up alongside, and five men emerged. They found targets above on the rooftops and at street level.

The inside of the limo was full of smoke, and Kate wasn't making any sound. Brad pulled the handle on the passenger side, and the door opened barely an inch. He kicked it hard several times as shots kept hitting the car. Finally, he protectively placed Kate's face on his chest, turned his back to the door, and pulled the orange handle near the floorboard. The charges blew the hinges, and the door panel fell onto the ground.

"Kate," he yelled, pulling on her shoulder to turn her over. She moved with a deep sound. "We have to get out of here. Can you move?"

She didn't respond. The Cartel's men took care of the street-level danger and were now concentrating on snipers from above. Brad knew the shots were hitting the other side of the car. He stepped out of the vehicle and onto the door. It rocked beneath his feet. He reached in and sat Kate up; then, he pulled her out. Her legs started to respond as she began to stand. Brad gathered her up in his arms and headed towards the private door opening in the wall not ten feet away.

Inside was a private courtyard. He lowered Kate to the ground and, grabbing his pistol, looked out the steel door and onto the street. A figure stood up on the roof of the building across the street, casting a familiar silhouette. It was a man with a grenade launcher on his shoulder, and he fired it at the limo.

Crouching on his knees, Brad pulled Kate close, placing her between himself and the steel door. He felt the concussion of the blast as it destroyed its target. The wall and door held. He lifted Kate again in his arms, ran to the residence's front door, and kicked it in, heading directly to the back of the house. Kate was moaning and trying to hold him around the neck, but one arm kept falling. Despite everything, she was coming back around.

"Can you walk?" he asked.

He put her down feet first, and she stood with one hand on a wall and the other arm to her forehead.

"Come on; we need to get out of here."

He pulled out his radio and said into the channel: "This is Danner, we are at the back entrance of a residence directly west of the limo, and we need exfil now."

Kate leaned against the wall and started to slide down to the floor, holding her upper arm. It was then that Brad saw it was bleeding profusely. He pulled the center runner from the table nearby and tore it to size. Wrapping it around her arm several times tight, he then ripped the end into two with his teeth and tied it in place.

Crouched down, he looked out the back window, his gun in a firing position.

"Brad?" Kate said.

"Sit still. You're going to be all right."

The G9 phone in his pocket buzzed. He pulled it out. On the screen were a map and the word "Destination." The pointer was about a block away, with another indicator showing his position. Brad looked at the screen. There was no sender, so he didn't know who sent it. But with the ultra-security, it could only be from the Cartel, he thought, but how would they know where we are? Kate was looking around, dazed. A woman came into the room screaming, followed by her husband. He saw the gun in Brad's hand.

Brad said, "Please get on the floor." The husband grabbed his wife by the arm and disappeared to the other end of the house.

"Can you get up?" Brad asked Kate.

"Yes," she said. "What's going on. Are you okay?"

"Yes," he said, still looking out on the street from the back window, looking for any signs of danger. "We need to get out of this location."

He took a step over Kate, put his arm around her waist, and pulled her up. They both went through the back door. He turned right, following the directions on the phone, and proceeded down the street. He heard another explosion coming from the other road, along with continuing gunfire.

Making their way along the sidewalk, he looked at the screen as they came upon the other screen marker. It was a modern multistory building with a metal roll-up door on the side for deliveries. Brad leaned Kate up against the door.

"Why are we stopping?" Kate said.

Brad wasn't sure what he was supposed to see or do. "I'm not sure," he said, looking at the G9 device. "It's right here."

"What's here?"

"I'm not sure."

Kate knew she wasn't completely clear, but the conversation didn't sound normal.

Then right next to them, a loud clattering signaled the metal delivery door starting to ascend. Kate felt the movement against her shoulder, thinking everything was just a little strange in her head. Brad cautiously walked them both through the opening into what looked like a large warehouse. It was full of barrels and boxes but devoid of any workers. He pulled Kate in, and they made their way over to a shipping table with some chairs where he sat Kate down. Brad heard the loud racket as by itself the rolling door started down to the closed position.

"Kate?" he said. She was out again and didn't respond, but was still upright in the chair. For the first time, he could see she had lost a lot of blood as her dress was soaked with small drips starting to hit the floor. He picked her up and laid her on the table just as the G9 device buzzed again. He reached for the device, and the screen said, "Stay." Brad had no problem staying put, as the warehouse and solid door offered better cover than the house. With time to think, he got on the radio and contacted the security team on the street.

"Penn, are you there? Anyone, are you there?"

"Yes," Penn responded. "Are you two okay? Tell me you're okay."

"Kate is hurt and needs medical attention. What about the team?"

"Two wounded but not seriously, but can't say the same for them. I thought you were in the car when the grenade hit; then I couldn't find you. I have your location on the device, and I'm in a car coming to you now. We should be there in about two minutes."

"We are behind a shipping roll-up door. Tell me when you are outside."

"Roger that. Stay on the line. After things are stable, we will extract everyone to the plane."

"What if they have that targeted already?" Brad asked.

"The security team we left behind to guard the plane has cleared the area. We should be good."

"Wait," Brad said. The G9 phone buzzed again, and a face was on the screen. "Mr. Danner, we are outside."

It was Danny, and it was a happy sight. He went over to the door and hit the big button on the wall. Danny came in with the medical kit, as he was the team's EMT.

"Is anyone else hurt?" he asked, looking at the blood exiting the wound at his jawline and landing on his shirt. Brad reached up and saw the blood on his hand.

"Kate has a serious wound on her arm. It's bleeding bad. Take care of her first."

"Right," Danny said, moving quickly over to where Kate was lying on the table. Danny checked her eyes, her pulse, and looked at the bandage. He was concerned about her soaked dress and checked for a leg or torso wound, but the arm appeared to be the only injury. Danny carefully removed Brad's makeshift bandage and ripped open a sterile package containing an Israeli bandage. Placing one end of the pad over the wound, he fed the other end through the pressure bar and finished by wrapping it around Kate's arm before looking up. "That will stop the hemorrhaging," he said.

Danny reached into his bag, brought out a large bandage, and placed it on Brad's neck. "Here, put pressure right here," he said, pointing at a spot on his face.

A man Brad didn't recognize, dressed as an EMT, appeared with a stretcher and said, "Let's get her up on this."

They both transferred her to the stretcher and moved her to the ambulance.

"Hold on," Brad said. "Who are you?"

"I'm with the ambulance just outside," he said.

Brad walked out to the sidewalk checking the man's story to find the ambulance driver standing next to the vehicle, holding a clipboard, and talking into his shoulder radio.

"Who is in charge?" the driver asked in German.

Penn, who just walked up, said, "I am."

"What is the destination? Krankenhaus Barmherzige Bruter (Hospital Brothers of Mercy) is the closest hospital," he said.

"Nice job on the ambulance, Hauer," Brad said.

Penn looked at the emergency vehicle with some curiosity and said, "Brad, we cannot go to a hospital. There will be a lot of bodies coming in, and the local authorities will have too many questions."

"We have to. Kate needs a doctor. I won't let her leave until we know she can safely make the flight, and we won't know that unless we get her to a hospital."

From inside the ambulance, Danny said, "She is talking."

Kate said in a weak voice, "Danny makes the call."

Danny was sitting inside next to Kate, finishing with an IV, and said, "I have everything I need in here. She is stable and will be all right. We need to take this to the plane."

"Okay, to the plane it is," Brad said. He got inside the ambulance as they shut the doors.

Penn spoke to the driver, telling him to follow them to the airport. They were wheels up in the Challenger 850 in about thirty-five minutes. A clean-up team had already finished at the ambush scene before the local police arrived, setting fire to the limo and removing any evidence that could link the incident back to the Cartel. The family they terrified when using their home was well compensated on the spot by a Cartel agent. They loaded the entire security team, the wounded, and the remaining SUVs into the C-130 that had flown them in.

In the Challenger, Brad was sitting across from Kate next to Danny. Avery was nervously standing with one hand on the ceiling. "She looks a lot better than when we brought her in."

Brad said, "How can we be sure?"

"Mr. Danner, she is going to be fine," Danny said. "It was just a graze, but it was deep enough to clip a smaller vessel close to the surface and, yes, she bled a lot, but her blood pressure is fine. She was definitely in shock when I got to her, but she has come around nicely."

"Brad?" Kate said. "I remember parts of it, and I need to say thank you."

"I was also trying to save myself, does that sound familiar? You said this wasn't going to be a habit."

She looked at him. "I lied," she said with a weak half-smile. "I will make it up to you somehow."

Avery said, "You'll be lucky she doesn't fire you." He looked at Brad's quizzical look and followed with, "Just kidding, old boy."

CHAPTER—37

IRGC COMMAND CENTER

Khiabani met with his top staff in the IRGC command center. He said, "I have met with the originators of the letter. Their demands are humiliating. If it was our intention to be treated with respect by the West, then so far, we have failed. Anticipating their arrogance, we planned a demonstration of our resolve after the meeting. We succeeded in destroying the vehicle in which one of our spotters said the two principals were riding."

Someone said, "Were there any casualties on our side?"

"I don't know. Information is still coming in," Khiabani lied.

Admiral Rahmani spoke up. "If I may ask who wrote the letter?"

Someone else asked, "Who did you meet?"

"It was strange," Khiabani said. "They claim to be an independent group and do not represent the US or any other country. It is a laughable position. If they do not represent the Americans, then who else could they be? They performed examples of their ability to force us to comply with their wishes, which is why we had power outages in Isfahan and here at headquarters. Who can tell me? What was the reaction of the administration to the blackout?"

Rahmani said, "There wasn't any explanation as power outages are not exactly uncommon except at headquarters. Someone is sure to have lost his job."

"Well, if they wanted to intimidate us, they failed," Khiabani said. He had purposely left out the freezing of his commanders' accounts. By the time they discovered the truth, the situation would be over and corrected.

"Their demands were we stop implementation of A'rafat faRdā.

It is deeply disturbing they know of our plans. I will deal with this grievous security breach later in a ruthless fashion. Right now, we need a demonstration of our strength and resolve.

"Admiral, did you confirm the presence of the US ships off the coast?"

"Yes, just as you said. It seems the US was going for numbers rather than firepower as most of the group is of secondary warships and support vessels. There are, however, two guided-missile destroyers and six coastal patrol boats. Some were in the general area, and others came in at flank speed from their base in Bahrain. They're currently cruising at twelve knots up and down the coast."

"Arrogant dogs," Khiabani spewed out. "Admiral, I want you to hit them and make them hurt. I mean, bloody their nose without getting into a full-out battle."

"Sir, we are not in a position to take on a force that size."

"Listen to me. I didn't say take it on. Pick out something and hit it fast. I want casualties but nothing that would trigger a war. Get it done now."

"Should we not get approval from the Guardian Council?"

Outwardly showing his impatience, he vigorously replied, "The protection of this nation is our responsibility. We must protect the purity of the revolution; the IRGC *is* the Guardian Council. I will take care of our Supreme Leader Ali Semnani and his lackeys."

Everyone was drawn back by the indifference Khiabani paid to the ruling elite and the ayatollah in particular. The feeling in the room was tense; the orders created irreversible situations in which all of them would eventually pay unless they were to stage a coup. Admiral Rahmani was starting to think that it was what Khiabani intended to do all along. He was in a quandary as to what to do.

Khiabani sensed it right away. "Do you have a problem following a direct order, Admiral? Let me answer with if you do, I can assign someone else to the task."

The inference was unmistakable; he would go the way of Nabavi, who currently sat in deep confinement without contact with his officers or his family.

"We will have detailed plans on your desk shortly."

"Good. You will now attend to those plans. We need to make a statement."

"Tell me, Abasi (Chief of Intelligence Capt. Musa Abasi), what do we know about this group? They denied affiliation with any country. How can they talk as though they're a force that can influence a sovereign country? At least that's what they said. They also had the irreverence to use a woman as a messenger." Khiabani paused, looking at Abasi and saying, "Well, do you have an answer?"

Abasi said, "Your statements indicate no association with any government. Yet they were able to control the shutdown of exact portions of our power grid and have, despite our immense efforts, managed to infiltrate our plans."

"Yes, a situation that I find very disturbing. What do you know?"

Abasi paused again, knowing the reaction his answer would provoke.

"Captain," Khiabani yelled, "I asked you a question."

"Yes, General, in the intelligence and security world, I might have heard of something like this."

"Something? Curse you, Abasi, out with it."

"There is an old rumor of a group or organization with substantial power both on the ground and in cyberspace, but it's just a rumor. My field is full of young, imaginative, talented people who worship those who flaunt the rules like comic-book characters. These rumors are always being spread."

"Do they have a name? Where are they?"

"They don't have a name. That's why I believe it's just a rumor. No one has ever proven they exist. And certainly, nobody knows where they are."

"I want you to find them and find them now."

"But, sir, the rumors are based on thirty years ago. Before some of those spreading the rumors were born. I just brought it up because what you said matched their supposed surveillance capability."

"This means they exist. Do you have another explanation? Find them. Get everything on them you can. You can go."

He turned to his new head of the Quds. "I want those stationed on the coast to be on alert. We don't know if they have Marines on those ships."

He then turned to the rest of the group. "You are all dismissed."

When they had all exited the room, he picked up the phone and selected the secure line directly to his house. His wife answered.

"Where is Fared?" he asked.

"He is in his bedroom studying. Why?" his wife answered.

"Massid, my driver, is coming to pick you up in thirty minutes. Quickly pack what you can; buy the rest when you arrive. They will take you to a private jet to Beirut, and I have taken care of customs. Check into the Movenpick in Beirut. Our off-shore accounts are frozen, so you must take the cash in the safe and all the gold at home. Leave it on the plane to avoid customs, and someone will remove it later. I will call you at the hotel as soon as I can and explain."

With great concern and confusion in her voice, she said, "Vahid, what are you saying?"

"Sepideh you must do this quickly. It is temporary, and as soon as things clear up, you will be back. My request is just a precaution. No more talking, just do it."

CHAPTER—38

GULF ATTACK

The phone rang next to the president's bed. He reached for it while finding his glasses.

"It's Devroe, sir. Sorry about the hour. I have some news out of the gulf."

"That's okay, Stephen," he said out of a dead sleep. "Let's have it."

"I might be stepping on DOD's toes here, but given that it involves the task force off the Iranian coast and your friends, I thought it might be good to discuss it with you first."

Stephen could hear the man pull himself to a sitting position.

"Okay, what are we looking at?"

"The Task Force 146 has come under fire."

"Shit, who is it?" the president said.

"This time, it's obviously the Iranians. Six of their fast-attack craft and a ninety-foot Iranian missile boat, the *Thondor*, went after the *Arcadia*, a supply ship trailing the task force. They specifically avoided bringing anything big and avoided any of our warships. The *Arcadia* took some .50 caliber fire and three 105mm rockets from the fast-attack crafts as the *Thondor* approached. The *Connolly*, who is still on patrol in the area, launched two Harpoons, which obliterated the *Thondor*. It also launched a UH-60, which hit one of the fast crafts with a Hellfire missile, and then the rest scattered back to the coast. The *Arcadia* quickly suppressed an onboard fire started by the missiles. Three suffered minor injuries fighting the fire. The *Arcadia* is fully functional and remains on station. The whole thing was over in minutes and, I'm sure, meant to send a signal."

"There is no doubt about that," the president said.

"We were to disperse the task force in a matter of hours,"

Stephen went on. "I would like to suggest we stay in position for another twelve hours so that it doesn't look like they drove us off."

The president thought for a second and said, "It's a good idea. Can you take care of it for me with Sec Def? We can go over this in the PDB. It's almost time to get up anyway. Try to contact your friends for an update on what they are up to before the PDB."

"My friends? Don't you mean Harper's friends?"

"Stephen, can you just call them?"

"Yes, Mr. President," he said in an official voice.

CHAPTER—39

CARTEL DEBRIEFING

The next morning, Kate sat at the conference table's head with her arm bandaged and held in a sling. Getting a full night's sleep had been difficult due to her arm. She had received stitches and been given the go-ahead for moderate activity. They also said she was going to have a scar. She was on over-the-counter pain relievers and very thankful for Danny's quick and effective work.

She knew the full Action Committee would be attending, and a full complement was sitting around the table. She looked around where Avery, Brad, Elena, Lauren, and Penn Hauer were seated. Several associates sat at chairs around the outside of the room.

Kate started. "Thank you, everybody, for being here. Let's waste no time in reviewing our efforts in Vienna."

She noticed Hauer's dour countenance. Looking directly at him, she said, "Penn, I think we should start with you as you look to have bad news."

"No, not bad news," he said, "but there has been something weighing on me. Ms. Adler, my staff and I are so sorry how events unfolded on the egress to the airport, and the fact that you were hurt. I'm beside myself. I must tender my resignation for placing you as well as several of our agents in such a situation."

Brad couldn't help himself. "Hauer," he said, "if it wasn't for the part of your plan that worked, meaning the steps taken in the event of exactly what happened, it could have been much worse."

Kate was genuinely surprised at Penn's comment. "Penn, I won't hear of it. In fact, tell your team they did a great job of covering the contingencies in a chaotic situation. Go back and tell them that. You made all of us look like heroes. Oh, and tell Danny and his needles I'm especially in his debt."

"Yes, ma'am," Penn said, looking at Avery and feeling quite relieved. He wasn't worried about his job as much as the effect his error might have had on Ms. Adler. She was someone he was starting to respect. It was apparent she was going to play a significant role in the future.

Kate noticed Penn looking toward Avery and said, "What was that all about?"

"I think Penn was expecting the kind of response I would have given," Avery said.

"And what would that be?" she said.

Smiling, Avery said, "Let's just say it would have been a little more detailed, emotional, and focused than what just transpired."

Penn couldn't hold back a laugh.

"However," Avery continued, "to my delight, I'm no longer directly in charge, and nothing could please me more."

Kate looked at Brad, who seemed amused at the exchange.

"So enough of that," she said. "Given Khiabani's reaction in Vienna, I assume the US deployed its ships as promised. So even with references to his family and the demonstrations, it did not convince him to stop. To say confronting him didn't work is an obvious understatement."

"Or we didn't go in with enough leverage," Avery said.

Brad said, "We threatened his family, for heaven's sake. Not sure what else it will take."

"That's my point," said Kate. "I don't believe there is a threshold we can cross that makes him see the light of day. The ambush, in daylight, in the middle of an international city known for diplomatic negotiations was a real surprise. The man went from ill-advised to reckless. I, for one, am not sure we can reason with him in any way. That means greater pressure will not be effective, which makes negotiation a nonstarter."

The door of the room opened, and Dr. Wilkerson from

intelligence along with two staffers entered.

"Sorry," he said to everyone as he shuffled through a stack of papers, "but there has been a development."

The doctor had everyone's attention and was surprised all eyes were on him as he looked up from his papers. "Oh," he said, unaware of the impact his statement had on those waiting. "The Iranians have fired on the task force the US assembled at our request."

"Incredible," Brad said. "That's stupid. However, Kate, it sure cements your take on this guy."

Wilkerson continued. "They went after the *USS Arcadia*, a supply ship trailing the main force with their fast-attack boats, and they also brought out an anti-ship missile boat. They're all forces under the IRGC naval command. They intended to sink or heavily damage the supply ship. Gunfire drove away the boats. There's more," he said, "oh, the task force sunk an IRGC missile boat. That's all we have right now."

"That's big," Penn said.

"It's Khiabani at it again," Brad said. "Penn, wouldn't they need a higher authority to direct fire at the US?"

"Yes, they must get the authority of the Guardian Council. Unless," he paused, "and it's a big unless, they felt directly threatened, in which case they have all the authority needed to respond in like kind."

"That proves he is acting independently," Kate said. "Our only shot at avoiding a war is talking directly to their Supreme Leader Ali Semnani."

Avery listened to Wilkerson present his information and knew things had changed. "It's going to be very hard to keep the US out of this now that they have a target. The military is going to be all over the president to take advantage of this opportunity."

"Yes," Kate said, "but it's not a target they can prove is responsible for any of the chaos. They came out shooting, and they slapped them down. That might be enough."

Brad said, "Yes, but I think we need to be in front of this."

Kate followed with, "Who have we been talking to in the States? Can we convince them to stay out of it for now?"

"Stephen Devroe has been our contact," Penn said. "He is director of National Intelligence. Everything in the Intel community is under him, including NSA and the CIA."

One of his assistants whispered in his ear. "It seems that the president and Devroe go back to roommates in college, so the connection is more than formal."

Kate said, "Let's figure out what our next plans are and then get them an update. We want to keep them out if we can. Otherwise, the dominoes are going to start to fall as they did in WWII. France covers Poland, the British cover the French, and it's a runaway situation. Here, America responds, NATO covers them, and we have a mess. If we can keep the international commitments in check, we have a chance of pulling this off."

"I can hear you already know what we are going to do," Brad said.

"Actually, given Khiabani's actions, I think there are a limited number of things we can do that would be remotely effective, and only one that will ultimately stop all of this."

Brad added, "That one solution is we need to *stop* the unstoppable general."

Silence followed the comment as the true meaning of that statement sunk in.

"I don't see another way out," Kate said. "His approving the ambush on the way to the airport just seals the fact we cannot negotiate with him. The government certainly didn't approve of an attack carried out in daylight and the middle of Vienna. That means we have a powerful rogue general with a very dangerous and compromised agenda. I'm not at all sure bringing down the West was his original plan. It could have been to demonstrate his power to disrupt the world and his own country unless Ali gave in to some list of demands. We might never know. The solution is the same."

Brad had a thought. "Doctor, can you get any information on where Khiabani's family is? If they have left the country, if he has sent them away, it means he is all in."

Wilkerson turned and briefly spoke to one of the assistants who came in with him. Sitting back, Meg silently worked her laptop hardwired into the G9 network since, for security reasons, there wasn't any wireless in the building.

"Per our usual operating procedure," Kate said, "we need to be invisible on this. To that end, I think we can get the Iranians to do it for us."

"Really? How do you plan on doing that?" Avery responded.

"By creating a situation where Ali Semnani thinks Khiabani is planning a coup. My briefing pointed out Ali's main concerns are his wealth and his political power. If we can demonstrate they're in jeopardy, he will have no choice but to protect his interests. The question is how do we go about it and how dug in is Khiabani."

Wilkerson felt a tap on his shoulder and turned around. He said to his assistant, "Meg, did you find something?"

"Yes," she said, "they're on an IRGC private jet to Beirut without filing a flight plan. A classifier has him calling his family on a secure internal line and telling his wife to leave the country without an explanation."

"That seals the deal for me," Penn said. "He is in all the way, and that puts the pressure on us to stop him before the US decides to go cowboy."

The outwardly demure Lauren, who had been torturing her laptop during the conversation, impulsively shouted a little too loudly, "I know how!"

Her outburst drew the entire table's attention, whereby she shrunk back down to her usual self while looking up at Elena.

Elena said, "Get it out, Lauren, before you burst."

Kate watched Lauren put her hand on the top of her laptop's screen and saw a transformation occur that answered the outward dichotomy of this wonderful, frail-looking creature occupying the position of head bombardier.

"During the meeting with Ali, we present a fake set of orders from Khiabani to his officers. It outlines several things that have already occurred for credibility and then, at the bottom, instructions for a coup. The first step of the coup plan will be mobilizing the IRGC for an attack on the headquarters building."

She glanced at her notes on the screen, then continued. "Ali probably won't believe it, but then I get Mom to shut the power to Ali's headquarters and leave it on at the IRGC. In building assaults, cutting the power is the first thing on the list, so given the warning in the fake set of orders, Ali will think they're going to attack.

"Then I have Mom deliver flash orders from Khiabani to mobilize the IRGC troops stationed at the former US Embassy.

The orders will bring them out, unwrapping and staging their equipment. This activity will appear to prove our point. The IRGC at the barracks will think it's just an exercise as there is no order to attack any target. Ali sees it as the start of the coup and would have to react by bringing the Quds Force, in effect the palace guard, out from their barracks at headquarters. Military doctrine states he should establish them in forward positions between him and the IRGC for protection. He would then order additional Quds Forces to surround the IRGC headquarters and Khiabani's office, keeping them in the compound. Khiabani will look out the window and see tanks and panic.

"Then all we need …," she paused with a smile, "is a match and … *boom*," she shouted. It was emphasized by clapping her hands together in front of her, then slowly moving them wider and wider apart, simulating an explosion. "Khiabani's dead. Problem solved."

Kate just stared at her.

Brad almost burst into laughter.

Penn and Wilkerson seemed unfazed.

Brad said, "Lauren, we are going to be great friends because I don't want to contemplate the alternative."

She looked at him, cocked her head slightly to one side, and said, "Mr. Danner, I don't think I understand."

Elena followed with a sly smile, saying, "I warned all of you."

Lauren was perplexed and looked at Elena. "Did I do something wrong?"

Avery said, "Brilliant, just brilliant."

Brad said, "Lauren, can you cause some sort of disturbance in the streets?"

She thought for a moment. "I could have Mom send a blanket message from Khiabani to every social site available that Ali has betrayed the revolution and the true believers are the IRGC. He will appeal for them to join in restoring the glorious promise blah blah blah," she said mockingly. "That will spread via text messages like wildfire. Many social sites are blocked, but Mom has never met a router's firewall she didn't kick in the ass. There, Mr. Danner, is your confusion and chaos in the streets."

Kate looked at Elena in disbelief.

Elena was silent for a moment and added, "She's older than she looks."

Avery said, "I think it's the basis for a plan."

"It's quick, and we need quick," Brad said.

"What does the rest of the table think? Penn?" Kate inquired.

He tapped his pencil on the yellow pad in front of him. "It keeps us physically out of the country, and that suits me just fine."

"Elena?"

"Go."

"Avery?

"Go."

"Brad?"

"I love it," he said.

"It's settled then," Kate said. "Penn, can you and Elena work out the details and establish a meeting place? Let's get the invite to Ali out later this afternoon. Have him confirm he can make the time."

"Wait," Lauren blurted out. She addressed her laptop again for a second, then said, "After the meeting, Ali will need to transfer to a means of transport from his helicopter. They're using the old C-130Es and still run the old Allison T56s, which are slower than hell. That makes the flight time about an hour and a half back to Tehran. That gets Ali back at around 1350 hours. By the time he lands, we can have this whole show on the road. As soon as he touches down, I can get Mom to cut the power to his escape airport near the palace—I can't remember the name. That means they can't pump fuel, which makes an escape by plane problematic. It also cuts off his escape route and will make him feel trapped along with everything else going on. We need to get the oven as hot as we can."

"Lauren," Kate said, "can I ask what established your dedication to this organization?"

Lauren seemed reluctant to answer, preferring to look at her computer screen.

Elena filled in. "Lauren's father was a four-star in the US Army and is a member here. He was also the former head of NATO."

"Is that a secret?" Kate asked.

"No," Lauren said. "It's just I was never able to talk about it and still find it hard to bring up." Still, her face then lit up as she added, "But my Dad, he is the greatest, and taught me a lot about covert operations and tactical planning."

"Well, I think we have the outline of a plan. Penn, can you work with Elena's team to get the sequence and timing right? We also need a place to meet. We need to get the invitation out by this afternoon. See if you can get a confirmation. We can't wait around and waste a day if he isn't going to show."

"Done," Penn said.

"Lauren, nice job again," Elena said.

"Let me be the first to second that, Lauren," Kate said. Everyone filed out of the room; most of them talked to Lauren, who was explaining the details of her plan.

Brad walked up to Penn. "Look, nice work today, or should I say today and yesterday. However, something has been bothering me about yesterday. Did you contact the ambulance company, getting them to show up at the right time in Vienna?"

"That bothered me too because I didn't make the call. I asked the driver, and he said he received a normal dispatch. He received instructions over his laptop from his office as usual."

"How do you explain that? Did someone from us make the call?"

"I haven't had the time to look into it yet, so I don't have an answer."

"Another thing," Brad said. "Right in the middle of all the gunfire, I was getting directions from the G9 phone to the location where you found us. I always figured that was you."

"Wrong again. I wish that were the case. Are you saying the phone just turned on and told you where to go?"

"That's about right."

Penn looked at Brad for a second before smiling and saying, "I will talk to Elena, and if there is an answer, she will find it."

"Great, let me know, okay?"

CHAPTER—40

INVITATION TO ALI

Nameed, secretary to Ali Semnani, the Supreme Leader of Iran, sat at his desk with a fresh cup of tea. He had just finished prayers and wasn't looking forward to the laborious tasks that lay before him.

Sitting down, he noticed his ancient Windows XL computer rebooting. That's strange, he thought. He waited until it finished and started to bring up the word processing program, but the keyboard was not responding. The screen went blank to black with a cursor in the upper left-hand corner. He had never seen this. He looked at it and then looked around the room at the other staff members at their desks. It appeared he was the only one having a problem. He tried his keyboard a second time without result. Then, by itself, his printer started printing. He looked again at the black screen and wondered what it could be printing. Because of the black screen and single cursor, he wasn't even sure the computer had finished its reboot.

Nameed pulled the printed document from the tray. In bold letters across the top, it read, 'Deliver to the Supreme Leader Immediately.' He didn't know what to do. The ayatollah never received letters he wasn't already expecting. Nameed put the papers into a folder. He would have to wait until the Supreme Leader returned through his private entrance before asking permission to enter the ayatollah's office. Nameed had expected the man a half hour ago but knew never to question his actions. A small light indicated the elevator door to his office had opened, indicating the republic's Supreme Leader had returned.

He waited a few minutes before moving forward and opening the door. Standing at the entrance to the office, he said, "Rahbar (leader), this is most unusual, but I feel it might be of great importance." Ali Semnani nodded his approval.

Nameed walked over and placed a folder on the desk, and turned to leave quickly.

Upon opening the folder, the ayatolla said, "Nameed, where did this come from?"

"My apologies, sir, my computer rebooted by itself, the screen went to black and proceeded to print this document automatically."

"Did you read this?"

"No, sir, when I saw the first line, I did not read any further and waited for you to return."

Ali Semnani turned his attention to the letter and started to read.

URGENT
DELIVER TO THE SUPREME LEADER IMMEDIATELY

Supreme leader Ali Semnani,
Maj. Gen. Khiabani of the IRGC deeply believes the current policy of concessions to the West has undermined the purpose of the revolution and the Shia Muslim doctrine of Wilayat-e Faqih. He has executed a covert series of events in the name of Iran to cripple the world's financial system. This must be stopped. It is believed Iran's present government is not aware of or participating. Hence, you're receiving this letter.

We are requesting a face-to-face meeting to take place tomorrow at 1200 hours to prevent the general's vision from becoming a reality. We must emphasize the importance of coming to a common understanding. It is the only way to avoid immediate action against your government and your personal wealth.

Knowing that you've never left your country in your life, we have arranged to meet on a yacht located directly at the edge of Iranian territorial waters. Send a helicopter with security personnel to inspect the facility to your satisfaction. Upon confirmation, you may arrive.

We suggest just you and an aide attend the meeting with a method of contacting your office. A simple yes emailed to the address below by 1500 hours today will confirm our appointment.

E6b8Ni@fmkl4983.EU

Meeting Location: 29.669503 49.625660
Meeting Time: 1200 hours.
Semnani looked at his watch, noting a time of 2:50.
We are a non-governmental group with an unprecedented ability to penetrate the most secure networks. The following actions will be taken if we have not received a positive reply by 1500 hours today.

LIST OF SANCTIONS
1. Rolling, eight-hour blackouts will occur, including the following cities and locations encompassing a total population of over 11 million people.
>*Mashhad*
>*Isfahan*
>*Kara*
>*Tabriz*

2. Morton-Roth BV will file a declaration temporarily dropping Iran's compliance rating due to its continuing inability to operate within statutes. As is the norm, the rest of the reinsurers will quickly follow until a review is conducted. This will result in the suspension of Iran's maritime insurance. Per the Marine Insurance Act of 1906, this will keep your fleet in port, limiting income from the sale of oil and the import of grain.
>*Participating insurance companies:*
>*Morton-Ross BV*
>*International Union Club*
>*Lloyd's of London*

3. The off-shore account in the Channel Isle of Jersey, under the name Independent Title PLC, will be frozen due to "transfer irregularities." This is only one of fourteen accounts in six tax havens controlled by your family that we can affect.

4. The mortgage of one of your properties, an office building located at 254 Burham Rd., London, will temporarily go into default and review. This is only one of the forty-three properties controlled by your family that we can affect.

5. We are also aware of your family's wide-reaching business connections, including interests in European manufacturers, African mobile phone companies, and international commodities markets.

238

We look forward to a productive meeting.

Semnani put down both sheets of paper, then took off his glasses and rubbed the bridge of his nose. He tried to understand the context under which an organization would send such a letter. The mysterious manner in which it arrived aside, it seemed beyond reason anyone would address a state and its leader in such a confident way, claiming such skills to manipulate events. Iran's relations with the Great Satan had never reached such a forthright tone as was used in this letter. Its claims were outlandish enough to be ignored entirely, except they concerned his personal fortune and his position as supreme leader, a power he needed to retain to protect his wealth.

He sat alone and silent, contemplating whether this required further attention or was a frivolous waste of time. Minutes went by, then he grabbed the phone and called his personal finance manager.

"Samir, I need you to do something for me."

"Of course," Samir said, "but first, I have troubling news. I have just received an email notification concerning the account we set up in the Channel Isle. The account is temporarily frozen due to what they're calling 'transfer irregularities.' They won't explain, and we are checking the other accounts as we speak."

"Samir, there is something else. Check on the status of the property at," Ali picked up the paper and read off, "254 Burham Rd., London. I want to know the status of the mortgage and quickly."

"Yes, sir," Samir said. "Right away."

Ali selected another line and called his minister of trade. "Javadi, I have been told that our merchant insurance has been negatively affected."

"Sir, I do not understand. What do you mean?"

"Has there been a change?"

"No, rahbar, what kind of change?"

"I was informed of a compliance filing today."

"Often, we won't know right away, as these things require multiple approvals. But I can tell you this would be highly unusual." A slight pause followed. "Dear leader, I have just received official notification that our compliance rating is indeed under review."

"What does this mean exactly?"

"Sir, it means no port will accept our tankers without proper proof of maritime insurance. They will have to turn back, but worse, it means we cannot ship oil until they complete the review."

Semnani said, "Do what you need to do to straighten this out."

"Yes, sir."

Semnani sat back in his chair and found it hard to believe that this group could possibly hold such power. More intriguing was why they thought they were immune to the natural retaliation reflex they were provoking with their attitude. The letter was steeped in the arrogance repeatedly displayed by Iran's greatest enemy, he thought. The unknown was of such force as to require great caution.

CHAPTER—41

DEVROE BRIEFED BY CARTEL

9:30 p.m.

Devroe was sitting in his home office, reading the response to a question he had posed to his head of signet. He asked why, with a budget of some $56 billion, someone else was able to intercept the LNG tanker, and they're in the dark.

It's just not possible, he thought. They spend billions, and the owners of some stupid brick phone pull off what appeared to be a slick, covert op.

There was the sound again. He reached down by his feet and grabbed his briefcase, pulling out the stupid phone.

After the protocols, he heard Penn's voice. "Dr. Devroe?"

"This is he," he said.

"This is agent 2062 with an update."

"Can you hold for a second?" Devroe got up and closed the door to his home office.

"I'm sorry, Mr. 2062, I had to create some privacy."

"The meeting with Khiabani did not go well," Penn said. "We have requested a meeting with the Iranian government in the next twenty-four hours."

"Why in the world would they meet with you when it would be a direct admission of their involvement? The meeting would be something the ayatollah would have to explain away to his people as he doesn't meet with Westerners."

"Thus, it would be in his best interest to keep this meeting secret, avoiding having to explain. The Ayatollah Ali Semnani's main objectives are retaining his sizable fortune and maintaining his grip on power in Iran so he can protect said fortune. We will have led him to believe—in fact, have demonstrated—both are in jeopardy without a meeting."

"So, who is at fault here?" Devroe said. "Who is the energy behind this mess? Semnani?"

"Not necessarily, Doctor."

"Look, the president is having some problems with Congress having approved the naval demonstration. There are questions as to what we are doing to stem this crisis. I have to say, up to date, damn little."

"If I may ask, what could you be doing? What are the options available to you, given internal evidence? What action will pass the filters and screens that are the basis of democracy? What you, on the whole, are experiencing is frustration. The Iranians have played a wonderful game."

"Listen," Devroe said, "if you've something that will incriminate the Iranians, why don't you give it to me and let us run with it. There has to be a way to nail this Ali bastard to the wall for what he has set in motion, and this could be a singular opportunity."

"Dr. Devroe, first I have to ask, what bastard? Do you know who is responsible? If we resolve this situation we find ourselves in, you may commence on any avenue you wish. It is, however, outside our interest and charter to further pursue this beyond the effects on the markets."

"Charter, what charter? Who are you guys anyway?"

"Just a group trying to keep things on an even keel so everyone can prosper."

"So, you're just a group. A few random people who over tea decided to confront, all by themselves, one the world's biggest pains in the ass and demand a meeting with its leader. I don't think so."

"Remember, we didn't do it alone, but with your help."

"Look, Mr. Agent; you know perfectly well what I mean. You have power but no footprint. How is this possible?"

"I can hear your growing frustration, but at this point, with the markets in turmoil, 'who' is rather unimportant if there is a solution."

Devroe asked, "How is it you know so much about what is occurring in Iran? Why don't you just let us know so we can prove it's them to the world and get on with it? It gives us the cover to take out something valuable and say more is coming unless they stop."

"Because your options are those that create wider conflicts and wars; our way gets to the core of the issue, reducing chaos, not adding to it. The eyes of the world will be on your every move; your method will involve many players obligated to respond in one form or another. Billions in financial losses later, the problem will have been dented but not solved. Keeping this quiet gives all of us a chance, at least, to solve the problem while keeping it off the radar."

Penn continued, hoping to calm an impatient counterpart. "Frankly, we are capable of performing acts that, as the obvious leader of the free world, you cannot even entertain. We prevented a catastrophe in Singapore that might have sent Wall Street's volatility index through the roof, stopping trading on all international boards. I suggest we stay with what has been working, Doctor, and keep our frustrations of inadequacy out of the mix because they're not productive. May I bring up that you were the one who contacted us? Forgive me for being blunt, Dr. Devroe, but you insist on being part of the problem, and the Western world needs you to be part of the solution."

Agent 2062 stopped talking and purposely waited for Devroe to respond.

Devroe clenched his jaw. Someone had just pushed him out of the school lunch line, and *he* was supposed to be the bully. Devroe had to both swallow hard and take a few deep breaths. "I will try and buy some time, getting us past your meeting," he said, a detectable tightness in his voice.

"Thank you. This conversation was an update as to our progress but not a detailed list of our plans. In the next twenty-four to thirty-six hours, we will complete everything.

"Doctor, your help in assembling a naval presence off the coast of Iran was invaluable. We are sorry they were bold enough to start shooting."

"Nothing we couldn't handle. This question might seem trivial, but how do I know something is being done on your end while we wait? The question is certainly going to need an answer."

"Well, there was the LNG tanker incident, and I'm sure you are aware of the shooting in Vienna. It was an ambush on our staff who was meeting with a high-level Iranian official."

"Where do we go from here?"

"Our next meeting will be with Semnani. We should have a full understanding of the situation after our discussion. I will get back to you with a full report. Like I said, after we correct the damage to trade and finances, we will conclude our participation."

CHAPTER—42

SEMNANI CONFRONTS KHIABANI

Saturday

As president of the Islamic Republic of Iran, Shahab Mohammadi was duty-bound to follow the supreme leader's instructions. He did not want to make this call to Khiabani, as he thoroughly detested the man. Khiabani had from the very beginning, and through the years, turned the IRGC into something the country didn't need. He had created a privately controlled center of power that rivaled the theocratic leadership. Everyone owed him favors, and he held everyone hostage as he provided everyone's security. He thought nothing of calling in the favors if it served his purpose, even if it meant the destruction of a man's career. No one knew where his ultimate goals lay, and many a late-night discussion failed to create a solution to his ruthless leadership.

The phone rang on his desk. His assistant said, "Mr. President, it seems, Maj. Gen. Khiabani is in a meeting with his generals and can't come to the phone."

The president recognized the slight and was not amused. "Thank you; I will take care of it." He hit the button connecting him to the line and said to whoever was listening: "This is President Mohammadi. Tell Maj. Gen. Khiabani that I wish to speak to him now, not later."

Less than a minute later, he could hear Khiabani say, "President Mohammadi, this is an honor."

"General, you've had a busy couple of days."

"No busier than the office of the president, I'm sure. A call from the highest levels of our government must mean something special."

"Yes, I have been asked by the supreme leader to find out if you directed the attack on the US naval forces yesterday."

"Of course. I'm the only one who can authorize such a response. The Great Satan was amassing substantial forces just off our shore, and I felt it was threatening our security."

"Our supreme leader wants to know how you could authorize this without the approval of the Guardian Council."

"Because, my dear president, we are tasked with protecting the supreme leader, our government, and the principles of the revolution. I acted per Article 105.3."

"This article is not without constraints, General. It states there must be an imminent danger behind any such decision. Otherwise, it requires council approval."

"It was my opinion that such a situation existed and hence my order. Are you questioning my judgment?"

"Do you actually think the Americans were preparing an invasion with such a small force?"

"We needed to make a statement to the arrogant bastards."

"This may be true, but a statement is much different than imminent danger."

"This was my decision; it was a military decision over which you have no control. May I suggest you occupy yourself with issues within your area of control?"

"Vahid, you cannot continue to act as though it's your own country to manage as you wish. There are checks and ..."

"May I remind you I have the full blessing of the ayatollah?"

"I'm sure you do," Mohammadi said. "Technically, we all do. You may return to your meeting," he said brusquely.

Mohammadi entered the office of the supreme leader, also located within the headquarters building in Tehran. He took a seat as requested, and Ali silently looked at him before asking, "So what did our dear Khiabani have to say?"

"He said he felt the country was in imminent danger and the basis of his decision. His point was he didn't need the council's approval."

"This was not unexpected, was it not?"

"No, but it brings to light once again a situation we face and cannot seem to resolve. The guard has come to dominate Iran in a very uncomfortable manner."

"This, too, is not a surprise. We are all in some way beholden to him. I rely on him for protecting the office of the supreme leader. You need him for the protection of the presidency. He suppressed the crowds in the green revolution without either of us getting our hands dirty. In an emergency, his responding forces only need to be ten minutes late to our rescue to be ineffective."

"I have delivered my message and offered my concerns again. I leave it happily with you, as just talking to Khiabani creates impure thoughts."

"Thank you, Shahab. As always, I value your opinion. I believe what lies before us are trials in which we must be victorious. Some extraordinary problems have come to light. I'm afraid they will require some extraordinary solutions."

CHAPTER—43

DEVROE CALLS DOD FOR OPTIONS

Saturday 10:00 a.m.

Devroe called his office. "Doris, can you discreetly assemble as many members of the National Security Council (NSC) group as possible for a secret meeting ASAP? Tell the president there is a situation that will need his attention. I'm on my way over."

"Doctor, right now he is tied up, and you know him. Even if it's an emergency, unless it concerns anything nuclear, he will want to keep to his previous schedule to avoid any alarm. On that note, he is meeting with a very visible German trade delegation for the next three hours."

"Shit," Devroe spat into the phone.

Doris's eyebrows raised, she said, "Doctor?"

"Sorry, Doris, call me when you know how many will attend the meeting? Then we can negotiate with him as to time. Can you do that for me?"

"Why, yes, Doctor," she said dryly. "I know it's not my place, but I would ask for a partial refund on that expensive Ivy League education you received."

"What?"

"Particularly the cost of any class you attended addressing the English language."

Devroe laughed. "I apologize. It slipped out."

"I accept your apology," she said with a completely straight face.

Devroe put the phone down, shaking his head at the unflappable Mrs. Heywood. Just minutes ago, he had received a call from Wakefield, the national security advisor, favorably reporting that the NSA had finally filtered out a conversation from one of the top

Iranian generals after it had worked its way through the system. The general was directing his family to leave the country and explicitly stating Khiabani was involved in at least the Singapore hijacking attempt. It proved the Iranians were behind this. We finally have cover to kick some ass, he thought. He had decided to go forward on options for the president and called Dennis over at DOD.

"Dennis, we have some new information proving the Iranians are behind the hijackings. We now have our legal case to take some action. I need, or the president will need, some options to make a statement that we are on top of this."

"I take it a threatening diplomatic release is not what you have in mind?" Dennis said.

"Hell no, we have been locked out of this thing since it started. Mrs. Heywood is going to call you to set up an NSC meeting with the president. The president is tied up for a few hours, so we have some time. I'm on my way to the White House, and I will see you there. But we need it fast."

Corwen put the phone down and knew that when Devroe got something under his bonnet, the hat lit up. He called the deputy secretary to research preplanned packages for kinetic aggression against Iran.

CHAPTER—44

MEETING WITH ALI SEMNANI

Saturday 11:00 a.m.

Kate and Brad were on the yacht *Katerina*'s bridge deck overlooking the white water of its wake rushing away into an ever-thinner trail toward the horizon. The *Katerina* was a fifty-four-meter beauty that stood four decks high, not including the flybridge. Yesterday they had flown directly into Dubai and then via helicopter to the vessel, landing on the helipad above them. At eighteen knots, the yacht headed toward the northern part of the Persian Gulf where they were going to meet Ali. They and the staff had already gone over the plans for the meeting. They were now waiting.

Kate looked down at the beach club two decks below and said, "I know this sounds small, especially after seeing the castle, but it takes being on this ship to realize how big, well-funded, and powerful this whole organization is. Did you even know the Cartel had a yacht?"

"Hardly. How would I know?" Brad said. "Besides, given the name, I would take a wild guess and say it is your father's. It doesn't matter as I think he had most of what he owned wrapped up in the organization anyway."

"But he never mentioned a yacht. I spent time going over the balance sheets and didn't see any mention of a yacht."

"That's simple; it's probably registered to Morton-Roth. Anyway, why would he mention something like a yacht when he never even told you about the Cartel?"

"Good point," she said. "It's not like I pounded down father's door to find out his secrets."

Brad looked down over the railing as he said, "Actually, my

coming-to-grips moment came when Penn outlined what we had done in Singapore and the equipment that the raiding team used. It's top-flight US equipment. Do you know how much a Black Hawk helicopter costs, let alone just getting your hands on one? I understand they used two along with a C-130 cargo plane. These people possess some serious capabilities."

"You sound like a little boy. Are you going to go all military ga gah on me? Besides, 'these' people are now us."

"You're not impressed because you haven't any idea what I just said. Do you remember the finance briefing with Paul Samson? He said the operating costs of the Cartel were over $2.6 billion a year. Well, I believe it. This boat certainly costs a couple of million a year to keep running. It's a good thing your father set up the trust, and the members have big, deep pockets."

Running her hand along the varnished teak rail, Kate said, "I have to say this is very nice."

"Well, it's all yours, cookie."

"Cookie?"

"Sure, the most powerful people get the weirdest names."

"You are seriously in need of some help, Danner." Still looking out to sea, she said, "You had dinner with Elena last night."

"Truth be known, it was the last two nights."

"Anything I need to know?"

"Like what, red or white, beef or chicken?"

Kate threw him one of her 'cut the crap' glances.

"Okay, I like her, and I think the feeling is mutual. Is that what you want to know?"

"Brad, I was trying to find out if you were happy."

"Well, I might be on the road to it, but, come on, it's been days. Besides, when Elena finds out I haven't solved the Hodge conjecture problem, or I don't do differential equations before breakfast, she will become bored with me anyway."

"Did you ever think she might be looking for someone who can't or doesn't?"

Brad looked at Kate for a second, realizing she might be right, then said, "Thanks, actually I hadn't thought of that."

There were a few seconds of silence between them, and then Brad said, "Katy?"

She continued to look out onto the water. "I know, Brad; it just

251

won't work, and, besides, this is the better of the two options."

"Who says?"

She closed the short distance between them. As Brad was bent over, resting on an elbow, she put an arm around him and rested her head on his back. "I'm quite into you, Brad Danner, but I don't want to complicate or ruin your life."

"You sure have a funny way of showing it."

"It's all so simple; if Elena shows any interest, then let her make you happy. And in return, you make her happy."

"Simple?" he said, obviously referring to her lack of a love life.

"Ok, so I'm not simple, but stay with me. I need you. Let's go inside and talk to the others."

Brad took a deep breath, "These are some of the shortest conversations we have."

"Would you like to ride *in* the boat or float *outside* the boat?"

"You know, you're not half as attractive when you're doing the boss thing." Brad jumped ahead and almost pantomimed opening the door, emphasizing a bow and saying, "After you, my wonderfully beautiful, brilliant, radiant lady-boss."

"That's better, much better," she said, walking through the door, giving him an artificial punch in the arm. They entered the main salon with its contemporary interior design. The walls, carpet, and seating were in light beige accented by the dark teak furnishings and cabinets. Next to the main salon was the dining area with a huge table that served as a conference room.

Brad looked for Elena. She was where he had last seen her at the morning meeting. She was dressed in a navy-blue suit with white insets, sitting in one of the salons' lounge chairs. On her crossed legs was an oversized iPad. That morning she and Penn had been in complete control, and the confidence that she exuded was palpable, almost intimidating. He and Kate passed Ali's two security guards, who had arrived earlier. They were standing outside the salon, dressed in Western business suits without ties. The curved glass salon doors automatically opened and closed behind Kate and Brad, maintaining the room temperature and keeping out the wind.

Penn looked at Kate and said, "Can we go over a few things? Ali's security team arrived earlier, and they're through with a full tour. They made a few small requests, but after determining no special forces team came aboard, they radioed back, and everything seems to be on schedule."

Avery walked in. "I think Brad should be in the meeting."

Kate didn't say anything.

Brad said, "Why?"

"Continuity. You were at the first meeting and can attest to what went down if required."

"And I can't?" Kate said.

"Sorry, Kate, facing the lay of the land, you are a woman and Semnani is a conservative Muslim. You could face some resistance on a couple of levels."

Penn said, "Avery, is that necessary?"

"Can it hurt?"

Kate said, "No, it can't, and Khiabani had a rather strong issue with that. He took it as a personal insult."

"No one asked me," Elena said, "but I'm with Avery."

"How long before we are in position?" Brad asked.

Penn looked at his watch and said, "Just about now."

Just then, everyone could hear the low hum of the engines fade to almost nothing. "We should be just on the edge of the Iranian declared waters, allowing each side to claim the meeting occurred in their preferred location."

"Interesting," Brad said. "I didn't even know that was engine noise. The sound just receded into the background."

Penn said, "We will be there in less than ten minutes, which makes us only a few minutes early. I didn't want to sit there for hours like a sitting duck, so it's more of a rendezvous. As we briefed before, the meeting will take place here, in the main salon. Both of his security people will stay outside the glass sliding doors, in full view of their charge. I don't see this taking over twenty minutes as there is very little to say."

Kate looked around. "Who has the letter?"

Penn tapped the folder on the glass-topped table. It sat between two large sofas and would serve to separate the two parties. "Right here," he said.

The radio lying on the table came alive with the captain's voice. "We are in position with GPS stabilization holding us steady. Hold on a second. We have one incoming helicopter asking for permission to land."

Penn said into the radio, "Good. Bring him in. I will send his security people up top."

"Should we meet him up there?" Kate asked.

"No," Penn said. "His people specifically asked that they bring him down."

Penn got up, walked outside, and spoke to Ali's men. They proceeded up the stairs.

Kate looked curiously at Avery, and he responded, saying, "Penn speaks Farsi."

"Okay," Elena said, "I'm out of here; let's hope everything works as planned."

Penn said, "I will leave as soon as he gets inside. Everyone should be standing when he enters the room, and there will be no handshaking."

"Good luck, everyone," Elena said as she and Lauren left the room.

Everyone stood as the first guard came into view, coming down the stairs, followed by the leader's staff. He entered the lounge and looked around. Seconds later, the supreme leader followed. The other guard stepped forward to open the automatic door.

Penn said in Farsi and then in English "May I introduce Ayatollah Ali Semnani, supreme leader of Iran."

Semnani made quite the impression as he entered the room dressed in a clerical outfit with its V-neck tunic and a cloak inspired by the Prophet Muhammad. He had a black and white checkered keffiyeh scarf under his other garment. His black, instead of white, turban indicated he was a direct decedent of the prophet. It was his uniform.

He silently motioned to the guards, who exited the room, leaving behind an aide and an interpreter.

Penn said in Farsi, "We welcome the supreme leader of the Iranian nation and hope that these discussions will bear fruit for all. Please be comfortable," he said, motioning toward a lounge chair.

Ali did not move and said, "I'm not happy to be here, but thank you for your gracious hospitality." As he sat, his aide sat next to him, and the interpreter pulled up the loose padded stool Penn had provided to be at his master's ear. The aide was young and appeared exceptionally bright as he scanned the room, absorbing everything. A crew member placed bottled water and glasses on the table.

Penn said, "Would you like anything else, sir?"

The ayatollah said, "May we begin?"

After Penn made the introductions of Brad, Kate, and Avery, he left the room.

The ayatollah said, "He must stay."

Penn replied, "Of course." He followed in English with, "Normally the ayatollah does not meet with Westerners. I believe my speaking Farsi is a cover for this technicality."

The interpreter whispered Penn's comment and pulled back.

Kate started with, "Thank you for being here. We hope to solve a problem that affects us both. We know Maj. Gen. Khiabani is behind the recent hijackings of tankers in the Gulf and Singapore's failed tanker attack. While this has caused obvious disruptions in the world markets, we have reason to believe his real agenda is to overthrow the current government—your government. We want to cooperate with you to ensure he fails in this regard."

The ayatollah did not show any reaction at first, then said, "You've brought harm to my nation with the blackouts as well as threatened my family in your letter. These threats are not a good start in any cooperation."

"We are very sorry for the tone of that letter, but time is critical. We needed to be absolutely sure you would attend this meeting. We needed to demonstrate we are worthy of your time. We are pleased you are here."

He looked at Kate for an extended second. "Who are you that I might believe such a dangerous accusation?"

"We are a nonaligned independent organization interested in maintaining balance in the world's economy so that all might prosper. We also have a certain level of influence in preserving this balance as we outlined in our letter."

"You're aligned with the Great Satan; this is obvious, and wish to influence and disrupt our country."

Kate shook her head. "As I have said, time is short. We have a matter of hours for us to solve this issue before the US steps in, and you will be battling an internal overthrow of your leadership *and* an external threat from the Americans at the same time. If, at this point, the ayatollah honestly does not believe we have the power to influence events and you lack the sincerity in wanting to solve a mutual problem, then this meeting should stop now, as we are wasting precious time.

"The blackouts will continue, and the rest of your accounts will be frozen and steps taken to reveal your holdings overseas, holdings that, I might add, have been estimated at ninety-five billion US dollars. It's an interesting number as it happens to be more than the Shah was worth before the revolution. Not something that you want public, I'm sure."

Brad winced internally; this was when Khiabani backed away from the table in a rage, toppling his chair.

The interpreter did not immediately start translating for fear of the language and lack of respect shown to his leader. The assistant told him to proceed. Ali leaned in to receive the translation. When completed, the ayatollah didn't move and looked at Kate with a steady and penetrating gaze.

Kate continued, "We, of course, do not think that will be necessary. As proof of our assessment, you have before you a letter provided to us by an anonymous source from inside the IRGC. It's a top-secret internal directive from Maj. Gen. Khiabani to his generals outlining the strategy behind the coup and specific orders to be carried out by several branches of the IRGC."

The aide reached for the letter. After a glance, he held it up to the light, recognized the IRGC watermark, and started reading the letter.

Kate waited a minute as they read the letter. "The instructions included proceeding with the coup after the hijackings and use of social media to create concern within the population that may spill out onto the streets.

"You must leave here and take control of events, especially the IRGC troops leaving their barracks and possibly attacking your Pasteur headquarters. You must stop Khiabani before the Americans take this to a level where war cannot be avoided. Please have your assistant check with your office to see if I'm telling the truth."

Immediately, the aide, without an interpretation, got up, dialing his phone, and walked out the sliding door.

The ayatollah, showing no sign of any emotion, said, "You spoke of cooperation, and this has not the aura of any give and take."

Kate said, "I know we are being very direct and have crossed the line of friendly diplomatic exchange, but you must believe the time to correct this situation is rapidly running out. The US could be planning a military strike on something of value in your country. I suspect it would be your Natanz facility."

Silence followed as they waited.

The hiss of the opening doors produced the aide who leaned down next to the ayatollah's ear.

The aide looked up and said in English, "Please, the supreme leader must excuse himself for a brief moment."

Both were on the deck, and the aide was visibly demonstrative but deferential, addressing the ayatollah. No doubt he had verified Lauren's cutting the power, sending the fraudulent orders to the embassy's billet commander, as well as the social media barrage. The ayatollah directed one of the guards up the stairs, and then they both came back inside.

He took a seat, turned to Kate, and in one of the greatest understatements in history, said, "We are willing to listen."

Kate said, "We are only the messenger and went through these steps to get your attention. It would be best if you restricted the actions of Maj. Gen. Khiabani to ensure we return to the calm before the disruptions. That's our sole objective. However, his plans for a coup would seem to put your interests in concert with ours. Upon resolution, we will reverse all the effects implemented in the invitation. We will inform the US of the positive actions taken and persuade them not to retaliate. We will then disappear. But again, time is short."

The radio Penn had in his hand came to life. It was the captain. "Sir, they're spinning up the helo."

Penn said into it, "Roger that."

The ayatollah silently sat, arranging his cloak. Steadfast in his need to not be dictated to by the West. He sat without displaying any emotion. Finally, he said, "We will continue to verify your claims and take any appropriate action we deem necessary within our country. Someone will be in contact."

"I have a better idea," Kate said as she held up a G9 phone. "This is a very secure cellphone with a single line." She was careful not to hand it to Ali but his aide. "You can contact us after you've taken those appropriate actions. We will give you a code to enter, and the phone will take care of the rest. It is virtually untraceable."

The aide thought, Who were these arrogant, unknown players who acquired this information and talked with such assured power? Regardless of his questions, the stakes were high, and actions were required. He needed to convey that to his supreme leader.

"We will now conclude this very unusual cooperation," Ali said. He then rose, and with a slow, deliberate cadence, he made his way to the doors, and the group watched him turn and ascend the stairs to the helipad.

The aide remained for a moment in the doorway and said in English, "I will contact you as soon as the general has been," he paused for just a second, then continued without a trace of irony on his face, "arrested."

Once they were gone, Kate said, "Penn?"

"Got it," he said. "I will get to Devroe and let him know the meeting was a success."

CHAPTER—45

POTUS DOUBLES DOWN

Saturday 11:45 a.m.

Devroe was going through security in the White House when his phone rang.

"Dr. Devroe," Doris said. "I handed the president a note an hour ago, and he managed to temporarily get himself out of the meeting before the reception starts. I have gathered the team, and they're outside his office now."

"You're wonderful, Doris. I'm downstairs and will be there in a sec." Two minutes later, Devroe walked past Doris. "Thank you," he said, "this was important." He then walked into the Oval Office.

Everyone was already seated. The president said, "Dr. Devroe, what is going on? I would hope something serious as we have a lot of high-powered salaries sitting around."

"Mr. President and gentlemen, we have had a breakthrough. We intercepted a message proving the Iranians are behind all the attacks. We now have the legal cover to strike a blow the Iranians will not forget and release to the world the reason behind the attacks. We can get everything back to normal before the dreaded bread lines."

The president said, "How conclusive is the evidence that they're at fault?"

"We have one of Khiabani's generals calling his wife and

telling her to get out of the country, and when she insisted on knowing why, he explained that the LNG tanker attack went bad."

Dennis Corwen (SecDef) said, "I read the entire transcript. It looks legit, but the question is: What we do now?"

"I agree," Wakefield said, "What are our options without starting a damn war?"

"What do we do?" Devroe replied. "We hit them hard. How can we contemplate letting them get away with this? Our situation is definitely not like removing Turkey's missiles in six months if the Russians withdraw theirs from Cuba. We don't have time. Dennis and I have been looking at options already designed. Dennis, can you go over the plans you brought?"

Dennis started with the information, but it was evident to those observing him that he wasn't exactly in love with the thought line.

"The obvious choice is to destroy or try to destroy their nuclear facility at Natanz," he said. "It seems the most viable plan, both militarily and politically. It would teach the Iranians a lesson on par with the global mess they have created. It entails the dispatch of two B-2 stealth bombers from Incirlik Air Base in Turkey with F-22 Fighter support. It would be dark when they arrive, and the Iranians would not know what hit them. The other option is to launch surface-to-surface missiles from off the coast. I don't like the idea because the ship and the missiles can be tracked. Also, the missiles don't carry enough firepower to do serious damage."

Devroe turned to the president after Dennis had finished. "A stealth hit on Natanz from Incirlik seems to be the best option. The equipment is there and waiting. No boots on the ground, no missiles that can be traced back to us, we fly in and out without being seen. We can take a chapter out of their own book and deny we were involved. The B-2 bombers have been armed, programmed, and are on the tarmac right now."

"Dennis," the president said, "what is this about planes being ready?"

"It's just a ready alert, Mr. President. They can be topped off and underway in fifteen minutes, but they're not going anywhere unless you say so."

"Let's be sure of that," the president said. "How do you think we are going to keep that a secret? Has anyone been to legal on this?"

"Yes," Devroe said. "NSA has passed it as a genuine target, given what has occurred, and Paul is here representing State. We will need to cover off NATO, the UK, and, of course, Turkey. But we could be in the air and take care of that."

"Stephen, why are you so hot to press the button on this?" the president asked.

Devroe looked genuinely perplexed. "Did I miss something here? Didn't they almost bring down the Western world and almost get away with it? They always manage to be devious and sidestep everything. They negotiate forever so they can continue doing whatever they damn well please. They're the best example of rope-a-dope since the Ali and Foreman fight. This situation is our chance to let them know they have to follow the rules like everyone else."

The president thought for a moment, then said, "Gentlemen, can Stephen and I have the room for a moment?"

It wasn't an unusual request, but also didn't happen every day. There were several curious looks as the men filed out the door. As the door closed, the president turned to Devroe and said, "Have you talked to our friends lately?"

"Yes, last night. They indicated they had met with the Iranians in a meeting that went south. They called to inform us they had established another meeting. Their real point was to hold us off from any unilateral action. They didn't give any details under the guise that if we knew, then we would be forced to do something about it."

"You mean like now?"

"Yes, but whoever they are, they have yet to be effective, and that was when we didn't have any legitimate reason to get involved. Now we can fight our own battles."

"There is one thing that has been bothering me. Why would Iran do this if the signals we have been getting were of cautious reproach? There has been a genuine dialog with some of the ayatollah's people. They have been abundantly clear they're not ready to take us to the prom, but realize they must become part of the mainstream world. They will have to bring the Muslim civilization into the twenty-first century because they cannot participate in the future and at the same time fight for the past. It's a tough road for them as everything in our society revolves around modern things, actions, and thoughts that are blasphemous acts against Allah. For them to then go out and pull this shit, doesn't make much sense."

"Mr. President, it's a good point, but they did, and we have proof."

He thought for a moment. "All right. Call everyone back in."

After everyone returned, the president got up and walked over to the front of his desk. Leaning on its edge, he said, "I wish things were more black and white, but the facts don't lie, and their egregious acts have caused inexpressible damage to billions. Dennis, get them in the air for Natanz. What is the time until over target?"

"Around two and a half hours, Mr. President," Dennis said. "Bomb release should be at 1515 hours."

"I'm still dealing with the delegation. I will meet you downstairs in the Situation Room where we can watch this unfold."

CHAPTER—46

GOLESTAN PALACE

Saturday 1:00 p.m.

On his return, Ali transferred from the helicopter to his private jet in Behbahan, about forty kilometers inland. En route, he called for his staff to make the trek across town from the headquarters building on Pasteur Street to the Golestan Palace, the new headquarters.

* * *

Upon arrival, Ali immediately went into a meeting and started reviewing orders he had given en route. He moved his hand, and the room fell silent.

"There is developing in this country a plan to remove the clergy from their responsibilities. We have a firm reason to believe Maj. Gen. Khiabani is not happy with the country's direction and has been tasking secret operations that have included the hijackings ascribed to us. These tasks include a failed attack on a tanker in the port of Singapore. The Great Satan and the world at large have accused us of initiating these attacks. The attacks have caused a significant disruption in the West. Be aware, all of you, I have ordered *no* such attacks. Nevertheless, we have proof that Maj. Gen. Khiabani has gone rogue and proceeded without authorization to an end we have just discovered.

"It seems that within the last hour, the IRGC army at the embassy has been mobilized with a communication blackout to restrict all but Khiabani's orders. The power was cut off at the Pasteur headquarters while remaining on at the IRGC headquarters. I have a report of messages circulated asking the population to follow him in overthrowing the ayatollah. There is no doubt Khiabani must be stopped and quickly.

"General Lajani, you will dispatch my Quds guard immediately and surround both the Pasteur building for protection and the IRGC headquarters. You are to arrest Khiabani. He must not escape, and you will bring him to me, if possible. If this is not possible, we must eliminate him as a threat to the republic. Also, you will proceed with sufficient force to the embassy barracks to keep the IRGC forces from deploying in the streets or toward the headquarters. Of course, you must employ reason and negotiation. However, if this requires force, you are authorized to apply what is necessary."

CHAPTER—47

WHITE HOUSE SITUATION ROOM

Saturday 1:00 p.m.

The White House Situation Room, located in the basement of the White House, is connected to all communication links available to the government. There are no cell phones allowed in the room, only direct connections to the secure network.

The president took his place at the end of the large conference table. It was a room, a complex, that Kennedy had constructed after the Cuban missile standoff. Kennedy had felt he didn't receive enough information during the crisis and wanted better communication with his government. Now, greatly expanded, it occupied over five thousand square feet. The staff were all gathered in the smaller main conference room.

The president started. "Dennis, how long until we are over the target?"

"One hour and fifteen minutes, Mr. President."

The president asked Paul Miller (SOS), "Have we gotten clearance from Turkey and NATO and covered off the other agencies?"

Paul said, "Sir, we have given GCHQ notification. We were going to wait one hour before we are over target to get to everyone else."

"Better get some coffee in here," the president said.

"What's the chance they will be detected?" the president asked Dennis.

"We are coming in over a low ceiling of cloud, so baring another plane making visual contact, close to none, sir."

"Then what about the one over Bosnia? Didn't we get a stealth jet shot down over there?"

"Yes, Mr. President. It was the result of a daylight eyeball sighting on a predictable flight path. Stealth only hides from radar. They had been utilizing the same flight path for several days. The Bosnians had people logging takeoffs at the airbase and timing the flight times and knew when the plane would be going down the same flight path. When it got there in daylight, they opened fire."

President Perez shook his head. "There are always screw-ups, and we are not immune from this being different.

CHAPTER—48

IRGC MILITARY COMMAND CENTER

Saturday 2:30 p.m.

Khiabani was now paranoid about security and insisted all phones be left outside and all electronics turned off within the center. Consequently, he was not aware of the ominous crowd drawing around the outside of the building.

Valid says, "Let's go over the Bern bank attack."

One of the generals interrupted. "Maj. Gen. Khiabani, sir, there has been an unusual occurrence. Most of us in this room, and some who have attended in the past, have had their assets frozen. General, this could not be a coincidence."

Khiabani snapped back. "I know nothing of this," he lied. "We can straighten this out after the task at hand is completed."

The generals said nothing but exchanged nervous glances.

Khiabani sensed the uneasiness in the room. "Is that understood?" he asked again, in the tone everyone knew and tried to avoid. "Soon, I will meet with the supreme leader and present the unprecedented opportunity to make the West respect our country. Then Ali can use the phantom attacks to demonstrate our power without ever addressing who was responsible. He will never again have to kowtow to the Great Satan. It will be a great day for our country."

His desk buzzed. "What?" he said harshly. "I told you not to bother me in this meeting."

"I know, general, but it's General Abasi (intelligence), and he says he must be allowed to report."

"Send him in."

Abasi entered the room out of breath; it was apparent he had been running. "General, Quds troops have taken positions around the building."

"What?"

"The building has been surrounded by a heavy infantry unit including tanks and troop carriers. I used a secondary underground entrance to get in."

Khiabani, taken by surprise, thought a moment. "This can't be possible."

Just then, the lights went out, and the room went dark until the backup lighting kicked in.

"What is happening?" Khiabani said to no one.

"General, those are General Lajani's troops."

"Yes, he is my friend. I will call him and find out what is going on." He reached for his phone, and it was dead. It was still in his hand when Khiabani realized something was seriously amiss. He turned to a general and said, "Send someone over to the embassy barracks. Make sure they know it is their job to protect the IRGC headquarters with their lives. Have them bring out everything and surround Lajani and his men."

"What is happening?" someone said. "Our accounts are frozen, and the ayatollah's guard troops are surrounding our headquarters? What have you done?"

"Shut up. I'm thinking."

Khiabani tried to work everything out in his head. Nothing made sense except that Ali had found out his plans and mistook them for something else before he had a chance to explain. "All of you go downstairs and reason with Lajani. Get this straightened out, now."

Khiabani worked through an explanation of events he could offer the supreme leader. After mulling over a few options, a cold reality swept over him. Nothing he could say would explain away events if presented to a skeptical mind. It was apparent Ali was now somewhat more than a skeptical mind.

Now alone, Khiabani reached into a drawer and grabbed a cellphone. He sent a text that activated a series of events. Next, he opened a safe, reaching in for a briefcase that contained several passports, cash, a set of civilian clothes, and a 9mm pistol. He walked into a personal bathroom accessed from inside his office. Reaching above his head toward the light over the sink, he pulled a lever hidden behind the shade. A hidden panel door popped open an inch. He grabbed the edge and opened it onto a narrow, dark set of stairs that led to the roof. Khiabani attacked the stairs as he ascended the two floors. He reached up at the top of the stairs, unlatching and opening a hatch in the ceiling that opened into the floor of the room above. He emerged inside one of two rooftop sheds housing the air conditioning equipment.

He cautiously opened the main door of the equipment room and looked outside. He could hear the sound of an approaching helicopter. Waiting inside, he wanted to identify the craft. When the copter's rushing air forced its way through the small opening, he looked out to see it was one of his personal pilots. Vahid could feel his body relax slightly as his escape helicopter came into view. It would take him to Mehrabad Airport and out of the country. As soon as it landed, he climbed in.

The helicopter lifted off. Khiabani looked down onto an empire he had built over thirty years that seemed to have disappeared in an instant. Someone had betrayed him with false information, setting him up for the greatest of misunderstandings. This person did not know a slow and tortured death awaited him due to these actions. Khiabani would find him or them and exact his revenge.

It wasn't ten minutes under the cloudy sky before the helicopter made its approach at the airport. It made a slow descent onto the tarmac, landing next to a cargo plane prepared for his escape. Two of his guards helped him down the step.

"Maj. Gen. Khiabani, sir, the electricity is cut off, making refueling the plane impossible. Our only option is to get to the Shahid Beheshti Air Base, where we must refuel before the rest of the journey."

They started walking him to the plane, which had already spun up its engines. The door opened on the forward section, and the stairs dropped slowly down. That was when Khiabani heard the shot and saw the man next to him jerk wildly and fall by his side. His men proceeded to return fire with deadly accuracy. Being wide open and unprotected on the tarmac's expanse, Khiabani hit the ground between the helicopter and the plane. More of his loyal troops emerged from a troop carrier and engaged in increasing fire coming from the hangar two hundred meters away. On his knees now, Valid felt an arm lift him up and toward the plane as the distinct sounds of bullets passing by filled the air. One of his men

269

was pulling him while firing a pistol, yelling that he must get to the plane. On his last word, the man spun around, crying out in pain, and fell back onto Khiabani. Freeing himself, Khiabani got halfway to his feet. Moving bent over, he headed to the plane. Ten meters from the stairs, he heard shots from a different direction. The sound made him look towards the plane's cockpit. He saw gunfire shatter the cockpit windows. Glass flew everywhere; he heard the pilots' cries from inside the plane. In the next split second, he heard a distinctive high-pitched ping to his right. Bullets hit the plane's spinning engines, causing an explosion. The blast hit him violently, throwing him into the air. The force of the explosion combined with burns and the impact when he hit the ground on his head and shoulder was more pain than he had ever felt.

Khiabani was on his side in the quiet provided by his blown eardrums, trying to assess his options. He tried to locate the briefcase with the pistol, but it was not around. This whole situation is just not happening, he thought. It cannot be happening. Yesterday he was the most powerful man in Iran and held the world in his hands. Unable to hear anything, he only felt the sequential points of instant, terrible pain as three rounds hit him from an automatic rifle. If he uttered a sound, he didn't hear it. His body went into painkilling shock. Rolling over onto his back, he looked up at the gray sky. Allah had made a great choice in his creation of the heavens. In his mind, the pain and the sky came together naturally. He saw images of his family on the soft gray background until it was obscured by soldiers standing over him. A final round ended the reign of one of the most influential individuals in the Iranian government.

Lt. Mazdaki from the Army special forces looked at the man lying on the ground. He wondered what could have happened to receive orders taking out one of the most powerful forces in his country. A medical technician had just checked Khiabani's pulse. He looked up at his superior officer and said, "Lieutenant?"

Mazdaki retreated from his thoughts, blinked twice, and said, "Right." He raised the radio to his ear, "This is Mazdaki; the target is terminated. I repeat, the target is terminated."

CHAPTER—49

GOLESTAN PALACE

Saturday 2:50 p.m.

Semnani's aide had the G9 phone in his hand. He walked over to the supreme leader and whispered in his ear. Ali nodded. Maj. Gen. Khiabani had been killed less than three hundred meters from the palace at the airport trying to board an escape plane.

Ali looked up at the aide and said, "Make the call we need to make."

The aide nodded and walked away to another room. Ali turned to those gathered and said, "We no longer have anything to fear from Maj. Gen. Khiabani, but those loyal to him are a different story. His top generals gave themselves up and are in custody, but there is fighting at the embassy. There is confusion about who issued what orders resulting in an intense firefight between the IRGC forces and our own Quds guard. We must wait for this to end before we know exactly what has occurred, and we can make any assessment."

Ali nodded and, for the first time, realized how close he had come to being overthrown. But the people on the yacht were a mystery.

CHAPTER—50

KATERINA

Saturday 3:00 p.m.

The *Katerina*, sailing on calm seas at twelve knots, was headed back to its homeport of Split in Croatia. The trip would take three days, with most leaving via helicopter at various times. Everyone gathered around the dining room table just off the main salon.

Wilkerson, staring at this laptop, said, "Vianden has intercepted a radio message stating Khiabani was killed at Mehrabad Airport. There appears to be continued fighting around the embassy between loyal IRGC troops and the palace guard."

Brad looked at Avery and said, "I wouldn't want to be in the middle of that mess."

"No," Avery said. "I wouldn't either, but we must remember we created it."

Wilkerson's laptop pinged with a notification. He looked down; it was a message from one of his people. "It appears the aide who had accompanied the ayatollah to the meeting just sent a message that verifies Khiabani being killed trying to escape in a waiting plane. Fighting continues between the IRGC forces at the embassy and the palace guards. It seems the embassy was taken by complete surprise when the shooting started. The IRGC headquarters is secured. The ayatollah is still in control of the country."

Kate spoke rather loudly when she said, "The first order of business is to get this information to this Devroe guy right away. Soon they will have the same information from the call to his wife. It will give them cover to bomb Iran."

Penn said, "I'll get right to it. This guy is pretty anxious to punish Iran for anything, and if they did intercept something giving them cover, he would press for action." Penn got up and left the room to place the call.

CHAPTER—51

FAILED CARTEL CALL TO DEVROE

Saturday 3:10 p.m.

The young Marine guard standing motionless outside the White House Situation Room thought he heard something faint and electronic but wasn't sure. He walked around the reception area right outside the Situation Room, trying to locate the sound.

Someone from NSA walked up and said, "Give this message to Paul Miller, who is in the meeting. It's important."

"Right away," the guard said. Slowly he opened the door and peered inside. He caught the attention of Devroe sitting next to the president and close to the door.

"Dr. Devroe, this is an important message for Secretary Miller."

Devroe grabbed the message and walked it down to Paul, who looked at it without comment.

The guard resumed his place outside the door and noted he could not hear the sound that previously bothered him.

CHAPTER—52

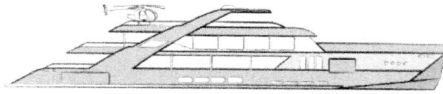

USA GOES COWBOY

Saturday 3:15 p.m.

Wilkerson, still at the dining table on the *Katerina*, interrupted the general conversations around the table with, "Hold on here, I have a POC report from Mom that two B-2 bombers and two F-22 stealth fighters lifted off from Incirlik at 1300 hours."

"It could be an exercise," Brad said.

"John," Elena said, "what is the flight time from there to Natanz?"

Wilkerson turned to Penn, who turned from his laptop to make notes on a tablet of paper.

"Working on it," Penn said. He looked at this watch and seconds later said, "If that's the target, it's two hours and twenty-eight minutes in the air. If they took off at 1300 then they will be bombs gone in fifteen minutes. The US just went cowboy."

Kate said, "If that happens, not only will all this have been for nothing, but we will have another full-fledged Middle Eastern war."

Penn pulled out his G9 phone and quickly set up another call to Devroe. Still standing, he started occasionally pacing, looking at the screen, making sure any delay was not the result of an error.

CHAPTER—53

WHITE HOUSE SITUATION ROOM

Saturday 3:20 p.m.

The Marine resumed his position outside the door, bringing his white gloves together at the waist. The sound he had heard previously was now gone. Two female staffers walked by and tried to start a conversation with him.

"I'm supposed to keep everyone away from the door," he said.

"Does that mean you can talk if we back away from the door?" One of them smiled.

"Well, it's better if you just pass by and keep going."

"I guess that's a no; Janet, it looks like the man doesn't want to come out and play."

The young Marine offered a stilted smile and said, "If you could just let me do my job." It was then he heard the noise again. His attention diverted, Susan, the other girl, said, "What's wrong?"

"Listen," the Marine said. "Do you hear that?"

"Hear what?" she said. "Oh, now I do."

"I need to find out what that is."

"We can help." They started looking around at things in a sitting area that contained a few chairs and a couch.

"It's faint," the guard said, "and it may be in the other room. Damn it."

Janet giggled. "Watch your mouth, soldier, or I will have to report you."

Susan looked next to a couch and pulled up a briefcase from between it and the lamp table. She held it up to her ear and said, "Found it."

The guard came over and looked at the ID tag. "Thanks a bunch" was all he said, and he hustled the case to the door.

Quietly opening the Sit Room door, he handed the case directly to Devroe, saying, "Sir, I think there is a phone ringing in your briefcase. I thought it might be important."

Devroe said, "Shit, I left it outside." He looked at the president, worried, and the president nodded to go outside.

Outside, he quickly opened the briefcase and grabbed the G9 phone. After the last ring, he promptly hit the acknowledge button and hoped the protocol delay wouldn't cause the caller to hang up.

"Is this Stephen Devroe?" the voice said quickly.

"Yes, it is. Thumb is on; you can scan now."

"Thank you." A few seconds passed, and the voice said, "Dr. Devroe, the problem is solved—call back the planes. Do not bomb the Iranians.

"How in the hell do you know we are sending in planes?"

"Jesus, who cares how we know. You're going to start a bloody war if you don't get them turned around. Khiabani is dead. The IRGC or Khiabani went rogue and were behind the hijackings, not the Iranian government. Ali is taking down the IRGC by force as we speak."

"Are you sure?" Devroe asked.

"Devroe, if you start a war, I will personally destroy your life because you had a warning. *Stop* the planes."

"Okay."

"I will stay on the line," Penn said. "Get back to me when you get it cleared."

Devroe put the phone down on the closed briefcase and rushed back into the Situation Room. "Don't touch that," he said, pointing to the phone as he passed the guard.

"Mr. President," Devroe said, coming into the room quicker than was necessary. The president was saying, "Dennis, how long before we are over target? When will we get video?"

Dennis looked at the countdown clock on the wall and said, "Twelve minutes, Mr. President. Video will start shortly. There it is," he said as the screen lit up.

Devroe said with a bit too much energy, "Mr. President, we must abort the mission. Call the planes back. The IRGC was responsible for the hijackings, not the clerics. Khiabani is dead, and Semnani is battling the IRGC as we speak. If we bomb them, they will have to retaliate. We don't need to bomb them now. Things have changed."

"How do you know?" the president said.

Devroe paused, "Reliable sources, Mr. President." He looked directly at him. "Your taxpayers' money at work," he said with a strained smile.

The president looked at him for a second and then turned to the table. "Call them back, Dennis, and quickly."

"Wait," Dennis said, a little more than annoyed. "Your reliable sources got us into this in the first place. When you put bombers in the air, they're not a yo-yo. I'm glad we are calling them back, but this is a perfect example of civilian authority tasking without full knowledge of the consequences."

Devroe, duly chastised, was looking for cover when the president said, "Gentlemen, let's stick with the fact we don't have to bomb anyone and be relieved, regardless of how we got here. This gives us time to validate the information. It doesn't keep us from making them pay later."

Dennis's eyes rolled at the comment.

"Abort the mission," the president said.

Dennis picked up a line and said, "This is SecDef, abort operation Eagle One. I repeat: Abort Eagle One, bring them back and put a blanket over it. The squadron stays in the air, tanker them to Sigonella, not Incirlik. I don't want anything out, understand?"

Devroe looked at the president and said quietly, "Excuse me, I will be back in a second."

"Where's he going?" Dennis asked, still irritated.

The president quickly came back with, "Mr. Corwen, I want you to cut the doctor a little slack. It's a personal request and not, as everyone in this room knows, because he is a friend. Now, unless I don't know how to play this game, this is a victory. Let's act like it. I'm ordering all of you to be happy, and I have more stripes and stars than anyone in the room."

Devroe was again outside and picked up the phone. "This is

Devroe. Are you still there?"

"Yes, I'm here."

"The bomb run has been canceled. The planes are on their way back."

"Look, Dr. Devroe, no one wanted to put you in a tight spot by having to bring them back, but we didn't ask you to send them. Did you get the intercept from the general to his wife?"

"Yes, with that, we had cause, and went with it. It's our job."

"I agree, but our phone calls were to give you a heads up. Being given the same courtesy would be nice. It would have avoided what must have been a messy mission recall."

"Well," Devroe thought for a moment. He didn't like giving up control to some ghost on the other end of a phone. "I will have to agree with you on that point. Anyway, what went down?"

"Fair enough, your facilities will get to the bottom of the story anyway. We had a face-to-face with Semnani and managed to trick him into thinking Khiabani's real reason for the hijackings was a coup, which made him a natural enemy."

"A coup? How in the hell did you do that?"

"We presented Ali with some forged orders from Khiabani to his generals saying that they were to execute the coup after the hijackings. Then we turned the power and network connections off at Ali's headquarters as though an assault was underway. Ali had no choice but to bring out the palace guard. Then, as a colleague of mine said, we just needed to light a match. That came by issuing official secret orders to the IRGC battalion at the embassy to mobilize, making it appear they were going to take Ali's headquarters. Khiabani was killed trying to escape at the Mehrabad, just a couple hundred meters from Ali himself. It pits the IRGC against the National Army, and it's going to be bloody, but Ali will win out and probably restructure the IRGC."

Devroe didn't want to say it, thus the delay after Penn stopped talking. "I have to hand it to you. That was a masterpiece of deception, lying, and bluffing, but a great alternative to bombs."

"That's always the preferred method, until next time. Keep the phone safe, and we must again follow written protocol on initial contact."

"Hold on—I still don't know who you are."

"Doctor, I'm surprised you would say that because, well, that's

279

the general idea, and it will stay that way. We only get involved when it's required."

"I don't get it," Devroe said. "How do you pull all this off? How did you know about Khiabani before we did? I guess I have to leave it classified as a mystery."

"Yes, it will have to remain a mystery, or we cannot be of service next time."

"Will we ever meet?"

"If we do, you will never know it happened."

CHAPTER—54

KATE CONTACTS ALI

Saturday 3:35 p.m.

Kate called the secure phone that was with Semnani's aide.

"Is Mr. Semnani available to come to this phone with an interpreter?" Kate said.

"Yes," the aide said. "Did you get my message regarding Khiabani?"

"Yes, we did. It is why I'm calling."

The aide whispered in Ali's ear and handed him the phone.

Kate could hear the muffled exchange.

In Farsi, Semnani said, "Yes."

Kate said, "I understand we are through with the … cooperation. Rest assured, we will reinstate all accounts without damage and, as agreed, keep it a secret. The internal battle taking place is unfortunate but seemed inevitable. Nevertheless, we avoided an irrational act by the Americans who were prepared to bomb Natanz."

"Without cause," Ali said.

"No, they had cause, the world had cause, and you know this. Through close contact with your country and patience on the American side, we do not have a war today. We do not expect you to love America, but wish for you to consider us neutral should there be any further contact."

Ali replied, "We have before us a long journey. Negotiations must be lengthy, and it is only the Americans who get impatient."

"I am thrilled that it is your battle and not mine. Thank you for your help, and good day."

The aide received the phone, and with Kate still on, he said, "How is it you can interfere at such a high level internationally?"

"I prefer the term 'assist.' Our group wishes to thank you for your assistance."

"Who are you?"

"I guess we will have to leave it as someone who helped when needed. Good day to you," Kate nodded.

Seconds later, the G9 phone vibrated intensely in the aide's hand as its batteries began overheating. Startled, he dropped the phone to the floor and observed the case starting to melt. The heat caused a small, contained fire, destroying the device.

Lauren still had her finger on the enter key as she said, "God, I love this stuff."

CHAPTER—55

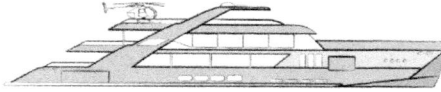

THE NEXT DAY ON THE YACHT

Sunday

Kate and Brad were sitting in the main deck lounge area finishing a light breakfast. Kate stopped talking and looked at Brad.

"What is it?" he said. "Do I have something on my tie?"

"You're not wearing one."

"Well, I guess it's not that then—what?"

Kate laughed, "I have a suggestion. Why don't you and Elena stay for a few days on the yacht and get to know one another?"

"Are you playing matchmaker?"

"Danner, how about you just let me help you for once? You can't tell me that a few days on this boat by yourself wouldn't be nice, let alone with Elena."

"Okay, I accept, but I'm not sure she will. What are you going to do?"

"Tomorrow, I go by helicopter to Abu Dhabi and via a Cartel jet to New York. I have some business I need to finish. I have already spoken to Avery."

"Monkey business, I hope. I think you need it."

"Maybe."

"What's his name?"

Brad hit the button that brought the typical reaction. "Ah, that would be none …" she said and stopped. Reconsidering, she said, "Darren Winton, he is into libraries," she said with a smile.

"Sure, libraries are the new hot pickup spots. I knew that already. When will you be back?"

"Just a couple of days, not sure, but I will be back. I will call you from the plane on the way back okay—deal?"

"It's a deal," he said.

CHAPTER—56

NEW YORK

Monday

Kate spoke into the phone. "Hello, is this Darren I'm speaking to?"

"Yes," Darren said, "is this Emily? We haven't spoken in a long time."

"No," Kate said.

"No? Then who is this? I don't recognize the voice."

"My name is Jane Doe."

Darren paused for a second, and Kate heard him speaking through the smile on his lips. "I don't know any Jane Doe. Wait— maybe I did once, but she threw me out of her hotel room after I spent a fortune on her."

"Yes, I have been thinking about that and have decided I need to make up for that little incident. How about you take me to the library like you promised, and I will pay this time."

He laughed. "How generous," he said. "Not until you tell me your real name."

"Meet me at the library on 42nd Street at eight, and I will tell you my name. Agreed?"

"I don't know." he said. "Is this another wild goose chase?"

"Are you calling me a goose?"

"That's not what I meant," he said.

"I know, but I couldn't pass it up."
"Well, at least now I know it's really you."
"What's that supposed to mean?" she asked.
"Be at the library, and I will tell you."

THE END

I live with my family in the Bay Area in Northern California and writing came to me late in life. It's now something I need to do every day. The comments I receive make it a labor of love. I would be very interested in what you think of this story and thank you for supporting my writing. You can find more information on my other books and a contact form, on my website.

www.richarddtaylor.com

Sign up for my newsletter for upcoming release dates and purchase information on my upcoming books: Primary Protocol, Islands of Peace and Brimstone Offensive.

https://landing.mailerlite.com/webforms/landing/n0o5d3

If you enjoyed reading this book, please let your friends know and consider writing an online review. Writers live by reviews as they help us evaluate the writing from the readers' comments and we get to see what you enjoyed in the story. The market for books is very competitive and the opinions shared by people are very important. If you would like to write a review you can type in the link below and it will take you directly to Amazon and a review form for this book.

Review link.
https://www.amazon.com/review/create-review?&asin=B07R66WJSB

Additional Books by Richard D. Taylor

Enjoy a sample of Primary Protocol.

PRIMARY PROTOCOL
A Kate Adler Book # 2

WITH 70,000 LIVES AT STAKE, KATE ADLER AND THE CARTEL RUSH TO STOP AN ATTACK ON THE FRENCH NATIONAL STADIUM

A page-turning suspense terrorist thriller that delivers constant surprises.

CHAPTER—1

Vianden Castle Luxembourg

The confidential referral was from *Tangent Day,* the code name for Martin Alejandro Perez, President of the United States. Brad Danner sat at his desk in Vianden Castle in Luxembourg, headquarters of the secretive Cartel, waiting for a call from the French ambassador to Mali. A unique referral was required before anyone could directly contact the Cartel, and *Tangent Day* was about as unique as it got.

The ambassador's call would almost certainly involve a problematic issue needing a somewhat unconventional solution.

The kind of solution where a national power would find their options limited due to the restrictions of law or convention. For the past two years, Brad managed the outside world's contacts for the organization as well as contributing as a special advisor to Kate Adler, the acting chair. Out of college, he joined the military for action, but his computer skills landed him in an intelligence tent at Bagram Air Base. The experience qualified him later to be a bodyguard to Kate in what was supposed to be an NSA intelligence center in Munich. The problem was Kate didn't know about the arrangement, which resulted in a rocky start to their relationship. Kate was his boss having taken over the Cartel two years ago fulfilling her late father's wish to further the group's agenda into the future. She was flying in today from New York. She would undoubtedly want an update on the ambassador's call.

The phone vibrated on the hard surface spinning on its axis as its bright screen lit the dark lampshade above it. He picked it up and entered the "one-time" code into the touchscreen.

"Hello, this is agent, 2810, can I help you?" Brad said in a balanced voice.

"This is Renee Magnant, French Ambassador to the Mali Republic."

"Madam Ambassador, I want to thank you for your call, and I must tell you this conversation will be recorded and available only to those in the Cartel."

"I would hope so because if it gets out, I'm dead. Who is this I'm calling? Who is the Cartel?"

"We are someone your referral thought could help in some way."

"Well, that was evasive enough," she said, "I will get right to it. I have information regarding a probable terrorist attack and have not been able to convince anyone it's real. I guess you are my last chance at avoiding a disaster."

"We will certainly do what we can to help."

"I don't need help. I need a miracle. As you know, the French military, at the request of the Mali government, came in, confronted, and defeated a terrorist group named Ansar Dine. They killed all the leaders except a man named Mokhtar Belmokhtar. I have it on good authority that Mokhtar's group, and several other offshoots located in Southern Libya, Tunisia, and the northern parts of Niger, have formed an alliance."

"What sort of an alliance?"

"An alliance to finance a vindictive response to Ansar Dine's humiliating defeat and a warning to the French to stay out of their area of operation."

"Did they say what form this response would take?"

"That I don't have. I just know, as a group, they have raised over thirty million euros, and revenge is their goal. I can guarantee it's going to be big, and a lot of French people are going to die somewhere."

"Why do you want us involved? Shouldn't you go to the French government?"

"Really, Mr. 2810? I have been in this business for a long time; don't you think that was my first thought? I called DGSI (French for General Directorate for Internal Security), and they could not find any chatter or Intel to support my alarm. All I got was they would investigate it, which means they didn't believe me. I called French President Maurice Jossart, who agreed to make some calls and also found DGSI didn't have anything to substantiate the claim. I know my sources here on the ground, and this is real. Mokhtar and his band of lowlifes are being very quiet about it. I insisted to Jossart that someone needed to do something or the prospect of dying Frenchmen was going to land in his lap. In confidence, he provided the information to contact US President Perez, who I have known for some time.

"Perez was very gracious but, after checking with his people, came to the same conclusion. I'm not exactly shy and probably pursued this a little aggressively with the President. I also hung on him the prospect of thousands of lives on his shoulders. He finally gave in providing me the method of contacting you people. By the way, who are you, and what's with the writing letters and this funny phone I have?"

Brad, who had been taking notes, replied, "I can assure you we have the same goals regarding your concerns. Innocent people should not have to suffer at the hands of a few who are radical in their beliefs. To my knowledge, we have not picked up any information regarding an attack on French soil. Who were your sources?"

"That's another problem I had with the DGSI, it's from previously used anonymous informants that I trust, having used them for years. Their information once saved my life during an assassination attempt. However, it's not the kind of information that the formalized institutions of my wonderful country consider the last word."

"Who did you talk to at DGSI?"

"I was given to a man named Durand. I was told he was high up, had access to all the information that would be available, and could make decisions. He was polite but didn't believe a word I said."

"Madam Ambassador, I want to thank you for providing this information. We have certain capabilities that we will incorporate to see if we can discover more information concerning your suspicions of an attack. I can assure you we will follow up on this. Please keep this phone in a safe place and tell no one of our conversations. I will get back to you with whatever we find. I will send you a meaningless text with a new code and a time on your mobile when we need to have an encrypted conversation. You will then repeat the procedures you used to make this call. Meanwhile, keep listening to your sources. If they have any updates, use the text feature of the G9 phone to get back."

"Well, Mr. 2810, this has been an interesting conversation. First, how do you know my mobile number? Second, I'm not used to sharing this kind of information with someone I don't trust or, in fact, know yet. Even if you find out what they're going to do, what can *you* do about it but wave another unnoticed flag?"

"As to your mobile number, well, as I said, we have our capabilities. Second, we don't publicly wave flags. If we find something vital that is not being addressed by the traditional authorities, we are capable of handling it."

With a challenge in her voice, she added, "A well-funded group bent on killing as many as possible somewhere in France?"

"Anywhere."

"As I said, this has been an interesting conversation. I will wait for your text."

Brad put the phone down and started filling out the call log on the screen. He could understand the ambassador's skepticism due to the unusual secrecy involved in her eventually making contact.

293

He didn't take the time to explain that the Cartel determines where to apply their resources in two ways. One is from a POC (Pattern of Concern) generated by Geneva9, also known as Mom, the Cartel's massive intelligence and surveillance asset. The other is information received from a secure phone conversation after receiving a written request for contact. All requests came in through letters re-posted several times to new addresses before arriving at the Cartel's headquarters and onto Brad's desk. In the age of computers, it turns out regular mail is the safest way to transfer information anonymously around the world without any digital trail. Each country's mail privacy laws and the sheer volume of mail within any country inhibited regular scrutiny. A letter is old fashioned and uncomplicated, but it is foolproof.

Look for Primary Protocol on Amazon soon by typing in:
https://landing.page.richarddtaylor.com/primary-protocol

Sign up for my newsletter and receive release dates and purchase information by typing in:
https://landing.mailerlite.com/webforms/landing/n0o5d3

Enjoy a sample of Islands of Peace

ISLANDS OF PEACE
A Kate Adler Book # 3

WILL ONE MAN, AVENGING HIS BROTHER'S DEATH, USE RISING TENSIONS BETWEEN THE USA AND RUSSIA TO START A WAR? CAN KATE ADLER AND THE CARTEL STOP HIS DEADLY PLAN IN TIME?

A mystery/thriller series full of unexpected twists and turns delivers nonstop action.

Enjoy a sample of Islands of Peace

CHAPTER 1

MOSCOW

Kate Adler entered her penthouse suite in Moscow's Ararat hotel and surveyed the utter chaos. Someone had ransacked her room while she attended a state dinner. Moving farther into the suite revealed a man ripping cushions apart. He looked back at her.

"What the hell are you doing here?" she asked, frozen.

Turning to escape, someone grabbed her from behind. She instinctively resisted but felt the grip tighten. Hearing heavy breathing and becoming overpowered, her body tensed. Angry at being accosted, she felt her high heel give way upon stabbing the man's foot.

"Bitch!" he yelled, reacting to the pain and violently throwing her on the floor.

Kate glanced off a couch and fell hard against the coffee table. An upward glare revealed a 9mm Glock held by a furious bald man with hollow eyes. Pumped on adrenalin from the struggle, he shouted in a thick Russian accent. "Where is the information from Tonkov?"

Kate frowned. "I can't help you and probably wouldn't even if I could. I'm sure you know by now whatever you want isn't here."

The other man pulled the purse from Kate's hands and dumped the contents onto the carpet. Looking down, he sifted the items with his shoe. The bald man put a finger to his ear-piece; receiving instructions, he said, "We can't stay any longer; we need to leave now." Still holding the gun, he looked intensely at Kate on the floor, the stare threatening and unmistakable. Both men turned and left.

In her thirty-five years, she had been shot at several times and survived a bombing, but never experienced a physical assault. She thought briefly about calling hotel security but then mused, This is Moscow. Instead, she reached for a specially designed secure phone lying on the carpet, along with the remains of her purse. Seconds after she hit the button, she heard Brad Danner's voice, a friend and associate.

"Hi, Kate," Brad said, "how was the dinner? Boring? I have you on speaker in the operations center. The team says hi."

"Hi, Brad, hi everyone; I have bigger concerns than the dinner at the moment. I came back to my room and look at what I found." She held the phone up to show a video of the disarray the men had left behind. Everyone in the center could see the images on one of the many large display screens on the walls.

"As I walked into the room, someone grabbed me and threw me to the floor, but I'm fine. I don't know what the men wanted, but I think it has something to do with Russian President Kozloff and my friend Aleksis. Tonight, after the dinner, Aleksis received a troubling phone call, and he told me to leave the country right away. I need the team to get me out of the hotel safely before someone else arrives."

Brad didn't need any more information, as this was as important as it got. His voice tightened, "Are you safe right now?"

"Yes, I have both entrances to the suite locked, and I have closed the curtains."

"Good, we will go to work on it and be right back." Three years ago, Kate had inherited her father's industrial empire, placing her high on the world's multi-billionaires' list. High society knew Kate as the very public face of the Helmut Adler Children's Fund, named in memory of her father. Only a handful knew she had also inherited her father's powerful covert organization called the Cartel.

Everyone in the Cartel's operations center heard her request, and in practiced precision, each addressed their specific assignments.

Elena and Lauren, the two with direct access to the Cartel's supercomputer affectionately known as Mom, queried for any Moscow police or security notifications out of the ordinary. In charge of field operations, Penn Hauer sent an alert to the Cartel's special operations group. He then brought up his contact list, looking for someone from his past. Another agent in the room placed the status of the Cartel's small fleet of private planes on a second screen.

Penn looked up. "We can't use her plane sitting at Moscow International airport. Whoever did this will already have it under surveillance. Someone call Captain Silanos on the plane and tell him to take off ASAP before they impound him and the plane, or worse. We will give him coordinates in the air."

A voice in the room answered, "I'm on that."

Penn found the name and reached for a secure phone. He heard a voice asking, "Hello, who is this?"

"Freddy, it's Penn Hauer. Where are you right now?"

"On my way to meet a few friends for a beer. Oh, by the way, it's nice to hear from you, too," the man said, outright laughing.

Freddy Faraday was more than just an old-time friend; he was a man of many talents, not all reputable. These talents made him extremely resourceful, depending on the need.

"Hold on a sec," Penn said to Freddy

"Lauren," he began, "I need a small airport well outside of Moscow that can take Captain Silanos and the Gulf Stream 650."

"Yes, I'm ahead of you. Kaluga is two hours or so outside of Moscow by car via the E101." Lauren queried the keyboard. "It has a 7,000-foot runway. The Gulf stream only needs 5,600 fully loaded."

"Great, get those coordinates to the Captain. Freddy, are you still there?"

"I'm here; where else would I be?"

"My principle could be in danger, and I need to get her out of Moscow—quietly. Can I count on you?"

"You always have; why stop believing now, brother?" Did you know I had dinner with Ms. Adler tonight?"

"No, I didn't, and don't know why you would. Hold on."

"Brad," Penn said. "Can you get to Kate and tell her a Freddy Faraday will call to escort her out of the hotel?"

"On it," Brad said.

"Freddy, I need you to pick up Ms. Adler at the Ararat Park hotel. I need you to go to her room and stay with her through the lobby and outside. Then I need you to drive her south toward an airport in Kaluga. Do you know where it is?"

"Hell no, I only live here—I was born in Cincinnati, remember? Send the directions to my phone. There went my beer and poker game with a few heavy rollers. You're going to owe me big time, my friend."

"Really, Freddy?" Penn had to crack a smile. "This is a hardship? When was the last time you had a beer?"

Freddy chuckled. "At lunch."

"That's what I thought. Freddy, take this seriously."

"You have that tone in your voice again. I know this is serious. I'm a highly respected psychologist in my spare time."

"What do you mean, my tone?"

"Every time you mention her name, you get all wobbly on me. You were going to introduce me to her sometime, but that never happened."

"Not in a million years would I introduce her to the likes of you," he said, laughing. "Besides, being concerned for her is my job, Freddy. She's a high-value target wherever she goes."

"Yeah, thanks for the company line. What's Ms. Adler's status? Is she ready? Do I go now?"

"How far away are you? More importantly, do you have a car more reliable than the one you had on my last trip out?"

"How about an Audi R8, their big guy? It's the baddest vehicle Audi makes. This thing is a rocket and chick magnet."

"How in the world …?"

"Some people just shouldn't play poker," Freddy laughed. "You declined last time here, smart man. Listen, I was already downtown, so I'm perhaps eight blocks away. I just hung a U-turn, and I'm on my way. Hey, Penn?"

"Yes."

"Not that it matters, but just how serious? It's a tactical question. What are we facing?"

"She attended a Kozloff state dinner, and when she got back to her room, someone had tossed it. Two thug types attacked her at gunpoint. Do you have a sidearm in the car?"

"In Moscow, it's not good when thugs come out of the woodwork, especially brandishing guns. That means it's serious. To answer your question, I always have one installed in a fake door panel, and the Audi is no different."

Coming soon look for Islands of Peace on Amazon by typing in:
https://landing.page.richarddtaylor.com/islands-of-peace

Sign up for my newsletter and receive release dates and purchase information by typing in:
https://landing.mailerlite.com/webforms/landing/n0o5d3

THE
BRIMSTONE OFFENSIVE

Never Underestimate Your Opponent
Coming soon The Brimstone Offensive on Amazon.

Sign up for my newsletter and receive release dates and purchase information by typing in:
https://landing.mailerlite.com/webforms/landing/n0o5d3

Coming in 2021

IMPORTANT CHARACTERS AND TERMS

CHARACTERS

Admiral Shahbazi — Head of IRGC Navy
Admiral Rahmani — IRGC
Ali Semnani— Supreme Leader of IRAN
Avery Stanton— CEO Adler Industries Chairman Cartel Steering committee
Brad Danner— Co-worker of Kate. Cartel communications, Security group, a friend of Kate.
Captain Carlino Bertucci—Captain of Montclair Star
Captain Hamid Mahmud—Captain of Yunes IRGC submarine
Captain Nadeem Petropoulou—Captain of the LNG tanker D.S. Serena
Captain Musa Abasi— IRGC Chief of Intelligence)
Colonel Langer—Former SAS commando, Cartel commander of Alpha Team 4
Danny—Cartel team EMT
Darren Winton— Possible love interest in New York City
Dan Tilde— Assistant Director CIA
Dennis Corwen— Secretary of Defense
Dr. Arsdale— Kate's Father's Doctor
Dr. John Wilkerson—Cartel head of intelligence and analysis. Dr. Stephen Devroe— Director of National Intelligence.
Dr. Stephen Austin Devroe— Director of National Intelligence (DNI)
Elena Maleeva— Manager of Geneva9 surveillance system (Mom) and security group.
Ethel Bannister— Manager of the safe house in Zurich.
Fared Khiabani—Khiabani'son
Gen. Karim Nabavi—IRGC Ground Forces
Gen. Hamid Lajani—Commander of Special Forces

Helmut Adler—Kate's father, founder Adler Industries and the Cartel.

Jake—Nursing assistant to Kate's father

Kate Adler (Katerina) — Protagonist, Executive Director of Cartel, Founder and Director of

Kira Vestrova—Business and romantic associate of Mr. Stanton

Konner Huston—Special assistant to U.S. president and Kate's love interest.

Lieutenant Ghasemi—Special forces led the attack on the D.S. Serena

Loren Sorrel— Assistant manager of Geneva 9 asset field operations. Directing the G9 asset in the real world

Major General Vahid Khiabani—Commander in Chief of the Iranian Revolutionary Guard Corps (IRGC), antagonist

Marc Henderson—Munich station manager

Martin Perez—President of the United States (POTUS).

Matthew Corbett—Acting Chairman of the Cartel steering committee

Mr. Anton Guerard—Cartel board member, former minister of finance in French President Navarre's administration

Mr. Gerrit Brouwer— Cartel board member Chairman of Cittel Oil PLC

Mr. Stovall— Cartel board member, Chairman of one of Europe's biggest banking houses

Mrs. Doris Hayward—Assistant to POTUS

Nazari—Iranian tech trying to penetrate Munich network

Paul Miller—Director of Central Intelligence Agency (CIA)

Penn Hauer—Director Cartel Field operations, security group.

President Kenneth Harper—Former president before Perez

Reyhan Lajani—Wife of Hamid Lajani,

Royce Wakefield—Secretary of State

Shahab Mohammadi—President of the Islamic Republic of Iran

Tangent Day—Cartel code name for POTUS

TERMS AND PLACES

A'rafat faRdā— (Blessing Tomorrow) name of IRGC operation to start a war.

Cartel—Secret private group promoting its agenda from the shadows.

DGSE—French Directorate General for External Security
Dragon—Anti tank missile launcher
Federico Damiano D'Argenio—Owner of Auberge Aal Veinen restaurant
GCHQ—Government Communication Headquarters) in the U.K.
Geneva 9—Cartel's surveillance computer
G9t phone—The Cartel's secure cell phone encrypted by Mom.
Helmut Adler Children's Fund—Created by Kate in memory of her father.
IRGC— Iranian Revolutionary Guard Corps
Kuala Belait—Cartel's special forces facility in Brunei
Mom—Cartel's surveillance computer
Morton Roth—Maritime management company. Part of Adler Industries"
Natanz—Iran's nuclear facility
POC—Pattern of Concern generated by Geneva9
Quds—IRGC para-military for assignment outside the country
Security Group—Brad, Penn, Elena, Lauren, and Kate.
Vianden Castle Luxembourg—Cartel headquarters

The Cartel

The Cartel is an ultra-secret, stateless organization addressing geopolitical problems that fall outside the control of typical nation states. The Cartel believes that free trade and stable economies in a terror-free environment are the solutions to economic prosperity and self-reliance. Acting in the shadows, it intervenes when bad actors try to exploit the status quo at the expense of others. Financed by Kate Adler and some of the wealthiest and most powerful individuals in the world, it utilizes a one-of-a-kind surveillance system and a highly skilled tier one ground force to further its agenda. Its asymmetrical capabilities and low profile make the Cartel a very effective alternative when conventional solutions are not an option.

The organization's offices are located in an old renovated castle in Vianden, Luxembourg, purchased from the King by Kate's father in 1975.

Katarina (Kate) Adler

Kate Adler inherited her father's companies two years ago making her a billionaire. She also inherited the Cartel, a covert organization created by her father to address geopolitical problems. During that time, Kate has grown into the Cartel's director's role, working closely with Brad Danner, her business partner and complicated romantic interest. To the world, Kate is recognized purely as a world-class socialite and philanthropist, but privately she also furthers the Cartel's agenda in a world where right and wrong is not always black and white.

Morton Roth
GLOBAL SHIPPING SERVICES

Morton Roth is an international container and bulk shipping company that also offers freight-forwarding broker and port services. It maintains offices in most major ports of the world.

Due to its long term and well-earned relationship with each port authority, it wields considerable influence in all manner of port procedures and business.

ADLER INDUSTRIES

Adler Industries was established in 1970 by Helmut Adler, Kate's father, in San Francisco California, and is one of the original Silicon Valley electronics companies. In addition to supplying low power processor chips for the world's cell phones, it is behind the design and construction of a unique super computer called Geneva9 but known to staff as Mom. It utilizes artificial intelligence to provide the Cartel with current information from penetrated networks and maintains a wide-ranging surveillance

304

regimen. When any situation reaches a level of concern, the system generates a POC or "Pattern of Concern" outlining possible situations that could concern the Cartel. Also, in certain situations, the Geneva9 computer inexplicably generates instructions to ensure Kate's safety. These emanate from an untouchable instruction set deep in the operating system called the Primary Protocol. The company's corporate offices are in New York city.

Printed in Great Britain
by Amazon